ALSO BY SCOTT MORGAN

PARADISE: THE LAST PLACE ON EARTH

THE BIG FRESH

SCOTT MORGAN

Livingston Press
The University of West Alabama

isbn 13 978-1931982-90-0 trade paper
isbn 13 978-1931982-89-4, library binding
Library of Congress Control Number 2007922088
Printed on acid-free paper.
Printed in the United States of America,
Publishers Graphics
Hardcover binding by: Heckman Bindery
Typesetting and page layout: Angela Brown
Proofreading: Barb Schwartz, Brittany Lovette,
Donmonique Gracie, Vilater Green
Cover Design: Jennifer Brown
Cover Layout: Jennifer Brown
Cover Photo: Tricia Taylor

Livingston Press
is part of The University of West Alabama,
at Livingston, ALabama.
It thereby has non-profit status, and all
donations are tax-deductible:
brothers and sisters, we need 'em.

first edition
6 5 4 3 3 2 1

For Shannon, Jeremy, Pete, Ryan, and Jay

THE BIG FRESH

PART 1

Do not be afraid. I am the First and the Last.
I am the Living One; I was dead, and behold
I am alive for ever and ever!

Revelation

PROLOGUE

Some two centuries or more before John Carter and the Cloud arrived in Siler City, a tomb was discovered in Ephesus, Turkey. It had been buried in nearly two thousand years of rubble. Outside the tomb were three dozen workers, sweating and picking at its skull for answers. It was calculated and openly predicted by Father Anthony Marcelino, an archaeologist and Catholic Priest, that the remains of the Virgin Mary were inside the tomb. Not only did this fact scare the hell out of the workers and Father Anthony Marcelino, but it also put back in them a fear of God. A fear that led to one slow, precise dig.

When the tomb was finally opened, Father Anthony Marcelino was the only one standing at its entrance. For two days he prayed for guidance then entered. That same day he reemerged carrying a bronze vessel. Above him, sitting impossibly low in the sky was a black ominous cloud. It not only gave Father Anthony Marcelino the feeling that what he was doing was divinely significant, it gave him the impression that what he was doing was divinely wrong. It made him stare upwards yet simultaneously inwards into himself, bringing his eyes eventually back to the bronze vessel. Upon its back were ancient inscriptions and a drawing of an ox standing on its hind legs facing a mountain with three crosses. A great phallus with scrotum hung from between the ox's legs. Upon the ox's back was an inscription that Father Anthony Marcelino translated: *Christ has died, Christ has risen, and Christ will come again*. He prayed two more days then returned to Rome with the bronze vessel.

THE GERMAN CONNECTION

Josef was a god, at least that is what he thought, staring at himself through a morning mirror. The papers and the people who worked with him never said it, but he knew. It just so happened that time and positioning had given him the opportunity to be more than mortal, if only for a while; and being more than mortal meant being a god. How special it must have felt.

Josef often stared at himself in the mirror, mostly in the mornings before stepping out into the world to do his godly duties. The mirror showed him how to look and when to split his lips to reveal the rows of pearls that lay as straight as any. Rows of pearls most commonly used to bite down upon themselves to anesthetize the abundant joy he received from performing what he called his *work*. It was this joy he inevitably confused as genius, and that genius that he confused for godliness. But history will eventually show he was not a genius at all.

In the mornings, though, he would stare at himself in the mirror—first naked then fully dressed, trancing on the beauty and intrinsic delicacies of his flesh, rubbing his cheeks and teeth, pulling at his earlobes like fleshy doorbells. "You're a beauty to look at," he would tell himself, then catch his words and laugh, as if God ever had to tell himself he was beautiful.

Straight from the womb he was naked, pink and wet, spitting out mucosal fluid like bad wine. He grew up on the fast track with little to obstruct his vision. Times were bad, yet he flourished, and the worse they got the better it was for Josef. He had a chiseled face that was somewhat perfect. He could see it as he worked his hair down around his temple with the fat of a thousand calves smeared in his hands. First the hands—always the hands—then a comb, then back to the mirror. It was perfect—as his wife had once told him. Not godly, but perfect. Josef eventually convinced himself that *perfect* was another word for God. As were the words *brilliant, intelligent*, and *gifted*. All these he would hear.

Suited, he was just as perfect. Nothing out of place. An immaculate deity. He would see this before leaving the mirror and would have a proud picture in his head for the remainder of the day as he performed his joyous and perfect work.

THE BIG FRESH

It was a very unusual Cloud to look at—fat and dimensional and absolutely immobile. It had rolled across the landscape the same day as John Carter, two days ago, and had refused to move ever since.

It was the belief of many in town that the Cloud was part of a larger meteorological event that was playing itself out across the world. A warming up of things, which was in direct correlation to the population and to the population's inability to control its own collective flatulence. "It was one big glorious fart that created us," joked some in town in response to the Cloud and the idea of global warming, "and one big glorious fart that will destroy us."

Most of the people in town didn't understand what they were trying to say. They took it literally, as always. They saw someone farting that huge Cloud up into the sky with the force of an atomic explosion and it made them laugh. It was fun to think that way. Unfortunately, for most people in town it wasn't an option to think any other way but that.

Ruby caught the last part of the joke and put the rest together as he stood staring up at the Cloud. It was unchanged from the last time he stared at it, but it gave him something to do and an inanimate object to do it with.

Few people at the Home made it outside to see the Cloud. They were either incapacitated or had lost the will to go out. Most had seen all they wanted of life—were unimpressed then and unimpressed now. They were dulled out by the senseless rotating shifts of day and night. It was much easier to just lie there with the eyes closed and let it all pass by like some lazy bullet with no concern for who shot it and who would be shot.

Ruby noted that the Cloud didn't give a shit about them either. It was disconnected from all that was below. It was an imperfect circle of frozen blackness, a gigantic chunk of sourdough jammed into the skyline. It was an impeccable display of nothing from the beginning—a meteorological awakening that sent a few to the Weather Channel, a few more to roll up their car windows, and a few more, one being the Reverend Alfonso King, to remotely question the Divinity. Of course, that was all in the beginning.

THE ISLAM CONNECTION

Jayln Amir lost her job as a nurse at the Home before the Cloud and John Carter arrived. The extent of her dismissal remains marred in the bureaucratic machine. It is known, though, that whatever transpired the day her employment was terminated, Ruben C. Riggs was involved. What isn't known is why Jayln Amir, wife and mother of two young boys, with a newly acquired citizenship to the United States and a brand new Volvo station wagon with payments, would so mysteriously feel the need to disappear from work for two or so hours then reappear stoned, stumbling drunk in her own words, hallucinating Allah.

It was a fact among all at the Home that her Middle-Eastern ways weren't understood or appreciated but that the strangely accelerated way in which she spun her English made her appear uptight to the locals. It was also a fact that she could become hostile very quickly if approached or petitioned wrong. Something Ruby did often.

It wasn't in Ruby's nature—or Jayln's for that matter—but something set the two sorely off the first time they met. Jayln never spoke of it to her colleagues and Ruby had no one to tell; they basically worked it out together in subliminal fashion. A cold war of the sort with neither fully understanding the whats and whys of their relationship.

Ruby had no problem with her crassness, and the accelerated way in which she spoke was a freshness within the stale ruins of the hall. No, it was the way she treated him. It was degrading and uncalled for. She brushed Ruby off as one of the rest even though he was remarkably more coherent and mobile than most of the staff. She routinely spoke to him and others like lost sheep, running through sentences scattered with parables for the sake of hearing herself speak. A very religious lady she was, and under different circumstances would have been an angel.

The day after being fired for apparent drug use on the job she and her husband showed up at the Home. They were driving the new Volvo station wagon and pulled it under the parking shelter directly in front of the two doors that opened into the lobby. She entered with her husband behind her in quiet respect. Rita Hymer, the Home's director, came out of her office when she saw them. Ruby was the only other person in the lobby; he was sitting in the corner facing the window. He was neatly dressed, slim, in slacks and shirt, his sleeves rolled up looking like a well-aged sportswriter. His right leg was crossed over his left and he held a cup of coffee in his hands. He did not fit the scene in which he was placed.

Jayln and Rita talked. First softly and then to the level of a low demanding scream. "He drugged me!" Jayln yelled after each burst of explanation, not seeing Ruby at first, then catching him from the corner of her eye. "That man!" she yelled, pointing a finger to the back of Ruby's head.

He could almost feel it. From across the room it touched him in inconceivable ways, but life had always done that. And why, on this ordinary Thursday, should he give a rat's ass what happens to Jayln? What he did to her, she had done numerous times to others, sometimes by accident. Ruby simply fed her the pills she fed to others. Tit for tat.

It was a persuasive plea Jayln gave, but one Ruby had given countless times himself with no result. Ruby took a drink of coffee and stared out the lobby window past the dead and dying grass, down the driveway that rolled awkwardly out and then down a small decline into the heart of the Brookwood Apartments. White two-story constructs, dilapidated and somewhat out of place, sat in long memorable rows like military crosses. There was a flight of stairs with steel railings for each building and an occasional oak tree that pierced through bare dirt ground in no particular order. There were always children in front of the apartments, usually Hispanic. They ran mad across the grassless mounds of dirt. They were cowboys and Indians in a time when the world needed neither.

Jayln's prayers and pleas went unanswered. It was out of Rita's hands now. Too many people had already established their own ideas about what had happened, and those first conceptual ideas are hard to change. There was no one way now to stop the unstoppable even if there were changes. Ruby knew this, but he also knew the pain and anger would eventually leave Jayln. It always does. It's the hardest irrevocable lesson of all. A lesson few people want to take.

Rita apologized for the situation and offered drug rehabilitation to Jayln and told her it was for the best. "The best for what?" Jayln asked in anger. "He drugged me! I know he did. It's because I caught him leaving the Home. You know that!"

Rita offered rehabilitation and a chance to go back to work, but Jayln was stung hard from her convictions. She wanted complete exoneration or nothing at all.

"Well, then it's better this way," Rita said.

Rita's words were harsh and well rehearsed. She had been saying them her whole life. A woman of the machine. A woman with a husband and kids herself. She thought of them when she talked, when she stared down into Jayln's eyes. And she knew it wasn't for the best. She knew Ruby had gotten to her somehow. But the complaints had been there on her desk, written out on standardized forms with *Sunbridge Psychiatric and Rehabilitation Center* stamped across the top. It was all legal. And somewhere out there someone possessed the yellow copy that had accompanied her white one, filed for just the occasion. Rita took this opportunity to do what she would have otherwise been unable to do. She took the burden from her shoulders and placed it on Ruby's. It was better this way, and in the long run everyone would be happy and smiling again, or so she said.

At that moment, Jayln made a run for Ruby. It was an uncomfortable attempt based solely upon rage—one Ruby refused to turn around for. She was stopped by her husband and escorted humbly out of the Home. She yelled Ruby's name. It sounded unfamiliar, and the syllables she had broken up in her accent and anger could not be put back together. She yelled it again, followed by this threat: "It's not over!"

An uncharacteristic remark from such a religious lady. She prayed five times a day as Muhammad had suggested and was active in the Muslim community. What she said reminded Ruby of something from television, something he rarely watched but was always exposed to at the Home. She was quoting Jerry Springer subconsciously now in a way only an American can.

It did nothing to Ruby though, and as for his coffee, it was already cold. As the doors shut and the lobby cleared out, the Volvo station wagon made its way down the driveway into the heart of the Brookwood Apartments. There were brake lights and then a left turn and it was over. As quick and as cold as that. It wasn't even nine o'clock in the morning and there had already been a murder.

THE BIG FRESH

There was nothing special about the Home. To Ruby it wasn't even a home. It was a house full of bricks and faces. Bricks that stayed and faded; faces that came and went. It was a construct full of misery, one he shut out and escaped from every chance he got. Ruby was transferred to the Home from a hospital in Wilmington about four months before the Cloud and John Carter arrived.

While laid up in a bed in Wilmington in a catatonic depressive state induced by the passing of his wife, he lost himself and everything around him. His broken legs and hip added to his state with complications that happened like this: He developed a series of clots. One lodged in his right leg causing pain and swelling; the other landed in a lung causing more pain and an unfortunate transient state of psychosis. The event lasted only a week, but it left him half the man he used to be with the half he hung onto painfully throbbing like an abscessed tooth. A month later, during his morning workout with physical therapy, Ruby had a seizure. It was not his first, but it was the first in decades. They had mysteriously stopped some time around the age of seventeen. A childhood illness that often left Ruby on the ground staring blank-faced up into the heavens. They were spiritual in nature with massive flashes of overexposed light, with voices and disequilibrium. They worked themselves out slowly, oftentimes without any lingering repercussions.

As an older man, the seizure weighed heavy. Ruby had felt it coming on and was immediately sucked back into the vortex of time to when it was commonplace to lie down and ride it out. His reflexes were slower though, and time has a way of making a man forget. He was bleeding from the forehead before he realized what should have happened. It was a complication far greater than his doctors had bargained for.

It was about this time Ruby was informed that his house had been foreclosed on by the bank. This left Ruby without a gun or country to fight for. Not only had he lost his house, but he also lost his freedom. He was no longer the man who could willingly do as he pleased. A very poorly thought-out bureaucratic system and a very poorly arranged sequence of events ensured that.

Ruby blamed all this on his wife. It was at her funeral after all that he decided to take the hearse and her body and run all-balls-out across the state. Running for the sake of running because he was confused, because he had spent so many years with her, because her flesh seemed more like his and losing that was like standing naked in front of an uncomfortable crowd. It was because of her that he couldn't let go, running the hearse to its grave like a wounded horse off an embankment two stories down before hitting rock bottom. Settling with the dust and silence on one cool Wednesday morning, with the sun barely breaking the horizon, with the casket in the back on its side with a quiet reverence, all made it easy for Ruby to cry. He was there with his wife for the last time—alone, undisturbed, waiting for the vultures of humanity to come with their lights and sirens to gather up the pieces and carry them off in different directions.

Ruby lay there with his back against a shattered windshield staring at the casket, working out his good-bye in his own way. It wasn't easy—after all the time, all the years and things said, all the promises. The closer he got to saying it the further he pushed himself away. He held her there—up and over the world—in silence, yet screaming to himself through the caverns of consciousness. The moment too much. The idea not prepared for. When he saw the headlights overhead and the blue lights flashing, he knew it was over.

THE BIG FRESH

The Sunbridge Psychiatric and Rehabilitation Center was the worst. As they wheeled Ruby in, he knew it was a nursing home even though he was told differently. He could smell it. All that he had tried hard not to think about as he passed through the years of adolescence and adulthood was now slapping him in the face like an insane clown. He was weary and worn. The trip from Wilmington to the Home in the back of the ambulance was like a giant parade down the main street of the world. Nobody waving and cheering him on, but a parade nonetheless, with all the fan and fare of a homicide.

It was humiliating staring out the back window of the ambulance at all the different cars that would nudge up to its bumper—everyone sneaking a peek at the unfortunate one in the back. Ruby thought of releasing himself out the rear doors into some unfamiliar town, maybe start a new game of life there, but his legs and torso were strapped to the stretcher. Ruby asked the attendant for the reason. "We don't want you to fall out," the attendant said.

Ruby told him that he had never fallen out of bed before and doubted seriously that he would fall out of the stretcher, but the attendant was adamant and things stayed as they were.

It was a long ride from Wilmington to Siler City, one in which most would have taken the time to contemplate matters of the higher order. But Ruby forced himself down none of those roads. No, he focused on the one behind him, the one that was sucking him ass-first through country towns that held little to no importance. And he watched his own town shrink and eventually explode into nothing.

It was a new landscape now and a new day. He was a relatively young man taking one unfortunate ride, and he was unsure now when he would be getting out. It was up to the state now, and it moves slower than one man's mind can allow. It said before he left Wilmington that he might be staying a few months. "These things take time," the social worker told Ruby.

"How much time?" he asked.

There was no answer. She left a blank there for Ruby to fill in at his leisure.

The four-lane highway he traveled for so many hours eventually turned into two lanes then into rural emptiness. The ambulance driver turned off onto a secondary road and drove ten miles before realizing he was lost. He spent the better part of the afternoon correcting the mistake. Ruby took this to be a bad sign even though it provided a good laugh. If a man can get lost while he's already lost then it makes it that much more difficult to be found.

Ruby was wheeled from the back of the ambulance onto the pavement, all the while explaining to the attendant that he was perfectly fine to walk—which he wasn't. "Consider it a free ride," the attendant said.

"I have," Ruby said, "and it's not."

The attendant laughed then spotted the tattoo on the right side of Ruby's chest. It was stretched and faded and barely worth mentioning, but the attendant felt it best to change the subject from the gurney ride, so he did. "It's the only thing my father ever gave me," Ruby answered.

The attendant laughed nervously and said something about it being a nice day and continued on with his job.

It was a sunny day; that was about all Ruby gave it. The sun was out over the Sunbridge Psychiatric and Rehabilitation Center. There was even a sun on the sign out front. It was a brick sign the size of a double-headed gravestone with two azalea bushes with young blossoms for each. The sun itself was an orange circle with orange dots placed symmetrically around the outer perimeter. It was symbolic of something. Someone's twisted mind at work. Propaganda at its worse. It was like putting a welcome mat at the foot of a guillotine. It mocked all of mankind and Ruby didn't like it. Maybe if the sun was depicted setting over the ocean, symbolic of some calm end—maybe then it would have been okay. But to give a full sun to a ship full of shipwrecked sailors was going too far. It provoked more madness than necessary.

The attendant wheeled Ruby through the doors and into the lobby. It was empty and smelled strongly of industrial cleaner. There were flowers on the curtains and chairs that reminded Ruby of a funeral parlor. Once in the hall Ruby began to see familiar things—things that had been at the hospital, like wheelchairs and linen baskets. They gave him strange comfort.

The story goes like this: Ruby was wheeled through the facility with no occurrences then was released from the stretcher into a bed. The sheets on the bed were pulled back expecting him. It was the middle of the day. The attendant would not let him stand so Ruby slid himself over, waited for the attendant to leave, then maneuvered himself to the side of the bed and placed his feet on the floor. Across the room a considerably older gentleman lay in another bed. His back was propped up with pillows and he was facing Ruby. Ruby said hello, but he did not answer. The man was *out there*, staring off at some distant wall, eyes open, full of matter. Ruby shuffled slowly and unsteadily over to his bed, holding onto the bedside table as he went, then looked down at the man in the bed. On his wrist was an armband. It read: *Thomas C. McNeil*, and below that a line of numbers: *1324469*. The Irishman was marked, though Ruby suspected he did not know.

Ruby stared at Thomas for a good while, contemplating the actual scale of misery one man can get caught up in. A scale that starts with birth then runs till the end—fast, slow, easy, hard, open, closed. It was all luck. Everything that happens and will ever happen is nothing but luck—dumb and irrevocable. How silly it is to have to play the game—to clock in every morning and run with it like some new flesh. There were options though, ones Ruby refused to consider. No matter how bad it got, no matter how many times he would fall down, no matter how many people got hurt, he would never quit. And under the circumstances, with nothing much left to lose, even Thomas, with his eyes open and out of focus, looked like a fighter. Ruby respected that.

THE BIG FRESH

For the next few months Ruby worked through the great depression that had hold of his spirit and concentrated on rehabilitation, working hard with the physical therapist at the exercises used to strengthen his legs, doubling them when he could with the idea that he would get better twice as fast. He stopped living while he did this, ate what was placed before him, and slept when there was nothing left to do.

Eventually he began to come around. He started getting up early on his own, washing and grooming himself, putting on the clothes and shoes he had abandoned. He kept to himself, developing a routine that made him feel more alive. He started back reading and drinking coffee in the mornings. He refused to lie down in the afternoons like most; instead, he worked his way outside and sat on the bench in front of the Sunbridge Psychiatric and Rehabilitation Center sign and stared off down the driveway into the vicinity of the Brookwood Apartments. It was there that he first saw Lisa pulling up and getting out of a silver Honda Accord. She was a lanky-framed woman with straight brown hair that lay over her shoulders. She moved fast in the early afternoon, loading up her arms with what looked to be Bibles then disappearing into one of the apartments. Ruby saw her often after that, from a distance, and found comfort in her routines. She moved the way Ruby wanted to. And most of all she had a car.

There was always something distracting going on inside the Home. The sheer engineeral design was distracting in itself, but add on top of that a mix of geriatric and middle-aged defects who whimpered and whined their way through every obstacle of the day and a nursing staff that had little to no tolerance for it, and you had bedlam. At night it was worse. The unit was shut down and still, the air hung stale and urine-soaked, lone voices—not human—moaning in the infinite night, creating visible bars for the already visible cage. And when the help tried to do something about it, they only made it worse. Ruby knew exactly when they pulled back the covers on someone, when they removed the pillows from behind the back and legs, when they grabbed the draw pad. The yells would always change dimensions—more violent and frightened. Infantile in nature.

The help always came into Ruby's room a few times at night to check on Thomas C. McNeil. They would pull back his covers, one on each side, strip off a urine-soaked diaper and replace it. Thomas never made a sound. Ruby listened. He just lay there with his eyes focused off on a distant landscape, possibly running Stravinsky through his head—most likely nothing. The help would turn him to his opposite side, replace the pillows behind his back and legs, cover him up, sling the old diaper in the trash, and be gone.

It made Ruby feel good when they came in. He had often considered taking the task on himself but never did. Some nights, though, he would sit up beside Thomas C. McNeil's bed listening to him breathe and watching his eyes and face. His face was always oily and his thin hair matted down.

Ruby tried talking with him one night. Small talk. Thomas never replied. "That's good," Ruby said. "I was thinking the same thing."

It was easier having him that way, and the world didn't seem to mind. Ruby got to where he could carry on conversations with Thomas and feel perfectly comfortable. Everything he possibly needed to say could be said to Thomas and afterwards Ruby would feel good about it. "Take care," Ruby would say as he left out in the mornings for breakfast.

The television was always on in the dining hall for breakfast and Reverend Alfonso King was always on it. A televangelist with a call-in show on the local cable channel, he was a favorite among the old, always running off the scripture like pumping gas, turning eyes and minds with his wild analogies and predictions. He fielded calls from all over Siler City and the surrounding area and was never afraid to answer one. Ruby overheard a kid ask him one morning about Jesus and if he was on Earth at this time and what did he look like. Reverend Alfonso King sat back in his chair and laughed as if the innocence of childhood deserved it, then cut into a well-thought-out answer to her question. "Of course not, dear," he said still laughing. "But his family is. They live on Raleigh Street out by the municipal park."

"Really?" the little girl said, over the crackly reception of the phone.

Reverend Alfonso King laughed again, "Really."

Ruby stared at the screen and at the reverend, not believing what he had heard. He looked around to see if anyone else had heard it, but no one seemed overly committed to anything. Some cut smiles and laughed, others just kept their heads down and ate.

Eventually Ruby realized that Reverend Alfonso King was cracked up one side and down the other. People watched him because they didn't know what he was going to say. They didn't know if this would be the day he completely lost it or not. And everyone seemed to want him to lose it.

The Reverend Alfonso King wasn't black either as the name implied. He was a white man through and through, but he often told people that he had black ancestors and that he was thirty percent black himself. It opened up his audience. The black community took him in as one of their own.

His sermons were often wild and audacious, inaudible at times, bordering on foreign language; he occasionally drifted from the scripture into his own prophecy about Armageddon and the Rapture. Ruby wasn't a religious man but often thought that the Reverend Alfonso King knew nothing of what he preached.

Every Thursday the reverend would visit the Home. He would fill the dining hall between meals with admirers. He would drive up in an old blue Mercedes smelling of diesel, his gut wading out of a three-piece suit, and his hair always wild and unnaturally combed. It stood straight up and back as if he had slept on his face all night. He would exit the blue Mercedes smiling a smile that was unbreakable and commence to shaking hands. He worked a crowd gracefully. Always on time with something: the right gesture, the right words, the right amount of silence between those words. He had a routine that was infallible and if ever he needed an out, he would just smile, place his hand on the shoulder in front of him and move on.

Ruby caught his act one Thursday in the dining hall. He sat in the back and drank his coffee and listened. The reverend was speaking of the *end of time*. He was quoting Revelation. " 'Fallen is Babylon the Great,' " he preached. " 'She has become a home for demons and a haunt for every evil spirit, a haunt for every unclean and detestable bird.' " He paused, looked out over the crowd. " 'For all the nations have drunk the maddening wine of her adulteries. The kings of the earth committed adultery with her, and the merchants of the earth grew rich from her excessive luxuries.' "

This confused Ruby. He did not understand why a bunch of geriatrics would need or want to hear about merchants and adultery. Not to mention the city of Babylon. But the people seemed to listen, more intensely than Ruby could have imagined. As if all this talk of the end of the world was comforting, as if it made them feel better. Ruby drank the last of his coffee and stood up. That's when the Reverend Alfonso King called upon him. "You, sir!" he said. "Do you believe in the coming of the Lord?"

Ruby looked around to see who the reverend was addressing then looked at the reverend. It took Ruby a moment to compose himself. He was not a religious man, never was, and it made him uncomfortable to have to address something he felt nothing about. He did feel as if the reverend was trying to get a rise out of him and that made him, in return, want to get one from the reverend as well. After a moment more Ruby spoke up. "No, I don't."

There was a weak gasp from the crowd and a few turned around to look at Ruby. Their faces were sadly angered but humble, and Ruby felt somewhat upset at himself for playing along with the reverend. It was truth the people were looking for, not mockery; and it didn't matter in the long run if the truth was not truth at all, as long as it took them where they needed to go.

Ruby broke away from their faces and started for the door when the reverend stopped him again. "Have you forgotten who you are? And do you remember where you came from?"

Ruby cut a quaint smile at the reverend and laughed to himself at the insinuating questions and called the reverend a bastard in his own mind before answering. "Yes, I do," then made it a few more steps toward the door before stopping again.

The reverend smiled back then asked Ruby his name. "Okay," Ruby said, almost in defeat. "My name is Ruben Riggs."

The reverend was pleased that Ruby answered. He bowed his head slightly in appreciation, all the while smiling. It was a strange moment to be caught in. One in which Ruby found himself somewhat connected to the reverend in a nondenominational kind of way. The geriatric dining room crowd felt it too. "Very good," the reverend said, then turned his attention to the crowd, ending his time with a closing prayer.

Ruby didn't stick around for the prayer; instead he worked his way outside and sat on the bench facing the Brookwood Apartments. The silver Honda Accord sat parked along the road out front of the apartments, and there were a half dozen or so Hispanic children playing around it. Ruby closed his eyes and thought about home and his house. Who lived in it now? And how upset would they be if he barged in one Sunday morning and made himself at home?

Ruby thought of that scenario often and found comfort in its insidious madness. The relief of holding what was his once more. He felt so removed from it now, so erased. Still it hung from him like a thin piece of flesh; he was unable to shake it, unable to take a razor and make that surgical slice, to bury it and forget. It was much easier back then just to live. The days seemed to click by with an almost automatic beauty. There was always money and food, and his wife was always willing to give him the love that made him feel somewhat above the rest.

Before her death and the accident, Ruby was a writer. A sportswriter for the *Wilmington Tribune*. It wasn't the best paying job and Ruby admittedly didn't enjoy sports as much as he should, but it worked itself out that he wrote there for some fifteen years. Looking back, it blew his mind to consider the idea of writing about Little Leagues and the World Series for such a long time. He had always had the idea of writing a book about something far more dramatic and uncivil, something like the Bible but with characters of the nonreligious sect. He was possibly aiming for a science fiction novel.

His wife, Kay, understood all this when he spoke about it. She read his sports columns like romance novels and knew he had the potential to do it. A humanitarian and loyalist, her job as a social worker at the hospital provided all the necessary extramarital satisfaction she needed and she felt that Ruby deserved the same. That was the reason she worked the long hours. She worked and Ruby wrote his columns. One to two a week, traveling as far as Charleston, South Carolina sometimes to do it. On the side he worked at drafting his novel, made numerous attempts at starting it—the language, the tense, the mood. It never seemed to work out though. There was always something to take his mind off of it or some complication or dislike of what he had done to that point. It just never felt right. So Ruby would stop for a week or a month, go watch and write about the 1A high school football regional championship in Raleigh or a boat race in Myrtle Beach. It was so easy to just hop in the car and drive, to sit and watch, to write what the mind had already written. It was automatic and disastrous but Ruby always found a way out. He had his book to fall back on. It was his ace in the hole. When collegiate sports got to him he would run back to the book, work with it for a week or two, then trash it.

It was this routine that ate into his adulthood. There was Kay, the house, and this and that. All the while it was easy.

The day he got the call from the hospital he was in the process of starting back on the book. He had not completely trashed the pages from the last session and was about to venture further than he had ever gone before. It was a momentous day. But when the hospital informed him that something had gone drastically wrong and that his wife was dead, the book took its proper place once more in the far back corner of his mind.

Certain things that should have been done that weren't came to life after Kay's death—no life insurance, poor medical insurance. Ruby was left dumbfounded at all the things he and his wife should have done to prepare for such an event. But how do you do that and why? They had everything they needed within themselves. Looking back, it was ignorant not to at least have something to fall back on; but life demanded more of them than just paying and banking for the secure comforts of painless death. They didn't think much about it because they didn't have to. And even now, after Kay's death, Ruby had a hard time believing that he too would someday pass. The hardest thing of all was believing that she actually died. Ruby had always considered her immortal with a beauty that could never die. An immortality that reached deep within him that made him feel open to breath and invulnerable to everything. Looking back from the bench in front of the Home he now realized how much of his strength was actually hers.

After some time, the Reverend Alfonso King made his way out the front doors of the Home and into the circle drive. A few geriatric fans followed, and he shook them off one by one till it was just him standing beside his blue Mercedes. It was warm and there was a bitter stale breeze that blew up from the direction of the Brookwood Apartments. He spotted Ruby on the bench wearing nothing but a pair of slacks and a polyester dress shirt with the sleeves rolled up, looking like a sportswriter. He walked up behind Ruby and gave him a friendly nudge on the back of the shoulder then came around the bench and sat down. "You don't belong here," he said to Ruby in an almost separate but recognizable voice. "You're too young and acute."

Ruby considered the words *young* and *acute*, then considered the source. The reverend laid his back on the bench and shot a quick glance into the sky. It was blue and cloudless. "Why do they call you Ruby?" he asked. "Isn't that a woman's name?"

"It doesn't matter," Ruby answered. "It's a nickname. After Babe Ruth."

"Did you play baseball?" the reverend asked.

"No." Ruby answered.

There was a silence and a car passed to their left and entered the circle drive. The reverend stood and stretched himself out. " 'Ruben' is a biblical name from Genesis," he said, as he started walking toward his car. "It means *Behold, a son.*"

Ruby did not look to see the reverend off. Instead, he watched the children in the street. They scattered as the reverend's blue Mercedes passed. When it reached the silver Honda Accord it stopped and the reverend blew the horn. In no time the young woman was out standing beside his window. Ruby could see her lips moving and smiling but was unable to make out what she was saying. After a few minutes she leaned into the car, gave the reverend what looked to be a hug, retracted her body from the car, then watched as the reverend drove off.

It was Ruby's first impression that the reverend was a swinger. A dirty old man that used God for his own personal gains and pleasures. It fit too stereotypically well, though. But why not?

Ruby was right in most of his assumptions. The reverend did use God for his personal gain, but it wasn't swinging he delved in. The truth is, the Reverend Alfonso King was a loyal and faithful man, although divorced and rather despised by his ex-wife for reasons beyond adultery. What he preached he believed, barring the fact that he did or did not know what he was talking about. The reverend's one weakness came in the form of a white serpent. Although the reverend would disagree that it was a serpent. The reverend's weakness was also his strength because it allowed him to perform the pastoral duties he so loved to do with a fire and passion like no other. If it was diesel that started his blue Mercedes, it was, most certainly, cocaine that drove it.

THE GERMAN CONNECTION

Josef's first task upon leaving his residence was to take a long pleasurable breath and look out across what had become his work. A devastated plot of land with barbed wire fences, two abreast, some ten feet apart, that carried charges of electricity through them. They sprung out from the ground symmetrically and parallel and gave Josef a warm feeling of maturity. Upon the outer fence posts were lights that burned throughout the evening and late into the morning. They illuminated the ground between the two fences, creating a river of light wrapped in barbed wire. Josef would often stand off in the distance and marvel at its alluring beauty. Inside the fences stood large, randomly placed institutions, two stories in height and made of brick. They ran out along the edge of the barbed wire like some precise invention. Other more subtly constructed buildings were laid among the larger ones with no particular correlation to anything. Josef often found himself working within the confines of one of these.

Above all this, off in the immediate distance just past the fences, stood tall slender spruces that cut through the gray morning sky like fragile veins. They held in their existence a form of quiet harmony, a piece of gentle art that broke up the concrete, the bricks, and the barbed wire. Josef was impartial to their existence. He would never run out and cut one down himself, but he wouldn't stop someone who wanted to.

It was the earliest of mornings that awoke his soul, and he would be up before the sun to catch it. Leaving his residence and walking out among what he had made and now had become his. It was a quiet undisturbed walk from his home to where he worked with the occasional distant echo of a far-off locomotive. Josef could imagine it making its way lazily across the landscape, its steel frame heated through and through pushing black smoke from the very depths of its heart into the sky. It was a piece of machinery he did not understand, but it helped fulfill needs within his work and he respected that. Maybe in another life he would have been in the position to tear one apart to see what it was made of and how it worked, just for the fun of it.

There were few people up as early as Josef. They stood pasted in the landscape like miniature toy soldiers. Others hurried about. As Josef passed they would stop in respect, salute, then go about their business. A lot of those were guards who had been up all night standing watch over Josef's work. They were protectors of the highest order, guardian angels and deities in their own right who had just finished their work and were now to hide away in their quarters and sleep. Josef was much more powerful than they, but like the locomotive, they played a key role in his work and he was grateful for that.

At the end of Josef's walk was a door. Always a door. On the other side of this particular door would eventually be his colleagues, the men who helped him perform his work. They were dedicated loyal men, mostly chosen by himself. Scientists, physicians, and anthropologists of the highest caliber. They rose in the morning with Josef for coffee and plates of bacon and eggs. They laughed and spoke cordially of their wives and girlfriends. They smoked cigarettes like locomotives across the landscape. They were joyous, stout men who held visions high above their own personal esteem. Calm and calculating under the most stringent of circumstances, they were the arms, legs, and heart to the machine of which Josef was master.

It was here in the mess hall before anyone else's arrival that Josef found himself alone. Across the hardwood floors and hardware, he could see the cooks and laborers dicing their daily vegetables and meats. Most were empty faces full of desperation and repetition. One in particular though always seemed to catch his eye. She was young and well nourished and had eyes like his mother's, which haunted him. She had a calmness about her and unlike the others, would sometimes greet his eyes with her own. He came to fancy her being there, the way one fancies an overweight cat stretched out on a couch.

Josef would get some coffee and then a seat, one he had chosen some years back. It was positioned by a large window that overlooked a courtyard, and it made him feel good to stare out at the work taking place. He would take his seat and then thumb for a cigarette in the breast pocket of his immaculately clean woolen jacket. Light it, inhale, and sit back. From out the window he could see Werner making his way across the courtyard. Werner was a stout man with a nervous tendency to take a drink at inappropriate times, and in his walk Josef could calculate his usefulness for the day. This morning he was straight and stringent, floating on an automatic cloud. He carried himself with unusual confidence. Josef took a drag off his cigarette and contemplated Werner, exhaling the smoke into his open fist, watching as it crawled its way out. The door swung open and Werner entered. "Good morning, Josef," Werner said.

Josef did not answer. Werner got himself some coffee and joined Josef by the window. "There's been a telegraph which arrived during the night from Istanbul." Werner said in his usual nervous voice. "A proposition."

"What kind of proposition?" Josef asked.

"It did not say. But they will be arriving this evening by train."

"With a proposition?"

"Yes," said Werner.

Josef took another drag from his cigarette then put it out. "It's good to see you in spirits, Werner."

THE BIG FRESH

Eventually, Ruby got to where he could move around pretty well by himself and he began taking walks. First, he would go out behind the Home where it was easy to slip off without anyone seeing him. After breakfast he would take his coffee out the front door, take a sharp left around a couple of holly bushes, and then out across a low stand of timber that wrapped around the back of the Home. It was always dark inside the stand, and it made Ruby feel somewhat new and mysterious. He often caught himself laughing nervously at the thought of something being new and mysterious, which was always accompanied by another thought of escape. He had always considered the idea of escape to be a relative one, but one that seemed desperate at times. Where would an aged convict of the social system with no money go? And what would he do when he got there?

The first question was the hardest to answer. From Siler City the world seemed distant and somewhat detached. There was a strange reality that engulfed the city. Not *backwoods* but definitely *backwards*. Ruby had difficulty associating and relating to the basic everyday conversation of the people. It was as if they had created a new language for themselves. Collectively, they seemed to concern themselves with unimportant things—ideas and thoughts that put no bread in the kitchen or butter in the soul. Tabloid issues. Oprah and Jerry Springer. Ruby denied this at first, believing all souls had a desire to strive for that higher level of interaction that he himself was a student of: conversation that led to enlightenment—not laughter and dirty jokes.

This pissed Ruby off because he liked a dirty joke just as much as the next, but for Christ's sake, to carry on a complete conversation using nothing but anecdotes and dirty jokes was too much. Ruby offended a lot of people before realizing it was better just to shut up and let the conversation run itself out. Eventually he was left alone and under certain situations would have felt bad, but under this one he was much happier. It reminded him of a line in a John Prine song: "Strangers had forced him to live in his head."

How true.

One day he decided to see where the woods came out and started walking. It wasn't fifteen minutes before he was clumsily trying to climb an oily embankment behind a Super Saver convenience store. A row of air-conditioning units was running, and it gave the task a rushed, awful feeling. Ruby slipped and fell to his knees a few times before making it to the top. Once there, though, he had a nice view of the surrounding area and saw a well-used path that cut around to the side of the oily incline. Ruby laughed.

The convenience store was on 3rd Street just down from the hospital. Ruby could vaguely make out the lettering on the brick sign in front of the hospital. It was a place he had never visited. That was a good thing. Out in front of the store there was one car at the gas pumps. A few other cars lined the front of the store. It had to have been around ten o'clock in the morning.

Ruby stood there contemplating escape. From the pavement it seemed unrealistic. Too many unfathomable miles of nothing to consider. The town was old and sat geographically in the middle of the state, four or five hours from Wilmington. Interstate driving most of the way. He could hitch a ride. That idea was not completely dead in the twenty-first century; it was a risky one though. The ethics of hitchhiking had vanished with the sixties, leaving one with a potluck's chance in hell of finding a good, safe ride.

Ruby brushed off his pants and straightened himself up. A great decision lay before him. He would have to get out of town quick if it were to happen. And if it were to happen it needed to be now. To the side of the store was a phone and Ruby used it to call an old friend from work. There were three rings before the friend's wife Sarah answered. Her voice was scratchy and nervous; Ruby hadn't liked it in the past and didn't like it now. The automated operator stated that it was a collect call and asked Ruby to state his name. Ruby did not answer. He listened instead to Sarah fumbling to light a cigarette. It was disconcerting and humorous altogether. A moment passed; then Sarah made an animalistic grunt and hung up. Ruby stayed to listen to the emptiness, the receiver against his ear, staring off into the direction of an old Purina dog food factory that stood in the lonely urban landscape, echoing a sad remembrance of the past, present, and future. He was interrupted by a heavy hand that slapped against his backside.

It was Geraldine Griffin, a social worker whose office was at the Home. Ruby had spoken to her many times before and felt more connection with her than with anyone else in town. She was fat and black and proud of it, carrying her weight like some glorious crucifix. "Ruben Riggs," she said, "what in God's name are you doing out here?"

There was a moment when Ruby felt concern but then it faded with the prospects that he could possibly talk his way out. "I had to make a call," he said, smiling somewhat to distract Geraldine from drawing any hasty conclusions.

"What's wrong with the phone in your room?" she asked.

"It's broken."

"And the one in the lobby?"

"Broke too."

There was a moment of silence; then Geraldine cut a smile and started laughing. "Broke," she said, in between the chuckles. Ruby joined in.

"Come on," she said, and started walking toward the Toyota Tercel parked beside the gas pumps.

Ruby made some adjustments to his pride then followed. As she pulled the car into the road and accelerated she told Ruby that it was okay and that she would take him back to the Home after she ran an errand. Ruby sat back in the seat relieved and stared at the old dog food factory as it passed to his left.

While driving, Geraldine spoke to Ruby cordially and it made him feel somewhat connected. She spoke of the town and of her life, rarely asking Ruby about his own. It did not matter, it was good to be out of the Home—traveling, seeing the world unfold again from behind a windshield. Ruby traveled a lot when he was writing sports columns, from one small town to the next. After a while they all began to look the same: miniature shopping malls and fast-food stands with the same colors and names, smelling of the same burnt flesh—chicken, pork, cow. A genocide of the sort. Industrialized and maximized for supreme efficiency. And beside every fast-food stand was a gas station and a car wash; and beside the car wash was a car lot. Geraldine spoke none of this. Her mind was on Saturday and a wedding. Names and faces she put to those names flashed by Ruby like the landscape outside the car. "Your son?" Ruby asked, politely spiking the conversation for interest.

"Lord, no. Grandson. You must not know how old I am?"

Ruby didn't know, but he quickly realized that Geraldine was probably older than he was. That made him feel awkward and useless. He thought of the Home and what he had become and almost cried. "Tyron is my oldest," Geraldine said, taking Ruby from his misery. "It's his son, Anthony, that's getting married. Marrying a girl that works at the hospital. She's a nurse. Her name is Jessie. Sweet girl. Skinny, though. Listen. Why is it you don't talk much? You too old to be shy," Geraldine said half serious.

"I want to get out of here," Ruby said bluntly.

"I figured as much," Geraldine said. "You're in a unique situation, you know? You could go home if you had a home to go to. But you don't. And, on top of that, you have no immediate family. It's a catch. Do you see the problem, Ruby? The state doesn't feel comfortable sending you out into the world with no place to go. Being in the situation you're in, the state takes it upon itself to do what it sees as right. What's right for them may not be right for you. It's messed up. I know it; you know it. But it's what we have and it's how it works. I apologize for saying it like this and I think it's a shame, but that's how it is. It's a damn shame that it's not perfect."

"It's okay," Ruby said.

"It's not okay," Geraldine said. "I see it too much—way too much."

Before taking Ruby back to the Home, Geraldine made a few stops. The last was to a trailer park heading west out of town. The trailers were single wide and dilapidated, placed in no particular order throughout a scant stand of young pines. Trash and old cars lay about them, and stray dogs wandered about freely digging in and under and around them both. A sign at the front entrance of the driveway said Pine Knoll Trailer Park. It was home to a large community of illegal immigrants who were promised lots of money if they came to America to work. In Siler City that work was in chicken plants. Large processing factories where chickens came in on the back of an eighteen-wheeler, caged and barely breathing, and left skinned or not in cellophane, ready to eat. It was within that process that the immigrants worked long, unforgivable hours in rubber boots and gloves, slipping around in guts and blood like ice skaters, decapitating, slicing open from breast to butt, pulling out handfuls of internal organs, and then running a hook through the chicken's hind legs and sending it on down the line. At shift's end they stream out of the plant like high school quarterbacks who just won the homecoming game. They pile into plant buses or Z28s and are gone.

Ruby wasn't surprised to see the squalor. He had seen it before in other towns. Some of the greatest baseball players in the world came from such dissonance. It did make him view his own situation with a little more prudence though, and if just for a moment, it gave him hope.

Geraldine maneuvered her car down the rugged, one-lane, dirt road that zigzagged its way through the trailers, going directly through the front yards of some. There was no grass, like back at the Home, but worse: exposed tree roots like petrified serpents jutted out here and there in the yards and along the road. The car would shift and sway as it rolled over them. All the trailers were faded, and random faces could be seen peering from curtainless windows. Young, expressionless faces, mostly girls and young women. Their eyes holding no dreams or hopes of ever dreaming. They reminded Ruby of most of the residents back at the Home. A startling comparison that forced Ruby to look at Geraldine for direction.

The car made its way systematically through all this and pulled up directly in front of a faded green trailer that sat somewhat away from the others. It was short, maybe forty feet in length with no more than ten for its width. The front door had no screen and looked as if it had been kicked in numerous times. It now stood some quarter of the way open. There were cinder blocks placed at the foot of the front door for steps and a trash can filled with white trash bags full of garbage. More lay all over and around the can itself. Many had been torn into and strewn about. Others were waiting.

Geraldine nudged her car up to the foot of the trash and blew the horn. A young Hispanic girl came to the door. In Spanish, Geraldine asked if Maia was there and if so to get her. The young girl nodded and disappeared. A moment later Maia came to the door with an infant no more than a few months old in her arms. In Spanish, Geraldine asked if her boyfriend, Roberto, was in the house. Maia humbly shook her head no. Geraldine asked if they were still seeing each other and she shook her head no again. Geraldine looked over at Ruby and shook her head. "She's lying."

Geraldine stuck her head back out the window and asked to see the baby. Maia brought the baby out to the car and held it out in front of the window for Geraldine to see. "Turn," Geraldine said, making a motion for Maia to turn the baby so she could see its backside. The baby was naked and flawless and Ruby stared at it like a raw jewel, thinking of how perfect and pure the world must seem from such vista. Geraldine said a few more words, and Maia took herself and the baby back inside. "It's a shame," Geraldine said. "Man beats her to death and she still has his baby."

Ruby did not reply; instead, he let Geraldine maneuver her

car out of the park and back to town.

They pulled up into the circle drive at the Home and what Ruby was expecting to happen never did. No cops. No nurses freaking out. No nothing. The Home was undisturbed by his absence. Ruby said his thank you and good-bye, and Geraldine reminded him that she was stuck here, too. During the walk through the lobby, Geraldine stopped Ruby and placed her hand on his shoulder. "Don't forget who you are," she said and walked off.

Ruby knew the trip to the trailer park was for him and he did appreciate it, but something kept telling him that the truth of his situation was more painful than the marked reality of others. He felt sorry for Maia and for the baby, but it was her choice to come to America not his. It was also her choice to continue on with the fatalistic love story. In hindsight Ruby would have rather had Geraldine tour him through a penitentiary with walls and bars more aesthetically visible than his own. He would have rather seen the young souls that fill the cages and heard their growls and whimpers. He'd rather have smelled the food they ate and the latrines in which they squatted. He needed real, defined cages that were sanctioned by the state and recommended by the country, closed to the normal ones. Maia had a chance. Once she learned some rudimentary English and the ways of America, she'd wise up; and the baby had odds like all the rest. So what if he had to start from the confines of a rusty mobile home; at least the door was open—if only a quarter of the way.

It did give Ruby something to think about and he was thankful for that. That night after Geraldine had taken him to the trailer park, he spoke at length with Thomas C. McNeil about it. Long uninterrupted periods of monologue that gave Ruby ideas not thought of or discussed in years. Thomas was a marvelous listener and that provided Ruby with the platform to let it all out—which he did. Afterwards, he took Thomas by the hand and thanked him.

After that, Ruby began frequent travels outside the Home. He had regained enough control of his left extremities that if he concentrated and took it slow he could make himself seem as normal as the rest. Of course, it took time, but time is what Ruby was made of at this point.

He now found himself walking off in all directions, even down the driveway that led into the Brookwood Apartments. It was an uninspiring walk—beyond the simple fact of walking itself—but one he had been wanting to take for some time. The silver Honda Accord was in its usual spot and Ruby walked up to it. In its back seat was a scattered stack of pamphlets. Ruby leaned forward for a better look. It was a stack of religious pamphlets with a suspended cross on the front and the title *Making the Connection* floating above it. Below the cross and words was the author's name: Reverend Alfonso King. At that moment a voice cut through the afternoon silence. Ruby straightened up to see the young woman leaning out of an apartment door. She looked distressed and bothered. "Is there a problem?" she said again, with Ruby hearing this time.

"No," Ruby exclaimed, playing dumb. "I was looking at your books here," pointing into the back seat.

She looked unimpressed and Ruby could have thought of a hundred different ways he would rather have met her. She was young and beautiful in a plain, natural way, and it made Ruby feel inferior. Her hair was straight and flat and reached comfortably down to her shoulders. She wore faded jeans and a white tank top that revealed little of her petite chest. She had no shoes or socks on, and that somehow made Ruby think of the reverend. "Look," he said, "I stay up there," pointing up the hill toward the Home. "I was just going out for a walk. I didn't mean to frighten you. Honestly, I was only looking at the—"

A telephone rang inside her apartment and she left. Ruby was angered at first; then he resolved himself to the fact that he at least tried.

At the bottom of the hill, the driveway intersected with Raleigh Road. To his left, he could see brick buildings in the distance—cars crawling slowly in and out of that framework like metallic cockroaches. This was the historic part of town. The forgotten part of town. Buildings that had survived a century of progress and decline, filled now with rare coffee shops and Hispanic record stores, smelling like mildew and bacon. Ruby could not see this from the road, but he did see the empty factories that lined the outskirts of its historic shell. Broken windows and boarded-up doors, railroad tracks with weeds from the summer past growing upon its back like hair. A church steeple pierced through it all to stand off and over it in the distance. No bells.

In front of Ruby across the road was a park dug into a wooded landscape. It was empty and rusted. To the right the highway was alone—a few houses but nothing more. It cut straight through the landscape then disappeared. Ruby went left.

Just as he made it to the sidewalk along the front of a Piggly Wiggly grocery store, Ruby was startled by a horn blowing close behind him. He turned around to see it was the silver Honda Accord and the young woman. She was smiling and remarkably more relaxed. "You need a ride?" she yelled. "I'm going to the library."

"Sure," Ruby answered.

"Where you headed?" she asked as Ruby took a seat.

"To the library," Ruby said, and she laughed.

"Look, about that business at the car," she said. "There's been some robberies lately around the neighborhood and I'm a little uptight about it."

"Understood," Ruby answered. "I'm fairly new in town. My name is Ruby."

"Ruby," she repeated. "That's a strange name for a man."

"Not really," Ruby replied. "It's a nickname. My real name is Ruben. Ruben Riggs."

"I'm Lisa."

Ruby stared into her eyes. They were green and infinite—neither sad, nor complicated. She smiled and he smiled and they rode silently on into the heart of the historic part of town toward the library.

The Wren Memorial Library was located across the street from the Dry Dock Seafood Restaurant. The library was named after a Mr. Richard Wren who owned one of the factories in the historic district that was now closed down. He eventually went insane, and spent many months, on and off, in the local hospital. Dementia had turned him into a babbling baby boy and eventually nothing. This fact struck Ruby as ironic for no good reason. A building down from the seafood restaurant was the First Baptist Church—a towering brick building whose front steps poured out into the street. From those steps one could look out across the street to the Town Hall and then to the left of it to the Sheriff's Department. Upon first inspection, the close proximity posed no immediate concern.

Ruby sat back, relaxed, and enjoyed the ride. Once at the library, he helped Lisa unload all the pamphlets and then faked as if the book he was looking for wasn't there. "How about another one?" she asked. "No need," he said.

Lisa bounced around about her business with a lazy enjoyment that made Ruby feel detached, and in return he himself bounced around with an almost childlike gaiety. On the way back they stopped off at Brownie Lue's for lunch, and Lisa insisted that she buy and would not take no for an answer.

It was the best meal he had had in months. Not for the food *per se*, although it was good, but more for the company. In the Home and at the other institution eating had always been a personal thing, not social like with his wife and friends. That took a while to adjust to. With Lisa, Ruby felt human—the same as with Geraldine, but on a more intimate level. Lisa was young, but she wasn't that young. Ruby estimated her to be in her mid-twenties. Old enough to know a few things without having the inconvenience of too much baggage. She was a woman, that's what Ruby told himself and that's what he believed, far beyond the thoughts of Kay and his house in Wilmington, and far beyond the accident and the institutions that transformed him into the man he now was. All had been erased, if only for the moment, and replaced with something good, something that was tangible yet unreal. It didn't matter how far it would go; it had exceeded his expectations already and every minute more was nothing but a bonus. Ruby was in the black for the first time in many months. He could feel his old self slipping back through the cracks of light. It was still there, even though he had lost faith—given up on it like he had to with his wife and everything she was part of. He thought his old self was buried along with her or in one of the institutions that housed his broken soul and bones for so long. Or maybe it had been burned and scattered over the harbor in which he once lived during some drunken exodus that he had never returned from. Ruby never blamed himself for his soul's absence. He knew it was the circumstances that had rid him of it. He just never thought he would see it again. Sitting across from Lisa talking of nothing in particular he could see it, and as the conversation stretched he felt as if she saw it too.

Ruby let himself go and talked freely about things that were once common. It was as if he had never missed a beat: the same old sportswriter with columns to revise and a book to formulate.

Lisa spoke freely too. She was not afraid to tell Ruby that he didn't look like someone from the Home. "You're cleaner," she said with a nervous grin, not wanting to offend him.

"Have you ever put a puzzle together?" Ruby asked. "Every piece having to fit just so for the rest of the puzzle to work?"

Lisa shook her head.

"The events that landed me where I am today were pieces of a puzzle. Unfortunately for me, they all fit. It's the craziest damn puzzle I've ever been a part of."

Lisa was not saddened by this, neither was Ruby, and during the course of the remainder of their meal he told her everything that had happened to him. On the way home she told Ruby she wished she were able to do something for him. Ruby felt heartened by the comment and thanked her. "Come by anytime," she said as Ruby got out of the car and started slowly up the incline to the Home. "We'll drink a beer."

THE BIG FRESH

A few days later he was sitting in Lisa's apartment drinking a beer. His third. The radio was on and Lisa was dancing around the living room showing Ruby the moves she used as a cheerleader in high school. It was a graceful dance that entranced him. Afterwards she fell down beside him on the couch laughing. The telephone rang and she ran to answer it. There was hasty dialogue, and then she returned. "It was my boyfriend," she said, standing over Ruby looking down.

"I don't care," he said extending out his hand.

They made love that afternoon in the apartment ... under warming skies ... with young Hispanic boys running circles out in the street ... with Reverend Alfonso King reciting Shakespeare and Genesis ... with Thomas C. McNeil staring down the walls ... with the help out back on the loading dock smoking cigarettes and laughing mad, unconcerned with Ruby—too much to think about, not enough time in the day. "Leave Ruby alone with his coffee," they probably would have said. "He's fine." Ruby—with nothing to say to anyone. Ruby—who can walk now, who should be helping the help, whose real name means *Behold, a son.*

It was good for Ruby to get out, to explore the flesh. And it was good for Lisa too. She did not tell Ruby at the time, but she had been drowning in the town as well. For her though, it seemed worse because she was free to go anywhere at any time. Her apartment had become her cage, with the few bars she had invented. It started in high school with a restlessness that drove her to cigarettes and beer, and then to hallucinogens when she could find them. She quit cheerleading because she couldn't stand the smell of football players, and constantly having to look up into the bleachers made her feel like a stripper. If she was getting paid that would have been all right, but she wasn't. She started giving her body to every car salesman that would take her. At seventeen, she could sleep with a forty-year-old man who was married and feel good about it. She had an abortion at eighteen and broke up a marriage in the process. She joined the Air Force to get away from it all but then never went. It was her father that got her out of that. She stayed around town after high school and became a faded porn star. People watched her deteriorate with the weather, like a bar of soap. She continued her promiscuous ways, was engaged, but then fucked that up. She finally moved out of her parent's house into the Brookwood Apartments, found love in a younger man named Christopher Riley, and started working for her father. She gave herself to Ruby for two reasons. First, she had not changed; it was still in her nature to be that girl that had caused her so much trouble, only the opportunities had diminished after high school. Second, Ruby was a charismatic man. He carried himself with a dignity not seen in younger men—Lisa had always been attracted to that. Ruby was lean and well maintained and his gray hair was masked by the blonde that still remained. Lisa saw him as a fugitive, an aged rebel now stuck in the system. She had compassion and a strange desire to make it all better for him. They started on the couch; then took it to the bed. They spent the afternoon there exploring each other's humanity and when the doorbell rang they did not stop. Only when Lisa heard the pounding fist did she realize her boyfriend, Christopher Riley, was standing outside.

She jumped off of Ruby and began frantically searching for her clothes. Ruby laid there until she waved him into action. "Come on!" she said in a hysterical whisper.

Ruby laughed to himself and then obeyed. Lisa ran into the living room and grabbed their clothes. Together they dressed. "Do you have a back door?" Ruby asked.

"Yes, damn it, but no steps."

Ruby put his clothes on and went to the back door. It was some five feet to the ground. He could not chance it. He closed the door and rejoined Lisa in the bedroom. Christopher Riley continued to knock. One long continuous knock. It had psychological effects. "Going out the back is out of the question," Ruby said.

"That's okay. Just sit on the couch and talk religion."

"Religion?"

"Yeah. Just act like you're a preacher."

When Lisa opened the door Christopher Riley shot forward into the living room. He was a young, well-built man of about twenty. He had strict round eyes and cropped hair—a cut Ruby had observed on many of the young men in town. He wore blue jeans with a red jersey T-shirt and sunglasses that made him look remarkably like a state trooper. Ruby sat on the couch with his legs crossed, unaffected by the young man's demeanor. As a young man Ruby had thrown enough fists to know he didn't mind doing it again if necessary.

Christopher walked through the living room without saying a word, looking around for something. He looked at Lisa, then at Ruby, then went into the kitchen, and came out. He conducted himself with an exacting discipline that seemed to Ruby to require some form of advanced training. Ruby sat on the couch with a disdained smirk on his face. Christopher came out of the kitchen and went into the bedroom, and then out. "Who is this?" he asked Lisa, pointing directly at Ruby.

"This is Reverend Riggs. He's new in town," Lisa said, smiling nervously.

"Reverend?" Christopher said. "Why did it take you so long to answer the door?"

There was a moment of uncertain silence then Ruby spoke up. "Praying," he said. "I was just about to leave and we were praying."

Christopher looked at Lisa and she nodded her head in agreement. Then Ruby stood up and extended his hand. "It was good to meet you, but I must be going."

Christopher hesitated; then extended his hand as well. They shook. Ruby said his good-byes and showed himself out the door.

Outside, the sun was warm and it hit Ruby's face like new medicine. He straightened his shirt and began the descent down the stairs. Inside he could hear Christopher's voice rising in argument. He thought of going back in, but then decided it was best to let Lisa handle the affair. All the way to the Home he thought of what he had gotten himself into and it only made him smile. It was a step in the right direction—one Ruby hoped to be making a lot more of.

THE ISLAM CONNECTION

Jayln Amir saw Ruby coming up the hill out of the heart of the Brookwood Apartments. She was sitting in the lobby waiting for him when he walked through the door. Ruby did not see her at first and then caught her out of the corner of his eye. He thought it best to keep walking but she called him down. Ruby stopped and walked over to her as if nothing had happened. "Mrs. Amir," Ruby said humbly.

She was not impressed. "It is against policy for a resident to be off property grounds. You cannot go off property grounds anymore."

Ruby played dumb and told her that he had only gone as far as the yard. "I watch you come up the hill," she said in response, and then stood up. "I will write this up as an incident."

She walked off, leaving Ruby to ponder the hidden severity of an *incident*.

Around five that afternoon, before leaving for home, Rita Hymer called Ruby into her office and discussed the incident. It was in the form of a standardized sheet of paper that added up to the equivalence of a very legal statement that could be used if necessary in a court of law. It sat in front of Rita on her desk. She was not interested in discussing it but was legally bound to do so just the same. She ran Ruby through company policy and then through her own philosophy, which was that she didn't care as long as no one got hurt. "I do not want to cage you up here, Ruby," she said, "but these policies are here for a reason. There have been many cases where residents have gotten lost. They have died out there, Ruby."

She spoke as if the world was cruel and indifferent to the nursing home resident—and in actuality it was—but Ruby sat high above the standard, placing himself there for his own protection. He did not need the protection of the Home or the State. His fate lay in his own hands, and it was his heart that kept it there. Ruby listened to what Rita had to say and gave her the respect she deserved.

When he got up Rita did the same and they extended hands. Then she said something that was worth being said and consequently heard: "Jayln is a good nurse, but she will get you into a lot of trouble."

Ruby smiled and it was over.

THE GERMAN CONNECTION

Josef finished breakfast and excused himself from the table. Outside, just off the steps, he pulled out a pair of white cotton gloves and placed them on his hands. They weren't so much for warmth as they were for looks; aesthetically, he thought they made him look good. In the afternoons he'd usually add a riding crop to the gloves to give his appearance a very strict, demanding appeal. He liked standing out in a crowd and as his wife said, he was perfect and chiseled.

The Institution was alive now with people and possibility, with the sun positioned just to the right of a beautiful black cloud that stained the landscape a tenuous dull gray, casting these playful shadows along the courtyard which made Josef feel all warm and giddy inside. It was an unexplainable response to an otherwise uneventful meteorological event. Of course, he let none of this be seen. Even to himself, it passed as quickly as it came.

Everyone stopped what they were doing as Josef passed by them in the courtyard. Many commented to themselves on how perfect the white cotton gloves fit the rest of his uniform. Others commented on his black leather boots that held an immaculate shine even in the dust. Others were struck by the way he walked and the depth and color of his eyes. He was a picture of perfection. An image of God.

Josef acknowledged their respect with a raised right hand and passed by gracefully. Before entering the Block, he took a walk around the back of the Institution where the trains came in. There were none docked at the time. He walked up to the tracks and looked down. Three sets of tracks butterflied out, converging just before reaching the main wall. There they joined as one and exited the Institution. Josef followed the one track with his eyes until it disappeared and then followed it back. It was smooth and precise and represented a lifeline to Josef's work. It was the jugular vein of the whole machine.

The gate in which the track passed to enter the Institution was a two-story brick building with the appeal of a fort. A tower stood another two stories above the track entrance. Aesthetically, it possessed intimidation far greater than Josef's riding crop could ever command. Josef liked this because he considered the gate an extension of himself. When he had his riding crop he would sometimes stand off in the distance and brush down the gate with impressive accuracy like a child placing his finger over the sun. He owned the gate and everything in it. But there were no trains to come through it this morning. Not yet.

Josef walked back into the heart of the Institution and entered the Block. He went to his office and placed his white cotton gloves and woolen jacket in their appropriate places and then covered his immaculate suit with a white lab coat, checking his face and dress in the mirror behind the door before leaving.

In the Lab, Werner and the others were already hard at work. They acknowledged Josef's presence then continued what they were doing. Josef stood back and observed with pride. The tables, the rooms, the instruments, everyone involved. It all created within Josef an uncontrollable urge to smile.

Werner was the first to break his concentration. Josef saw him from across the room. He was standing over a surgical table with a young vassal laid out before him silently moaning. Werner had a look of confusion and disgust upon his face. Josef walked over to the table and stared down. The vassal lay supine and naked, his finger and toes gangrenous, the right side of his abdomen punctured, spurting blood. The blood ran from the table onto the floor and splattered graciously onto Josef's shiny black boots. "Christ, Werner," he said, staring down at his boots.

Herta walked over and asked what the problem was. He saw the blood on Josef's boots and looked at Werner and shook his head. Herta liked Werner but thought that the pressure of being a scientist and surgeon had turned him into a sloppy drunk.

Werner was stone-faced staring out over the young vassal as if he were an ocean to cross, unaware that blood had so meticulously splattered on the boss's boots. Others in the room stopped what they were doing and gathered around. Carl, a professor and gynecologist, pulled up behind Herta and asked what was going on. "It looks as if Werner popped another liver," he whispered over his shoulder.

"Certainly," Carl said, staring over at Josef then down to his boots.

"You need to prepare for these things," Josef demanded, as he walked over to the glass medicine cabinet.

He opened it and pulled out a vial of phenol hexobarbitone—it was almost empty. Josef took a syringe and pulled out its contents, advanced the plunger, shook out the air bubbles and then advanced the plunger farther until a precise stream of solution shot from the bevel of the needle. Josef walked calmly over to Werner. "Be more careful next time," he said, giving Werner a grin then ramming the needle into the young vassal's heart and injecting the solution.

"We do not have time to waste," Josef said, staring over the young vassal whose chest was barely rising now. "If you have a problem with a subject then go on to the next. I have said this over and over. There is more than enough work to do here."

Horst, Carl, and Herta stood shaking their heads in agreement. Even Werner, who could not deny the unquestionable truth of what Josef was saying eventually found his head shaking in agreement as well.

Josef walked off leaving everyone to stare at the young vassal, the needle still stuck in his heart.

The Block laid out flat and open, full of air and madness. It was surgical in nature with the aura of infection. The interior walls were painted white and from them hung massive highways of piping and radiators, windows with bars, and the ever-present eye chart for the blind. Surgical tables lined down the side of the wall, each exposed to the other. No need for curtains. Upon them lay vassals of a wide assortment, thin and frail with the eyes of Jesus. Most were silent, staring out straight ahead or straight up into the ceiling; others found it hard to sit quietly—they yelled and squirmed, prayed for their misery to end. Some with gangrenous toes and feet, others with typhus, tuberculosis, scarlet fever, hepatitis, or diarrhea. They lay one next to the other in one long miserable line of catastrophe.

They were brought to the Institution by circumstance in rail cars and trucks, dispatched out among the barbed wire to live. Their homes—somewhere out there—had been given up to refugees, no need for luxury now, no comfort for the soul. There were bombs to be considered and a tallyman to consider them.

Outside the Institution was the barbed wire that seemed to cross the great scapes of land, over mountains and miles. There was a war—the greatest of wars—that all the world held as its own. There were bombs and bombers, flesh frozen in shrapnel; there were arms and armor and a bullet for every man that stood up for it. There was no more control than what one single individual could give to himself. The institute of law and understanding had dissolved in the pits and barrels of blood that now drenched the land like some unwanted shower. No more the day of equality; no more the prudent and worthy. If there was a sign for the time, then it was over the entrance to the Institution in which the vassals now lived. It read "Work will set you free." It was that duty that sickened them and eventually brought them to Josef.

Upon arrival to the Institution the vassals were asked to give up their possessions and positions in life, which they did. Their possessions in a pile; their positions like smoke. They exchanged their names for numbers which were tattooed upon their skin. Their hair was cut and sold to industry. They were placed in barracks and given salami and asked not to pray out loud. In the mornings they were given another piece of salami and work duty. Some were placed in fields to dig massive holes; others worked the crematoriums where unfortunate vassals were taken and burned and released into the atmosphere like dirty snowflakes. Others found themselves working alongside the owners of the Institution performing sacrilegious duties upon their own kind.

Josef had his own help but rarely used them except for cleanup. In his precise business of medicine and experimentation only the most skillful of hands were needed. Rarely did he ever see them working. Josef had become a myth among the vassals, and most did their best to stay as far away from him as possible. Back at the barracks, late into the evening, they would tell stories to the others of his horrific nature. Mad, unwinding tales of a man who sought misery out like one would a flower. "It's the truth," a vassal would say to a group of disbelievers. "As I was mopping the floor he came in polished from boots to hair. There was a man on the table who had broken his foot during work duty. His foot was twisted out of shape. The Doctor grabbed it and twisted it farther till it was turned almost completely around. The man yelled and the Doctor summoned me and two others to hold him down. We did. We laid him flat and the Doctor told me to come hold his foot. 'Pull it,' he said, and I did. He then took a razor and began cutting down between the bone until the foot came off and I was left holding it. The man passed out and was left to bleed on the table. I was told to take the foot to the crematorium, which I did."

Others had stories too. Wild and seemingly inventful ones about the Doctor and his mad deeds. Stories of his dissecting live infants and sticking needles in eyes and of unanesthetized castrations and dissections of breast and other bodily organs and limbs. There were stories of his collections of bones and body parts and the wildest of all: a pair of Siamese twins that he had ripped apart then sewn back together. "I saw it," a vassal said to the others, "as cold as the morning he did it."

"No!" said most.

"Yes," the vassal insisted. "He cut them then sewed them together."

"No!"

"Yes! And they lived."

THE BIG FRESH

John Carter arrived late one Thursday morning. They brought him in an unmarked ambulance. No lights or sirens flashing. It was a soft, uneventful journey up the drive through the Brookwood Apartments into the circle out front the Sunbridge Psychiatric and Rehabilitation Center. The driver stopped in front of the doors, left the ambulance idling in park, and got out. Ruby had just come from Lisa's apartment and was sitting out front on the bench. He was not moved by these particular actions, but when the driver and his assistant opened the rear doors of the ambulance and a great holler went out across the parking lot, he got off the bench and walked over to the front of the ambulance. Through the front windshield he could see back to the rear where the two ambulance attendants stood looking in with a somewhat not-so-surprised look on their faces (as if the man in the back had hollered all the way to the Home). Ruby could only make out the back of the man's head in the ambulance. He had wild grayish blonde hair full of tangles and curls, which yanked and swayed like a new language.

The ambulance attendants stood guard until a nurse and her assistant joined them. The nurse was Elnora Brown, a fake Buddhistic nurse with cavities for a soul; and her assistant was Julius Holmes, fat and proud and somewhat paranoid all at once. Julius saw John Carter first and backed off. "What the hell is wrong with him?" he asked the attendants. "Why's he jerking like that?"

There was no answer from the attendants. John Carter smiled. "You're a chubby, little, fat fuck, aren't you?" John Carter said, kicking his head from side to side wildly, with a tendency toward the insane.

"That's enough," Elnora said, motioning for the attendants to pull him out.

John Carter laughed. "Ah, the sister in charge. The one with the keys. The one who holds my dick like a drumstick. I'll dream of you tonight, baby."

Ruby moved around to the side of the ambulance to where Julius stood. Julius saw Ruby and nudged him. "You people are all crazy."

"You're just now figuring that out?" Ruby responded.

They rolled John Carter out the back of the ambulance then

raised the stretcher waist height. John Carter was smiling mad, staring at Elnora like an old lover. Ruby was unimpressed with his demeanor but felt somewhat connected to his madness. He had felt it before on his ride from Wilmington, and although he did not display his disapproval for the situation as John Carter did, it was an option he had considered.

When the stretcher wheeled around John Carter saw Ruby for the first time. There was a moment of adjustment—silence, that is—as their eyes dissected each other and then met. There was a strange familiarity about the moment, and it made Ruby feel weak and unimportant. He felt the intimidation Julius had felt and was disappointed at himself for not being able to control it. John Carter had been taken back too. He stopped laughing and jerking, and was not smiling now. He stared at Ruby with quiet contemplation and concern, breaking off only when the stretcher lunged forward. Halfway through the door he yelled, "Wait!"

He raised his hands over his head and turned back to look at Ruby. "Behold. A son," he said, opening his mouth to a wide slicing grin.

The attendants were amused by this but proceeded to push the stretcher on through the door. Ruby thought of what the Reverend Alfonso King had said to him earlier and what John Carter had repeated and was unimpressed at the correlation—at best they were both religious fanatics with too much time on their hands. He followed the stretcher into the lobby and out the other side and watched as they wheeled John Carter down the hall and out of sight. "Enjoy," Ruby said to John Carter, thinking of his own ride through the halls some months back. Years it seemed now. He, a veteran, pitying others as others had pitied him. What a difference a few months made. Ruby went to the cafeteria and got a cup of coffee then walked back outside.

They wheeled John Carter about halfway down the main hall then maneuvered the stretcher into a room where there was an older gentleman sitting up on the side of his bed in a somewhat meditative position. His name was Charles Apple. He stood up respectfully when the stretcher rolled through the door. He saw John Carter and was immediately frightened.

John Carter was a tall, lanky man with eyes blue, dark, and defiant—sunken into a face that demanded attention. And even in his state of invalidation and detention, he possessed an unholy demeanor that sent Charles Apple to stand behind his bed.

They rolled John Carter into the room and placed his stretcher parallel to the bed closest to the door. Elnora Brown and Julius Holmes followed closely behind. "You may want to step out for a minute, Charlie," Elnora said to Charles Apple.

Charles had a problem with speaking—a dyslexic impediment that forced him to repeat what he heard and speak entirely in third person. It was cute at first but eventually drove people away from him. "Charlie may want to step out for a minute," he said, smiling at Elnora nervously as he made his way past the stretcher.

John Carter felt his nervousness and when Charles got close enough to the stretcher John Carter lunged forward and began to bark like a dog. Charles let out a terrifying yelp and ran out the door. "That's why you're tied down," Elnora said. "You can't control yourself."

It was the truth. John Carter had a problem with control. It stemmed from a rare medical condition that few physicians knew or wanted to know anything about. He was antisocial in nature and bordered on schizophrenic. Most physicians, for the sake of argument, just called it Alzheimer's.

John Carter had been institutionalized many years for it. He had become a ward of the state. No family. No friends. Nothing to call his own. He moved from Home to Home like some geriatric gypsy. When one Home got tired of his evil ways they would move him off to the next. Dozens he had stayed in and dozens he had destroyed in one fashion or the other. Most kept him tied down in a back room away from the staff and residents, walked him two or three times a day for posterity, gave him three meals a day and a television, and dosed him with Risperdal in the mornings and afternoons and Haldol at night—which, in theory, was meant to put him to sleep.

Like Charles Apple, Julius Holmes was also frightened of John Carter. There was something not right about the man, something evil and undetermined. There was an unpredictability there, under his skin, that razed the common man. Elnora, on the other hand, felt completely comfortable around him. She found John Carter hilarious, a harmless monster of the sort tied down and displayed for her own experimental pleasures. She not only accepted the responsibility of taking care of such a man, she reveled in it.

Once the stretcher was in place beside the bed, they locked the wheels and lowered the side rails. "Now, Mr. Carter," Elnora said.

"Please, please, please," John Carter said, interrupting Elnora, "don't call me mister; that's so, so formal."

"Okay," Elnora said, playing along. "What would you like for me to call you?"

"Call me Jesus," John Carter said.

Both the ambulance attendants lost it and began to laugh. Elnora began to but then restrained herself. Julius was stone-faced horrified. What would his father, a preacher at the First Baptist Church, say about such blasphemy? "That's enough," Elnora said to the ambulance drivers. "Let's get him over."

They began to untie his hands and feet when John Carter spoke up in a very rational and believable voice. "Wouldn't it be easier to lower the bed and let me walk over? I mean, it's four of you against one of me; there's no way out."

"Nothing funny," Elnora said.

"Nothing funny," John Carter replied.

Elnora gave a signal for the ambulance drivers to do what he said. They unlocked the stretcher wheels and pulled it away from the bed then lowered the bed and stretcher. Elnora leaned over and untied John Carter's feet while the drivers untied his hands. Then John Carter swung his feet off the side of the stretcher and extended his back until he was sitting straight. He smiled, raised his hands in the air, and stretched out his back some more. He rotated his neck from side to side as if warming up for exercise. The ambulance drivers stood off behind the stretcher while Julius stood over by the door. Elnora was the only one within arm's length of him.

It was a disaster from the beginning. When John Carter stood up he faked as if he were falling forward; Elnora instinctively reached to grab him. When she did, John Carter straightened up, grabbed her, pulled her forward, and thrust her back against the wall, delivering a violent thud. Julius Holmes saw all this but was unable to register it quickly enough. He had instantly been pulled back into that incomprehensible realm of shock and now stood motionless with a blank stare on his face. Even when John Carter shouldered him into the wall, he was unable to react. John Carter cleared the door and was gone.

From behind, his ass was pale and emaciated, totally exposed for the world to see. All he had on was a light green hospital gown patterned with a wide assortment of flowers and a pair of black polyester dress socks that bunched up around his ankles. His hair waved as he jogged down the hall, and the whole scene laid itself out as one bizarre portrait.

Elnora was the first out of the room and saw him heading

toward the nurses' station. His movements were slow but agile, and Elnora was impressed at his ability to move at all, especially after being tied down for so long. She could hear him laughing, and as she took off after him found it very hard not to just let him go.

As John Carter passed by each open door, he looked in and laughed. Rooms filled with homely, forgotten faces, shivering at the mad laugh coming from outside their door. It was a shock to their geriatric systems, a breakup of their sedentary routines. Many made it to their doors and shut them while others stuck their heads out and took the chance. "It's okay," Elnora said to each of them as she passed. It wasn't, and they knew it.

John Carter made it to the nurses' station and instead of running around it, he ran straight through it, purposefully knocking over a computer screen as he went. Daisy Moore was sitting behind the desk when John Carter came through but did not realize what was happening until he was out the other side. She dropped what she was doing and joined Elnora in the chase.

By this time Julius and the ambulance attendants were well out the door and in the chase as well. From the nurses' station John Carter cut down a short hall into the cafeteria where he slung salt and pepper shakers over the buffet line into the kitchen at the kitchen staff. When Elnora and Daisy entered, he took off out a far door down another hall that led to the front lobby. He entered the lobby and then exited through the double doors. Ruby was sitting on the bench drinking his coffee when John Carter came jogging by. He was not startled and he did not get up. He had already resolved himself to the fact that John Carter was going to be trouble. He watched as John Carter passed, his ass swinging in the wind. John Carter ran down the drive and into the heart of the Brookwood Apartments. Some Hispanic kids that had been playing in the streets saw him and took off screaming for the back of the apartments. Ruby watched as the ambulance drivers ran down the hill after him. Elnora and Daisy ran as far as the bench Ruby was sitting on and then stopped. They were breathlessly laughing at each other and the situation. Daisy said something about a geriatric marathon and Elnora cracked up laughing even harder. Ruby heard most of the joke and pieced the rest together. He looked down the hill at John Carter's bare-boned ass waving in the wind and laughed himself. It was a fact that no one could deny: an elderly man running semi-naked down a highway was hilarious to see.

The ambulance attendants caught up with John Carter near the bottom of the hill. Both reached out to grab his shoulders and one stumbled, tripping all three. They fell to the pavement and rolled to a stop.

Ruby could hear John Carter's vulgar mouth all the way up the hill. He was cursing at the ambulance attendants for knocking him down. Elnora and Daisy stopped laughing, and when the ambulance attendants brought John Carter to his feet they took off walking down the hill.

Far off in the eastern sky Ruby saw the Cloud for the first time. A grayish black line of strange evolution that barely broke the fringe of the horizon. It appeared in the distance like an untouchable entity, removed from what was real. One great razor's edge of mystery. It had been quite a summer: hot and muggy, ninety plus degrees for days on end. It had not only been that way in Siler City but all across the state. An unseasonable summer with an unseasonable winter preceding it. Old timers around town called that an *omen*. Ruby called it luck. The town was due for a summer shower, a great dusting off of the soul. But for some reason Ruby felt that the Cloud had nothing to offer that the town wanted. Ruby drank his coffee and pondered over it while periodically switching to the action coming up the hill.

John Carter passed by Ruby smiling. "How long has it been?" He asked Ruby.

"Quite awhile," Ruby replied, thinking John Carter was referring to the giant Cloud looming off in the distance.

"Yes it has," John Carter said. "It certainly has."

Elnora followed John Carter and the ambulance attendants through the double doors into the lobby of the Home. The ambulance sat in the circle drive still idling. The low rumbling of the engine broke up the madness John Carter had created and dispersed it out into the atmosphere. The children in the Brookwood Apartments came back out into the streets and the lazy buzz of the afternoon continued. Ruby finished his coffee and stood up. He was going in to check on Thomas C. McNeil when he saw Lisa's beautiful face peering out the front door of her apartment and then her hand waving him down to her. Ruby smiled, looked back at the Home, then to Lisa, and then took off walking slowly down the driveway into the heart of Brookwood Apartments.

John Carter was escorted back to his room and placed into his bed where they tied down each of his arms and legs until they figured out what to do with him. “Is that too tight for you, Jesus?” Elnora said to John Carter with Daisy and Julius behind her.

“You’re a harsh bitch, you are,” John Carter replied, holding his head off the pillow, looking down at his feet. It was his duty to see what kind of restraints were being used and how they were being tied. After many years of being periodically tied down, he had developed a certain science for escape, a science that required observation.

“If you’re Jesus,” Daisy asked, “why is your mouth so foul?”

John Carter watched as Elnora and Julius placed the restraints. “It’s all a cover-up,” he replied. “Plans get destroyed otherwise. People take you too seriously. Got to keep people limber if you’re going to move them.”

Elnora looked over at the door and saw Charles Apple peering in. His eyes were strained and tired. He had a pathetic look on his face—one that suggested worry. “Charlie, go to the dining room and eat,” Elnora said as she hurriedly tied John Carter down.

“Charlie go to dining room and eat,” Charles Apple said. “That where Charlie go before plans get destroyed.”

Once Elnora and Julius finished, they stood above John Carter and stared down, mostly in relief but somewhat in amazement. John Carter lay strapped to the bed, rotating his head to each of the four corners, mumbling indistinguishable words of disapproval. After a moment, he laid his head on the pillow, took a long resolving breath, and then cut his eyes to Elnora. “How ’bout that blowjob now,” he said as serious as everything.

Elnora looked at Daisy and they laughed and then walked out. All the way up the hall Daisy made fun of the fact that Jesus had just asked Elnora for a blow job and she turned him down.

Sex with Lisa was unexpectedly refreshing, something Ruby could have never imagined; and it became a routine like brushing his teeth—and he liked that. There was something real and human about it, and Ruby could hold onto it. It made him feel like his old self again. There was a heart beating, and it was his. He felt the connection with the Earth and Moon and everything around him like mad youth and it ran like fire through his veins. It gave him purpose and direction and a release of energy. And with it, there was no ridiculous talk of understandings or misunderstandings; no commitment made or lost. Lisa did not press Ruby for love and in return Ruby did not pressure her. They spoke like friends, they loved like lovers, and they both left each other happy. No questions asked.

That afternoon as they rejoined for a second time Ruby felt even more enthralled. It was out of control, and he liked it. As he was leaving she gave him a hug and a kiss. "What about tomorrow around noon?" she said.

"Sure," Ruby said. "We'll go to the library."

Lisa laughed and went back inside. On the way up the hill Ruby remembered John Carter and how insane he had acted, and he felt some concern for his roommate who was unable to defend himself. Ruby thought of ways of getting rid of John Carter if he needed to. Nothing tragic, of course. At the top of the hill he turned to see if Lisa had slipped back outside. She hadn't. But the Cloud he had observed earlier, out over the eastern fringe of the horizon, had moved its way closer to town and was now sitting just over the tree line. Ruby turned completely around and stopped in the middle of the street to look at it. It was thick and grayish-black and sat low in the sky. It made Ruby feel as if the world was closing in on itself.

When he got back to the Home he went to the activities room where the television was always on. It was on when he went in, and the Reverend Alfonso King was on it, preaching about retribution and taxation of the soul. Ruby ignored what the reverend was saying and turned the television to the Weather Channel. There were a few grunts of disapproval from the residents while he waited for the local weather, but none of them disrupted him. Most of them knew Ruby was the healthiest of the lot and that he could take anyone of them if he needed to. It wasn't a threat; it was just the truth.

When the local weather scrolled by it said, *Sunny and 96*. Ruby considered this old news then turned the television back to the Reverend Alfonso King. "Get ready!" the reverend yelled as Ruby was leaving the room.

After supper Ruby went outside and sat on the bench to check on the Cloud. Its edge was over the Brookwood Apartments, creating a haunting line of light and dark. There was no rain though, no moisture, no wind or pre-shower rumbling of thunder. The Cloud just sat there, and if Ruby concentrated hard enough he could see it move. It was moving and he knew it and by morning he was sure it would be gone. That was the plan. Or rather that was Ruby's plan. By morning the Cloud would be gone and he would be halfway to Lisa's apartment. No rain, no blackness to concern himself with.

Ruby sat out on the bench awhile longer then went in for the night. On the way to his room he stopped by John Carter's. Charles Apple was standing out by the door. Ruby leaned over his shoulder and looked in. John Carter was in the bed closest to the door. His feet and hands were untied at the time and he was awake, staring off across the room, mumbling incoherently. He was having a conversation with himself, but Ruby could not make it out. "Go to bed," Ruby said to Charles Apple, and then walked off.

Thomas C. McNeil was staring at his own wall when Ruby walked in. "How's it going, Thomas?" Ruby asked as he sat down on his bed and began taking off his shoes. Thomas said nothing.

"Can't complain," Ruby said. "No, it certainly has been worse."

Ruby took off his clothes down to his underwear and walked over to Thomas's bed. "What are you thinking about, old man?" Ruby asked him.

There was no reply. Thomas just stared off into nowhere, blinking intermittently between breaths. Ruby waited a few minutes for a reply then turned off the lights and went to bed.

The next morning after breakfast Ruby walked outside to discover that not only had the Cloud not moved on overnight but it had settled in over the town. There was a quietness about it that Ruby had felt before. It was during a snowstorm years ago just outside of Atlanta. He had driven all day in it, fighting it back, trying to break free before it took him under. Eventually he had to stop and get a room. That night after it had stopped snowing, he walked outside the motel in hopes of leaving.

Everything was covered and nothing moved. There was an external quietness that felt like an internal chill, and no matter how much noise Ruby made he could not shake it. It was four days before he was able to leave. When he finally left, he drove all the way home with the windows down and the radio blaring. It was his way of getting back what he had lost.

The Cloud was dark, but it wasn't completely dark. More like a dusk-kind-of-dark without the impending thoughts of night. Ruby could see the outer boundaries of the Cloud off in the distance; they were consistently well defined all the way around, as if someone had premeditatedly set the Cloud over the city. Ruby watched it for the next few hours and it went nowhere. This puzzled him.

THE GERMAN CONNECTION

Josef had a hypodermic needle stuck in a vassal's eye when he first heard the whistle—one long, glorious squeal that sent euphoric shivers running all out across his skin. It made him flinch and tear open the vassal's cornea causing fluid to squirt out onto his white lab coat. When he saw this he flinched some more, causing the needle to lunge forward through the vassal's eye into his skull. Josef released the needle in surprise. "Shit!" he said, somewhat irritated at himself, stepping back, looking down at his lab coat. "Shit! Shit! Shit!"

In response to all this, the vassal slumped over, then fell off the table. Josef looked around to see if anyone saw what had happened. No one had. He removed the needle from the vassal's eye, then took off his lab coat. On his way out the door he stopped by his office and picked up his wool coat, his white cotton gloves, and his riding crop.

From outside the Block he could hear an orchestra in the distance. They had set up along the kitchen wall under the direct orders from the high command. Aesthetically and perceptively it was an eerie thing to hear, especially for the vassals, who under the circumstances could easily give or take the honky-tonk versions of Wagner and Schubert and Beethoven they were being subjected to. But for Josef, it put pep in his step as he jaunted across the courtyard toward the loading planks. He whistled along with the melodies and found himself thinking back to old lovers and Münich, where he was taught the fine art of medicine and surgery. He found himself thinking of Russia and the First War and the Iron Cross that hung from his chest because of it—and now this war, just as gruesome and as long as the first. He was older now and more in control of his emotions—at least that's what he told himself. He wasn't a hungry foot soldier in this one, fighting off Russian bullets on the front line, dragging wounded soldiers like bags of potatoes through mine fields to surgical tents full of mud to dig with hands and heart through flesh to find shrapnel like hidden eggs. He had no white gloves back then. He knew not what a riding crop was. All of that came later, much later, after he had taken all he needed from his masters and mentors, transferred to Berlin, and became Haupsturmführer. There he met the people that would transform him. He picked up the gloves shortly after that and the smile came naturally.

It was a new time with new and exciting philosophies to revel in, and Josef worked his way through it to become someone to admire and salute. He liked the attention, and the new uniform didn't hurt his pride much either. Once the Second War started he had already completed his transformation. He was now calculating and cruel with an edge of brilliance. He had the eyes and the chiseled perfection that resembled a razor, and he was everything his Führer had told him he would be. There was a Master Plan now and he was part of it and it was his duty to see it through. A Master Plan with a Master and a Master Race to think about. He could no longer concern himself with emotion. He was to act accordingly. It was awkward at first—in his younger days—testing out the long arm of command. As a young commander there were cracks, visible and painful, for Josef to work through. That all changed once he arrived at the Institution. He was given supreme control of his work. His gloves fit much better. There was no one there to question him and no reason to ask any questions.

The first week, he was approached in his office by a young female vassal. She had just arrived at the Institution and was complaining of stomach pains. Josef was busy and somewhat irritated at the fact that this vassal assumed she could just walk into his office and start complaining. He sat back in his chair and stared at her. She was young with unmistakable beauty. He told her to drop her dress and she did. Her stomach was flat and pale and her pubic hairs were long and bushy. Josef stared at her crotch for some time and then her eyes. She was not nervous. "Are you used to getting what you want?" Josef asked her. Her soft eyes flinching none as he spoke.

The young vassal paused for a moment then answered yes in hopes that the truth was what he wanted to hear.

Josef smiled and the vassal smiled. He reached into his desk and brought out a black marker. He gave it to her and asked her to mark on her stomach where the pain was. She took the marker and did as he said; a confident X along the lower right quadrant of her abdomen. Josef then called Werner into his office. "I want you to take this young lady out to a table and make an incision over the mark on her stomach," he said, pointing to where the mark had been made. "Take a look and see if you see anything wrong."

The young vassal let out a pitiful moan at hearing this. "It's better," she pleaded. "I swear. It's better."

"Take out her uterus while you're at it," Josef said to Werner. There was a long pitiful cry from the vassal and then silence.

It was Josef's first taste of real success. Not the monetary kind—he had always been rich. No, it was something else, something that made him sit back, fix his eyes on the door, and think about it. It was visceral and unnatural and was composed of a rare emotion. He liked that. And it venerated what his dear Führer had written years before: "A State which, in an epoch of racial adulteration, devotes itself to the duty of preserving the best elements of its racial stock must one day become ruler of the Earth."

That's what Josef was doing; that was what he was working for. He was preserving. And in a state of war, that act of preservation required rare, raw emotion. It required nothing more from Josef than the most common, basic acts of preservation itself. Nothing more. Nothing less. What started out easy at the Institution remained that way, and that's what made Josef who he was—one mean motherfucker.

Josef made it to the Gate before the train. Other officers and guardsmen were gathering too. It was routine.

He stepped up onto the track and looked down through the brick and barbed wire across the landscape to the miniature locomotive that was making its way toward him under the shawl of the beautiful cloud he had examined earlier. He stood there with his legs straddling the tracks with the riding crop gripped in both hands, forgetting about everything else. It was the train he wanted now and the contents within.

He stood like this as the train cowered up to the entrance of the maw then slowly proceeded through it. When it was about five meters away he stepped off the tracks. He could feel the heat from the engines as the locomotive passed. Then there were the eyes, the deprived, naked eyes that glared wantonly from the cracks and barred windows of the cattle cars. They stared out and beyond, across the hills of the far off distance then back to the barbed wire of the Institution, down cobblestone pathways that led to uncertainty, to the bricked building and chimneys that spewed gray smoke, to the vassals that hid their faces when they passed, to the suited ones with pistols and rifles, to dogs that cracked open the moment with ferocious barks, and finally, to Josef—the handsome one with immaculate taste for cleanliness. He seemed the least of their worries at the time. One man. One pair of eyes. A witness, a clean witness, nothing more.

That was their first impression. But when the train came to a stop along the plank and the cattle car doors swung open—one at a time—and the vassals were led out down the plank, they soon learned that Josef was more than a man, more than an immaculate dresser. He stood at the end of the plank at the exit on a raised platform that put him a good foot over the tallest vassal. He stood there straight and pure and stared down at each vassal as they descended off the plank. And when the vassals reached the bottom where Josef was standing, he would look down at them and point with his riding crop: left or right.

At first, this didn't seem strange to the vassals, but then they realized that he was dividing them between the weak and strong, young and old. The immaculately dressed man was the Grim Reaper himself.

Josef understood the importance of the job, which is why he took it upon himself to do it. Others had not the conviction he did. As the vassals dropped from the plank he would look each in the eye and down, staring at the throat and arms, the chest, and then the feet. He could usually tell sickness through the eyes—if they were yellow or weak. Sick eyes went to the right. Emaciated bodies went to the right. The old went to the right. Anyone that looked sick went to the right.

It was a long process—one that sickened most—watching the cattle cars unload, the faces, the sure enormity of the moment. It was the war itself that made Werner a drunk. But it was the Institution that made him a sloppy one.

The lifestyle wasn't for everyone. The Führer himself said that there would be weakness among the ranks—that some would rise to the occasion while others fell into their dutiful places. There would be those to lead and others to follow. Some would run while others walked.

It was true. Josef had heard it straight from the Führer's mouth many times at rallies when he lived in Berlin. He would sit out in the crowd and watch his Führer, thousands of people cheering him on, his words dancing across the open rooms and streets like rain. Josef would watch other people and their reactions. He had not seen such devotion, ever. It made him believe in the Führer and what he was doing.

Standing on the plank now, over the hundreds—no thousands—of vassals unloading off the train, Josef was the man they saw and the man they respected and feared. He stood firm and focused, picking over the flesh as if he were searching for a new pair of shoes. He had a weakness for twins and could spot them even if they weren't together. He would pull them out of the crowd and have guards stand watch over them.

It was his belief that the secrets of genetic engineering were locked somewhere within those identical faces. His commission at the Institution was based upon that fact. It was his job to duplicate the Master Race and eradicate the inferior ones. Josef didn't have a problem with this. No, he had thought it out and was damn well sure it could be done. All he needed to do was find the door and open it. His Führer had said it and he believed it. They both wanted to create a Super Race.

Once he had picked over the whole lot, sending a few to work and the others to death, Josef ordered the guards to take all the twins to his Block and have them cleaned and disinfected.

Josef stayed behind and watched as the train maneuvered its way back out through the maw. A precise duty it was: one track, one train, one man to charge it. Josef took his riding crop and placed it over the nose of the locomotive. "You are free to go," he said to himself, loud enough to be heard if anyone was listening.

No one was, of course, as they were too afraid to be near him. They had heard the stories, seen him in action with his riding crop and sometimes with the butt of his pistol. They knew his personality was split—one minute a Hyde, the next a Jekyll. Mostly Hyde. They didn't take the chance. It was best to stay back a good distance, never make eye contact, watch him from behind. Even those with equal or higher command felt that was a good policy to follow. And they did. That made Josef feel even better. Fear and respect were synonymous in his vocabulary. The same results applied.

Back at the Block, the twins were cleaned and disinfected and arranged along a white wall for inspection. When Josef returned he looked them over and picked the most suitable pair to start with. He had the others sent away for clothes and food.

The first line of business was to get an accurate height and weight and other anthropological measurements. This he had his assistants perform painlessly. After this was completed, blood samples and X-rays were taken. Afterwards, Josef reentered the room and examined their ears, noses, and throats. He was looking for anything peculiar that linked them genetically, some mysterious tool that coexisted within them both. He did not find it in their ears, noses, or throats.

Next, he went to the mouth. He had the twins strapped

down and their mouths pried open. He searched their teeth and tongues then ran a hose into their stomachs and had them pumped. Nothing looked out of place. Nothing there but stomach juices. He then had some teeth extracted and he studied them. Nothing. His assistants rolled the twins over and he examined their backsides from scalp to the toe. He went back to the rectums and ran tubes and pumped them. Nothing. "What makes you special?" Josef asked one of the twins whose system had already begun to shut down and was too messed up to talk.

"Yes," Josef said. "That's right. You aren't special."

He had them put to sleep; then he made enormous incisions down their torsos and opened them up. He could see their intestines turning and their hearts pumping. He reached out and grabbed one and held it in place till it almost stopped beating then let it go. It was nothing he had not seen before. He stepped back and thought for a moment. "What could it be?" he asked himself. "And where?"

Josef had his assistants draw up two syringes of chloroform and he injected each twin's heart with a syringe. Within a moment, they died and Josef left them for his assistants to remove. It was getting late and he had not had any lunch.

THE BIG FRESH

Ruby methodically watched the Cloud for two days and noted to himself that in those two days it had not moved. The same thing, just a different day—black with runs of dim light around the outer edges, sitting there with nothing better to do than look like rain. But of course, it hadn't rained and that was one of the things that bothered Ruby and the rest of the town the most. That and the fact that no one could do anything about it.

Ruby was beginning to feel the effects of it too. Subtle yet palpable changes that made him detest the Cloud. For one, his morning coffee didn't taste the same. It had less of that workingman's Maxwell House taste and more vanilla bean. He checked with the cafeteria supervisor to make sure they hadn't switched brands on him, and they had not. He made the cafeteria supervisor taste it, which she did and laughingly agreed with Ruby's assessment. She told him someone in the back could have made some home-brew at one point and contaminated the system. "It'll work itself out, honey," she said to Ruby.

And he had no scientific proof to back up this statement, but he felt as if his coffee didn't stay warm as long as it used to. Being an older gentleman, he had come to develop certain eccentricities that allowed him to get the most out of the things he enjoyed—all this being subconscious, of course. One of those things had become drinking coffee on the bench out front of the Home. Others things like sex, he felt were natural. It was natural to want to preserve the moment as long as possible. Lisa liked that about him. Ten minutes was not too much time to ask for a cup of coffee to stay somewhat warm outside in the weather—give or take the season. The first time his coffee went cold Ruby considered it a fluke, went back to the dining hall, and got another cup. The second time it made him think, stick his finger in the cup, and swirl it around. Not only was it not warm, but it was to the point of cold. This puzzled Ruby because even in the early morning out on the bench the temperature could easily be in the eighties Fahrenheit. This frustrated Ruby the most, and that frustration was easily reflected off onto the Cloud.

Other things changed too, subtly but easily recognizable to those who had the time and patience to notice. The view from the bench down the drive into the Brookwood Apartments wasn't as romantically stable. The Hispanic kids still did their little song and dance in the street, but Ruby could tell that they were just as preoccupied with the Cloud as everyone else. Lisa seemed okay with it at first, other than being completely irritated by the local chatter over it. "Why talk of something you have no control of?" she would say.

Ruby had mistakenly brought it up while they were lying around in bed. She sensed his uneasiness and reassured him that it was everyone else in town, not him, that was making her feel this way. "Do you know," she said to Ruby, "that some of the local farmers have asked the town council for legal representation because they are afraid to water their crops with that thing hanging over their fields. They think the state should reimburse them if it doesn't rain and their crops die."

Ruby considered what Lisa said and thought it sounded a little far-fetched. The word *ignorant* came to mind. He thought if that Cloud had been hanging over Wilmington back in his paper days he would have had a lot more time to work on his book. And that, he could say, was one of the better things that came from the Cloud. It gave him ideas.

It felt good to think about the book again. It had been dead for so long. He told himself that maybe this was it, the situation he needed for a jump-start. Sure, why not? "Do you have any money?" he asked Lisa.

"Sure, but why should I help a bunch of tobacco farmers who don't know when to water their crops?"

"No. I need some paper and pens."

"What for?" she asked, snuggling up to Ruby as if he were a mystery.

"The book," he said.

"You're writing a book?"

"Why not?"

This seemed very romantic to Lisa. She immediately got out of bed and began digging through the closet. Within no time she brought out an old Smith-Corona word processor and placed it on the bed. "I used it to write papers in high school. It still works."

Ruby looked it over and then got out of bed and got dressed. They drove into town and Lisa bought the paper he needed. On the way back they stopped by the library and Lisa put out some more pamphlets. While they were there Ruby got a library card using Lisa's address and checked out a couple of books. One was *Slaughterhouse-Five* by Kurt Vonnegut and the other was *Heart of Darkness* by Joseph Conrad. He had read them both in the past and was impressed with their styles and wanted to use them to get ideas for his own book.

In the parking lot, while waiting for Lisa, Ruby watched all the old people piling slowly out of their cars into the parking lot at the Dry Dock Seafood Restaurant. It was four, four-thirty at the most, and it looked as if the restaurant had just opened. Ruby was overwhelmed by the complete feeling of disconnection he felt with the people and the scene. He wasn't one of them. Even at the Home, he would stroll into the dining hall at the latest possible moment before they closed. But it was more than that. He never felt the age, watching them silently pile out of their Lincolns and Chevy Capris, smudging up the world in clothes Ruby could smell from across the street. To Ruby, they seemed attached to everything but the world itself, and that made him feel out of place, as if he had missed something somewhere along the way, some mandatory class on aging and ethics. He watched as they walked in silence across the parking lot, all in couple form, one in front of the other, all somewhat older than Ruby. They glanced up at the Cloud as they walked, some with umbrellas out, wearing their fear like flashlights taped to their heads.

It was the Home that had Ruby thinking about this. The Home and his wife. Those people were older than Ruby, but they had freedoms he could hardly imagine now. It made him bitter and thankful that he and his wife would never have the opportunity to look as foolish. On the way by the restaurant he asked Lisa to blow the horn and she did. It changed nothing, but it made him feel somewhat better.

All the way back to the apartment Ruby stared out at the Cloud and at everyone on the street. They all seemed preoccupied by it in some fashion or other. Groups of men congregated like school boys around a cigarette, staring up, pointing this way and that, silently moving their mouths in response or argument to what another had said.

Ruby seemed to tolerate this a lot better. At least it represented life. Real or otherwise. Lisa placed her hand on his leg, sensing some change in his mood for the better. She liked that; he could tell.

In the beginning of their relationship Ruby felt that showing too much emotion could be detrimental, that her youth might not be able to tolerate it, but she made it easy for him to be real. And if real meant being pissed off for a few minutes at a bunch of geriatrics who liked fish and chips at four-thirty in the afternoon, then so be it. She didn't mind.

Ruby zoned out on the Cloud the rest of the way to the apartment. It was an easy thing to do and the next best thing to talking about it. When they got to the apartment Ruby grabbed the paper and word processor, gave Lisa a kiss, and made his way back to the Home. Rita saw him in the lobby carrying the typewriter and paper. She pretended to be upset and suspicious but quickly faded off into other work. Ruby took the word processor to his room and placed it on the bedside table, said hello to Thomas C. McNeil, then left.

John Carter was tied to his bed, mumbling about rivers and railroads, when Ruby walked in. Ruby grabbed a chair and pulled it alongside the bed facing John Carter, then took a seat. John Carter did not acknowledge him immediately. He stared off like Thomas C. McNeil into nowhere, mumbling inaudible nothings over and over. The more Ruby listened the clearer it got: "Take the highway to the river, man, river man . . . build yourself a boat, man, boat man . . . take it to the ocean, man, ocean man . . . buy yourself a ticket, man, ticket man . . . on the next train home . . . on the next . . . train . . . home."

John Carter repeated this a few times, each with the same sloppy cadence as the last, laughing here and there in between phrases, smacking his lips, licking his teeth. Ruby watched this with some intensity then cut a grin, wanting to laugh but not. He was amazed that this was the same man that had run half-naked down the driveway a few days earlier. The same man that had kept Charles Apple out of his bed for three days, sleeping in the activity room on one of the couches.

Ruby stopped grinning and leaned forward. He examined John Carter's face. "What is it?" Ruby said.

John Carter continued to mumble.

"You're pure evil," Ruby said.

At that moment, John Carter stopped what he was doing and turned to Ruby and looked him in the eyes. "Are you the One?" he asked.

"One what?" Ruby answered.

"The One?"

Ruby sat back and laughed.

"He laughs because he doesn't know," John Carter said. "All ignorant men laugh. All men are ignorant of something. Can you save the world like I can?"

Ruby repositioned himself in the chair. "Are you in any

position to save the world?"

John Carter raised his right wrist until the restraint became taut. He looked down at it then laughed. "Surely you don't see this as a problem, do you? I'm Jesus, for Christ's sake!"

"Let's see you get out then," Ruby said.

John Carter laughed then took to mumbling his song, staring off as before, ignoring Ruby. "Take the highway to the river, man . . . "

Ruby got up, replaced the chair, and left. Outside the door Charles Apple stood waiting, the same scared puppy-dog look on his face. "It's fine," Ruby said. "He won't hurt you."

"He won't hurt Charles?"

"No."

Ruby took Charles by the arm, drug him through the door, and forced him to sit on his bed. Charles looked over at John Carter then up at Ruby. Ruby reassured him once more that John Carter wasn't going to hurt him then let his arm go. Charles sat back on his bed and ran his fingers across the bedcover. He looked over at John Carter again then to Ruby, cutting a nervous grin at them both. "He won't hurt Charles?" he said.

"No," Ruby said. "I promise."

That night Ruby had a dream. It was a dream he had many times before: he was covered in blood and naked, standing in front of a crowd of catatonic people. His hands were raised and he was pleading for mercy.

It was a short dream and one that rather disturbed him, usually ending with him sitting up in bed gasping for air. When he awoke this time though, he was unable to move. His shoulders were pinned down under the covers. His bedside light was on and John Carter stood over him with a mad grin, his hair dangling wildly down over his face. "Are you the one?"

"No," Ruby said, not knowing what the question meant, only knowing that *no* seemed the safer answer.

"You don't even know, do you?" John Carter said.

"Know what?" Ruby pleaded.

John Carter pulled back the bed covers exposing Ruby's torso and arms. On the right side of his chest was a tattoo, and John Carter stared at it intensely then slung the covers over Ruby's head. By the time Ruby got out from under them, John Carter was gone. He sat up on the side of the bed and got dressed. Thomas C. McNeil was facing the other direction, but Ruby could see the covers rise and fall with each breath. It was the first thing he looked for.

The halls were empty and dimly lit. There were a few stray wheelchairs and carts full of linen placed here and there. The door to John Carter's room was a quarter of the way open, but Ruby did not go in. He passed it and went on to the nurses' station.

Rosa Hurley was sitting by herself when Ruby walked up. She was a rather depressive young nurse who, according to the other staff, was working on her fifth child. Her stomach was well rounded, and Ruby gave her two weeks. When she saw Ruby she did not respond. Ruby leaned against the desk and waited. After a few seconds she asked Ruby what was wrong. "Your man, John Carter, is loose again."

There was a moment of awkwardness as Rosa Hurley pulled herself from her book and reacclimated herself to the Home. Once she did though, she was on her swollen feet yelling for Walter Rhoe. Walter was an older gentleman who worked nights as a nurse's assistant. He was quiet and feeble, and when Ruby saw him come from around the corner, eyes still matted together from sleep, he knew Walter was going to be no help at all.

Rosa Hurley grabbed a flashlight; then they all three walked down the hall and entered John Carter's room. Charles Apple was sitting up where Ruby had left him and John Carter lay in his bed. Rosa looked over at Ruby. Ruby looked at John Carter. He walked over to his bed and slung back the covers. "Hey, what are you doing?" Rosa demanded, grabbing Ruby by his wrist.

"Check his hands," Ruby said.

They both looked down to see all the restraints in place and tied. "What's going on?" Rosa asked Ruby, replacing the covers over John Carter whose eyes were closed.

"This man was in my room," Ruby said, pointing down to John Carter.

"I can't see how," Rosa said. "He's tied down."

"I know," Ruby said. "I know."

Rosa and Walter left the room. Ruby walked over to Charles Apple's bed and instructed him to stand up, pull back the covers, and then instructed him to lie down—which Charles did. He walked over to John Carter's bed and leaned over. "If you come into my room again, I'll break your legs."

There was no response and Ruby left.

THE BUDDHIST CONNECTION

Of course, Elnora Brown wasn't a Buddhist in the truest sense of the fashion, but she did adhere to some of the basic beliefs of the religion. She was a young, ineffectual woman who valued the state of *nirvana* and sought to achieve it as much and as often as possible. She had also memorized some proverbs and used them occasionally when the thought hit her. Once, when a resident had passed away, she leaned over him and chanted this verse: " 'As a star at dawn, a bubble in a stream. A flash of lightning in a summer cloud. A flickering lamp, a phantom and a dream.' "

It did nothing for the resident, but it disturbed Julius Holmes, who was only there to tag and bag the guy.

Elnora's cousin, on the other hand, was extremely well versed in the religion. She had just completed a story on the subject for the paper where she worked. Her name was Neena Moore and she worked for *The Globe*, a tabloid newspaper out of New York. The story was about a man in Russellville, Arkansas, who claimed to be the reincarnated Buddha. He weighed 457 pounds, and by the time Neena reached him he had gotten some neighborhood kids to rub him down with quick tanning cream—the kind that leaves the body a faked-out bronzed yellow. When she walked into his house he was perched up on three beanbags, naked, rubbed down in baby oil, truly looking like Buddha himself. The pictures alone got her a commission, but she went further than that. She created a living and breathing story around what he told her. She wrote it up in religious fashion, made him look even more authentic. When the story was released, the man became famous. The town was ransacked with religious tourists seeking translation and transcendence. When the man couldn't deliver he was rebuffed and declared a fraud. The story was dead by that time, and Neena longed moved on to bigger and better things.

She routinely spoke with Elnora over the phone during the late afternoons, before supper and before the afternoon pills when the Home was on autopilot. The day Neena told Elnora about the fat man in Russellville and how she wished she could stumble onto something like that again, Elnora, in a flurry of unmitigated excitement, interrupted. "I have a Jesus."

"A Jesus?"

"Yes."

Neena let Elnora calm down. "They're a dime a dozen," she said.

"True," Elnora said, "but this one has a foul mouth."

"As in rotten teeth?"

"No . . . no. He cusses a lot. Extremely foul. And we've got him tied down."

The more Elnora spoke, the less Neena was convinced. But Elnora was convincing herself, and that made her sell it even harder—she was in search of *nirvana*.

"I don't think so, girl," Neena said, "but thanks."

Then Elnora stumbled upon brilliance. "There is a Cloud," she said.

"A Cloud?"

"Yes. A really dark cloud, and it has not moved for days."

"What does that have to do with your foul-mouthed Jesus?" Neena asked.

"They showed up on the same day."

"Really?"

"Really," Elnora said.

There was a moment for silent digestion. Then Neena said it was interesting but that it probably wouldn't work because of logistical reasons. "Some other time," she said. "Good-bye."

THE BIG FRESH

Ruby did not sleep the rest of the night. He sat up in the chair, stared at the word processor and Thomas C. McNeil. He turned Thomas so he would be facing him and at some point traced out with his finger to the wall the exact point at which Thomas C. McNeil was staring. Ruby also stared at that section of the wall, examining it with his fingers, trying to find some method or motive in Thomas's actions. Of course there was none and that disappointed Ruby at first, but he resolved himself to the fact that Thomas was probably doing the best he could. Ruby took a picture—supposedly of Thomas's wife—off the dresser and tacked it to the very spot at which Thomas C. McNeil was looking, adjusted it with the consideration of the angle at which he was laying, and then took a seat. "Not bad," Ruby said to Thomas.

It was John Carter Ruby was thinking about, though—the lunatic Jesus that had pinned him down in bed, dripping verbal madness from his jowls. He wasn't frightened of him. No, it was the intolerable act of being held down in bed, and of not particularly liking the fact that someone came into his room while he was sleeping. Ruby wanted to dismantle the man piece by piece and send him back to where he came from.

But most of all, Ruby was just sitting in his room considering his own life and thinking of all the blanks he would like to fill in by writing his book. Occasionally, he would type a few lines then stop, read what he had written, and then turn to talk to Thomas. He would turn back to reread what was written and then trash it.

Every time he started, he would stop. That bothered him. Something wasn't right and had never been right. Back then it was Kay or his job or maybe the season; now, it was John Carter and the Cloud and the fact that his hands weren't as conditioned as they used to be. He needed a cigarette—but hadn't smoked in years—and a cup of coffee would have been nice. He tried speaking with Thomas but found it hard to fool himself anymore that night. He thought about Lisa and tried to call her. He got the front desk. It was Rosa Hurley. "No calls after eleven, Mr. Riggs."

He waited thirty minutes then took off for the lobby. When he swung the double doors open, a silent alarm went off at the nurses' station. It brought Rosa Hurley out of her own little world, made her grunt and growl like an angry dog. She sent Walter Rhoe out, and he caught Ruby just on the other side of the bench. Ruby could see where the darkness met the streetlights, and he was heading for it. Walter Rhoe tittered up behind Ruby and started talking about Rosa's temperament. "Checking on the Cloud," Ruby said. "That's all."

"Yeah. She's looking like rain," Walter said.

Ruby wanted to tell him that the Cloud had no rain to give and that no back country euphemisms were going to bring rain. He knew he could talk Walter into letting him go down the hill, but he was too frustrated. What he wanted was easy, and nothing all night had been. He stood there with Walter a few more minutes shooting the crap then went back inside. When he got to his room he pulled the chair up to the word processor and began typing. No looking back. Hour after hour, into the morning he typed—flinching none when the staff came checking on Thomas C. McNeil, none when they asked Ruby what he was doing and told him that it was time to eat. He sat there typing, maintaining a constant pace for hours on end way into the afternoon. When he finally stopped, he stood up, straightened out his shirt and pants, and walked silently to the dining hall for supper. He inhaled a great meal of potatoes, squash, and meat loaf, and then took a cup of coffee back to his room, and resumed typing.

The coffee was cold by the time he got to it, but it served its purpose and he drank it anyway. He typed on into the next morning never looking back, never looking too far ahead either, only typing what he felt and how he felt it at the time. Around four in the morning he dragged himself to bed and fell asleep, clothes and all.

Julius Holmes woke him some time around ten. "Ruby," he said a few times in a nervous attempt to transform Ruby into the only man he knew him as.

Ruby opened his eyes to see Julius staring down at him then closed them. "You look rough," Julius said.

"So do you," Ruby answered. "What time is it?"

"Around ten."

"Can you get me some coffee?"

"I think I can find you some," Julius said.

Ruby thanked him, got to his feet and put on his shoes, took off his shirt, and went to the bathroom to splash some water on his face. He caught a faint glimpse of himself in the mirror: slender with a few days' growth on his face. He turned away quickly. Too much to do. He went to his closet, put on a clean shirt, sat down, and started typing. After about thirty minutes Julius came in with a large cup of coffee. "Ruby-sized," Ruby said when he saw the large Styrofoam cup Julius was carrying.

"Only for you, baby," Julius said, laughing.

Julius saw what Ruby was doing and began asking questions. "Memoirs?"

"Not even close," Ruby said. "I'll fill you in later. Is the Cloud still hanging around?"

"You know it."

"I'll talk to you later," Ruby said.

Julius took the hint and left.

Outside, the Cloud was still around, darker than ever, hanging persistently low, pulling everything somewhat closer together—even if it didn't want to be. It was hot and muggy and the air had stagnated. Mosquitoes and gnats made feverish love in the tropical conditions and spit out their offspring like machine guns. There were packs of dogs running wild—getting run over left and right—and large birds flew in from the south to attend to the carnage. The town folks were losing patience; they wanted the Cloud to dance, to dribble rain from its puffy cheeks. They had talked about it enough—no more jokes to be made, no more laughing. And unlike Ruby's coffee, the city water had become warm. There were engineers brought in from Raleigh to investigate. "It's warm," they attested, then commented on the Cloud, and left.

Nights became unbearable because they were so long, and with each morning came the disappointment of another day with the Cloud. What started out as a change in the daily routine turned quickly into something far more ugly and intolerable.

Christopher Riley was also feeling it, but his concerns lay less with the weather and more with Lisa. She hadn't called him back for some time now, and every time he would go over to the apartment she wouldn't answer the door. It was a twisted Cloud indeed, but she was a twisted girl, and the Reverend Riggs didn't seem much like a reverend to Christopher Riley.

Ruby continued to write through the afternoon, through the thoughts of the Cloud, of Lisa, through the television down the hall with the visions and voice of the Reverend Alfonso King ringing throughout the Home. He wrote into the afternoon and broke for lunch. He ate, then went outside with his coffee, and walked down the hill. Lisa was at home and when she answered the door she laughed because Ruby looked so ragged. She stripped off her clothes, then stripped off his, and put them in the washer. They took a long, warm shower and made love while their clothes were drying. Ruby told her of the book and how well it was going and that he loved her for being such a good person. She cried—not because of him saying he loved her, but because of the Cloud and how uninspired she had become since it came to town and how she didn't feel like a good person. "It needs to leave," she said.

"It will," Ruby replied, not knowing if it would or not.

"There's no truth in it," she said. "I've watched it. It tells nothing but lies. It has everything so fucked up because it tells nothing but lies."

Ruby took his clothes out of the dryer and put them on then threw Lisa a shirt. They stood at the door for some time staring off into the blackness. "I thought you didn't like to talk about things you can do nothing about?" Ruby said.

There was a silence, and the air between them was stagnant yet he could still feel her. It was a question he shouldn't have asked. "That was then," she replied, and as Ruby descended the steps she called for him. "Should we do something about it?"

Ruby smiled, then ascended the hill to the Home, and went through the double doors into the lobby. He thought of Lisa all the way to his room—past the geriatrics and wheelchairs. He said hello to Thomas C. McNeil, sat down behind the word processor, and began typing.

THE NIRVANA CONNECTION

Elnora was contemplating untying John Carter when Neena called back. It was a day after their last conversation. "Is that Jesus of yours still there?" Neena asked Elnora.

"Where else would he be?" Elnora said.

"I ran your idea by my boss, for shits and giggles, of course."

"Of course," Elnora said.

"Well, he thought I should do it."

Elnora let out a laugh. "So, you're coming down?"

"Yes," said Neena. "In a couple of days. I want to take care of a few things up here first so I can spend some time with the family."

Neena and Elnora said their good-byes and that was it.

Elnora decided to leave John Carter tied down until Neena got there and she called her family to let them know that their blackest of black sheep, Neena, was coming home.

When she told them, the question of why was asked. For Neena had, in the past, found many more reasons to stay in New York than to come home and visit with the family. "She's doing a story," Elnora said then went into the whole spiel of John Carter and the Cloud.

After Elnora finished telling her family, she told everyone at work, and everyone at work was excited. It was *The Globe*, the national tabloid that donned every checkout station in every supermarket in America. They went home that afternoon and told all their family, and their families went out and told all their friends. By the following afternoon the story was well on its way to becoming folklore. Even Ruby, who was still writing madly, heard the news from Julius. He laughed and shrugged it off. "That's all that freak needs."

Julius also made the mistake of telling his father, the Reverend Frederick Holmes. "Blasphemy!" his father yelled across the dining room table.

He immediately called his deacons to see if they heard anything. They had, of course, and that only made the reverend madder.

Rita Hymer had heard about it too. But whereas the Reverend Frederick Holmes was concerned about the moral and spiritual implications, she was merely concerned with the legal ones. If

John Carter was a ward of the state, was it up to the state to decide if he could be interviewed? Or did it matter? What if the names of all the characters were changed just for the day, until Neena left? Things like that.

Rita did not know, and all the calls she placed to the Home office in Charleston, South Carolina were disconnected in one fashion or another.

It was Daisy Moore who told Geraldine Griffin just as Geraldine was leaving the Home, and it was Geraldine who told the Reverend Alfonso King in passing at the hospital. "Sister," the reverend said to Geraldine, "this is no new news to me. I saw the coming of the glory of the Lord months ago. With rain there will be shine."

"Are we talking about the same thing here?" Geraldine asked, wondering—not for the first time—if the reverend was all there.

"We most certainly are," the reverend said, kissing Geraldine on her hand.

He left the hospital and went over to the Home. He ran into Rita, who was trying to leave. She voiced her concerns about the situation, and he reassured her that it was all in the Master Plan. All Rita could see was her ass in that plan, and it didn't seem that masterful, but she promised the reverend that she would do her best. "Hallelujah!" he yelled out through the lobby. "Hallelujah to the highest!"

He was overly exuberant and Rita withdrew into herself as he outwardly practiced his madness. "Hallelujah, indeed," she said, backing out the double doors.

The reverend went into the Home and spoke to a few residents. When he passed by Ruby's room he stopped and stared in. Ruby was hunched over the word processor typing some one hundred words a minute—thereabout. The reverend chanted a holy incantation, smiled, then left.

The news of Neena Moore and Jesus spread throughout the town, and for the most part it was received as a pleasant distraction from the Cloud. It did not bother most that some lunatic was impersonating the Messiah—at least there was a joke there. Others though, like the Reverend Frederick Holmes, were unable to let it go half-heartedly. It is one thing to say you're something you're not—that happens all the time—and the reverend could excuse that, but to say it to the world?

No, the reverend just could not have it. Not like that.

THE BAPTIST CONNECTION

The next day, Sunday, church was in session. The First Baptist Church across the street from the police station was packed out to overflowing with angry God-fearing citizens who had heard the story of the blasphemous Jesus and had heard of their beloved reverend's crusade to clear their Messiah's name. Upon reaching the pulpit, the Reverend Frederick Holmes did little to quiet their anger. On the contrary, he put the ever-loving fear of God into them—firing them up with words, reading passages from Mark, Luke, and John, from Genesis and finally Revelation—quoting the Bible in ways few had ever heard. He was trying to keep the Beast from his Flock, while subconsciously turning his Flock into the Beast.

And his words did not lie. They rang out true throughout the holy church and the holy street, words heard many times before by all but now somehow more relevant in a visceral, uncontrollable way. They were words of action, not just words to ponder and pray over. They rang and then rang some more.

Along the back wall of the sanctuary, standing in unconventional lines behind the last pew was a row of healthy, impressionable, young men. Included in that row was Christopher Riley. He stood strong and proud as the Reverend Frederick Holmes delivered his words, thinking of Lisa and the Reverend Riggs and the blasphemous Jesus. And while doing this, he devised within himself a plan of action to accomplish what the reverend had so eloquently, if not subconsciously, requested of him and those around him: "Put words and will to motion and let God's work be done. Amen."

Amen, indeed.

Two blocks over, down Third Street, the Reverend Alfonso King was telling a different story to a relatively different Flock of Sunday worshippers. Using Mark, John, Luke, Genesis, and finally Revelation, he used his words to color in between the lines of a picture that had been sketched out centuries ago. A picture full of bountiful deliverance and rejoicing. He spoke to his people in terms of beauty not beast, of a time when no one would suffer or need anything. He spoke up and out into the heavens and waved his arms over the congregation like a desperate rejoicing angel. He spoke fast and deliberate and never stumbled once upon a word. When he finished, tithes were collected, a hymn was sung, and the congregation exited the church in an orderly fashion. Outside, the Cloud was as black and heavy as ever, but they did not fear it nor did they attribute it to the Jesus down the street. It was the black Cloud of deliverance that they stared upon. Hallelujah, Hallelujah.

At about the same time, the doors swung open at Reverend Holmes's First Baptist Church. Seething unorthodox creatures, gnarling at the Cloud and all the biblical connotations it represented, emerged. They filed out into the streets with no order, speaking loudly and boisterously about the need for correction. They hovered in packs around parked cars and street posts, their hands in their pockets or running through their hair, staring collectively at the Cloud and the police station across the street with discernment. They asked themselves why the police couldn't just pull the heathen Christ from his throne, take him outside the town, give him a walking stick, and tell him to head west.

Christopher Riley and his friends pondered these questions as well. And as they stood on the top steps of the church staring down into the Sunday stew, Christopher Riley put the final touches upon his brilliant plan. He let his friends in on it and they agreed: "It will be a statement, one of biblical proportions, one that everyone will see and not be able to destroy easily."

It was juvenile and exciting altogether and possessed within it a completely relevant and profound nature—one that made Christopher Riley smile, smile, smile.

THE GERMAN CONNECTION

Josef ate his lunch alone with a slow, methodical dissection that let everyone around him know he did not want to be bothered. He was thinking of his work, and as he ate he stared out the window into the courtyard at the vassals as they scurried about. He shook his head at their ignorance. So feeble and forgetful. Bumping into each other with their necks broken, staring at the ground, their spines prideless, their eyes crossed and useless.

It was within this foundation of clumsy flesh that Josef searched for the key to immortality and the Super Race. It made him wonder. The odds were great, but demand superseded practicality and supply. And at this point of the war, certainly there warranted a demand.

But how to turn that invisible key to greatness? And which way? Josef had the visions of the Immaculate Man. He dreamed many times in the past of standing in front of an army of perfect flesh with perfect hair and perfect eyes and a perfect glow that made him swell from the inside out; and the more he stared upon them the more brilliant they seemed and everything bad was wiped clear by their presence. It was the flesh that mattered and the blood that put color to it and gave it life. It was the flesh that made the mind and the man. And there were no substitutes for greatness.

Josef did not understand the finer points of genetics or genetic engineering—as his successors wouldn't some fifty years later. But like them, Josef had a miraculous and uncanny ability to overcome such handicap. Like them he learned to concentrate on what was essential. That meant that it did not matter that mathematical equations oftentimes did not add up or that pain hurt and flesh seldom would die before an idea was born. No, in his situation it did not matter. Josef had counseled himself many times in the past over such trivia and somewhere, somehow found the ability to forget it, or even better, to hide it away inside his Work. It became reflexive, then automatic, then it was gone. There was no god on the side of good. Righteousness always prevailed. There were rules; then there were none.

But how to turn that invisible key? That was the question. Just once, that was all he needed, to the right or left, then open, then remember—yes, one must remember. He had all the subjects he needed for the experiments—too many at times. He had access to the most modern of medicines and a boatload of surgical equipment at his disposal to perform unheard of operations—some mad, others madly brilliant. And he often performed them with admirable precision. He was a genius within his ranks. But still he could not help but ask himself for more. It was the *wheres*, the *whys*, and the *hows* that transferred over into his physical demeanor, sitting there chewing his food repeatedly, more than necessary, pulverizing and eliminating the scientific process all at once in its most infantile state.

When he first came to the Institution he was told by the others in the Block to start small. "Work your ideas up slowly," they said. He took this advice only for a short time, quickly becoming disheartened at the aptitude of patience one needed to sustain such slow pace. He watched the other physicians and was repeatedly amused and then enraged by their method of discernment: it was delicate, with a range of compassion that suggested an unwillingness to take whatever measures necessary to complete the job.

He had no use for their sympathies and knew his Führer wouldn't either. He found inventful ways to have his colleagues removed from their positions. Some went to jail, while others were simply murdered right outside the Block against the brick wall that outlined the bottom edges of a quiet, country scene. Josef would stand there behind the firing squad with his white gloves and riding crop, gritting his immortal loving teeth, staring the guilty and condemned straight in the eyes. Sometimes he was lucky enough to have them stare at him all the way up to the point of the bullet's impact. Josef reveled in the awkwardness. The guilty hung in his mercilessness, there against the wall, their hands tied behind their backs, their mouths silent in the wisp of torture, a thousand things to say but with no way of knowing how to say them. Josef felt it. He knew they felt it too. It made him smile, smile, smile.

This created a terrible amount of uneasiness among his colleagues, but their power to do anything singularly or collectively about it had been taken away—almost immediately upon Josef's arrival. Those who had a problem not only had to deal with Josef, but they had to deal with the high command, and Josef was looked at very favorably among the ranks of the highest in command. It was their belief that he was exactly what the Master Race needed—a strong disciplined machine with precision and overall loyalty to its Führer.

After lunch Josef took a leisurely stroll past the crematorium and contemplated immortality. In the distance he could hear the rumblings of another train. It made him smile. It was the little things he had forgotten about over lunch. He remembered now what Werner had told him before breakfast. A certain individual from Istanbul with a certain proposition was coming to visit.

THE BIG FRESH

Walter Rhoe was the first to see it, some time around 6:30 in the morning, just before the day staff dragged their tired bodies into work. It stood off to the right of the circle drive in front of the Home, directly in the middle of the asphalt parking lot. It was made of constructural steel and welded meticulously and geometrically to form what Walter Rhoe immediately identified as a Cross. Not the dogwood kind with carpenter's cuts and splinters but the more industrial, twenty-first-century kind that could easily be recycled into a skyscraper if necessary. Walter Rhoe stared upon it with his sleepy eyes then went back inside the Home and forgot all about it.

Elnora reacted about the same as she pulled up early for work. She walked up to it and thought how odd a piece of yard art it was. She noticed that it had been cemented at the base and that the cement was still somewhat wet. She placed her hand on the Cross and gave it a nudge. It did not move and it did not care.

All morning people walked by it or saw it from off in the distance, never paying it that much attention, never bringing it up as an oddity in conversation. It stood there unabated, straight, strong, and deliberate. A crucifix with modern hardware. The Cloud sat above it, accentuating its roughness, pulling it somewhat closer to everything else.

In close proximity to the Cross was the Sunbridge Psychiatric and Rehabilitation sign. It still had its sun and still represented nothing of what went on inside the Home. It was a painted clown's face and the Home was one sad clown.

The Reverend Alfonso King saw none of this as he drove up the hill through the Brookwood Apartments into the circle drive. When he got out of his car he did see the Cross and acknowledged it with a "Praise the Lord" and a smile, and then went into the Home. Nothing out of place. Nothing unusual.

Ruby was hunched down over the word processor typing away when the reverend walked into his room. "So you're going to do it?" the reverend said in a somewhat out-of-breath fashion, probing Ruby's shoulders with his hands as if warming Ruby up for a prizefight.

"Do what?" Ruby asked, still typing.

"You know, the interview."

"What interview?" Ruby asked.

"What do you mean?" the reverend said, somewhat irritated at Ruby's lack of enthusiasm. "You know, the interview."

"Oh, the interview," Ruby said.

"Yes. Yes," said the reverend.

"I know nothing about it," Ruby said.

"What?" the reverend said, confused.

"Not me. Try room 62."

The reverend stood behind Ruby, silent and perplexed. The energy that had been in his face all morning was now gone, and a look of confusion had taken over it. The plans and puzzles he had put together were a wash. "Isn't that queer," he said, taking his eyes off the back of Ruby's head, looking around the room at Thomas C. McNeil and beyond, then over Ruby's shoulder onto the face of the word processor.

Ruby stopped what he was doing and turned to see what the reverend was up to. The reverend straightened his back and said good-bye and then left.

John Carter lay in room 62, his head raised some thirty degrees off the bed. A breakfast tray sat untouched in front of him. He was wide-awake when the reverend stuck his head into the room. Charles Apple sat on his bed, feet to the floor. The reverend looked at Charles Apple first, sizing him up, then switched his attention to John Carter. Neither fit the image he had acquired over the years of a modern-day Messiah. No, he had adopted a particular image, and even though Ruby did not fit it either, the reverend found him much less disappointing.

"Hello, misser preacher man," John Carter said.

The reverend stepped into the room and stood over John Carter's bed. "Morning," he said hesitantly but politely.

"Praise be," John Carter said.

"Yes," replied the reverend, "Praise . . . be . . ."

"Good morning, misser Charles Apple," Charles Apple said then giggled.

John Carter was a slender-faced man with wild, grayish hair who demanded immediate attention, the kind one gave to a band of street musicians at 2:30 in the morning. The reverend was not struck immediately by anything out of the ordinary, nor was he intimidated by the restraints that held John Carter to the bed. He had seen them before, many times and often in more violent situations. He assessed John Carter as being confused. Confused in the sense that he was not functioning on the same level as most. He was confused but not dangerous, at least that's what the reverend thought. The reverend still played it safe though and maintained a comfortable distance from the bed.

"Misser preacher man. Hee . . . hee," John Carter said. "The people living in darkness have seen a great light."

The reverend immediately understood this to be scripture. It was from Matthew. He had used it in sermons and speeches many times himself. "'On those living in the land of the shadows of death a light has dawned,'" the reverend said, completing the sixteenth verse of Matthew.

"I am the Son of David," John Carter said. "The Lord Almighty. Healer of the blind and mute. The crucified Jerusalem."

The reverend stepped forward with an overwhelming feeling of empathy. "You poor lost soul," he said then quoted from Matthew. " 'Enter through the narrow gate, for wide is the gate and broad is the road that leads to destruction.' "

John Carter laughed and swung his arms and legs violently, causing the bed to convulse and rattle. The reverend did not move nor did he show any weakness to what he was now calling a Demon.

"Fallen is Babylon!" John Carter yelled.

"Yes!" yelled Charles Apple, jumping up and down on his bed as if he were watching some great comical play.

"Fallen are the angels with phallic wings hard as teenage cocks," John Carter yelled.

"Blasphemy!" the reverend yelled.

"Hallelujah," John Carter said. "Some say tomato, some say tomata. I saw an angel standing in the sun and her cunt was dripping love. She smiled and I fucked her with my mind. Woe is Babylon. Woe is man. Woe are the eggs and the bacon and the 2% milk."

"Woe is Charles Apple," Charles Apple laughed.

"You are a demon," the reverend said. "Pure and evil."

John Carter stopped laughing, as if hurt by the reverend's comment. He then quoted the first line of Dante's *Inferno*: " 'In the midway of this our mortal life, I found me in a gloomy wood, astray, gone from the path direct.'"

The reverend thought about this then determined what John Carter was saying was not biblical but babble. He walked over to the side of John Carter's bed and placed his right hand on his forehead. "Lord, Father in Heaven, please help and direct this unfortunate soul for he is lost, lost, lost."

"Charles Apple need help too," Charles Apple said.

"Amen," John Carter said.

"Amen," said the reverend.

"Amen," said Charles Apple.

The reverend finished his prayer then looked down at John Carter. From under the white bed linen he could see urine expanding out like a great flood. "And the red sea parted," John Carter said laughing.

"Damn it, man," the reverend said.

"Do not forsake me in my hour of need," John Carter said, "you fucking idiot. Preachers are all the same—full of cum and glory with no guts for the good stuff."

The reverend stared down at John Carter queerly, completely confused and irritated by what he saw. He left John Carter still babbling. All the way down the hall and out into the lobby he tried to shake it off. Residents walked up and extended their hands in hopes of a cordial shake, but the reverend was in no state for it. He couldn't even smile. His round, wrinkled face sat sadly down upon itself making him look altogether uncomfortable. What he needed was a bump. A little something, something to pull his mind out of the wash. There was a restroom in the lobby and he went for it. He opened out his stash right there on the counter sink. No concerns. A little bump, that was all. He took out a credit card and sliced the stuff down until it was a fine powder. Overhead there was a speaker and it was playing some easy-listening Top 40 Muzak. The reverend did not recognize the song and didn't particularly like it, but it took his mind off Ruby and John Carter for the moment. He licked the credit card and put it away and pulled out a two-inch straw from the inner folds of his wallet. It was an instrument he used to perform his daily duties. He crouched down behind the powder and put the straw to his nose then inhaled. There was a moment of uncertainty, then a sting, then the reverend straightened up and looked at himself in the mirror. The hair on his head was finely gray, waxed down and beautiful. There was a strand that had fallen out of place and he fixed it. "Immaculate Savior," he said to himself, taking another bump then replacing the straw in his wallet. He ran some water and dribbled a few drops into his nostrils then washed his face, straightened his shirt, and left.

Outside, the Cloud hung low and heavy and it was the first thing the reverend saw. He repeated to himself what John Carter had said: "The people living in darkness have seen a great light."

The reverend was confused. It was Ruby he had aspirations for. Why? He had asked himself that question before and could only rely on divinity for the answer. It was in the cards and in the face that he held. When Geraldine Griffin told him about Neena Moore coming to town to interview a divine one his first thought was Ruby. It was a given. He was the most undeniably convincing member of the Home. He had not been shut down by the hard times; he had words and he used them. Any betting man would have placed money on him. The reverend was struck by an odd mysticism the first time he saw Ruby during his sermon in the dining hall. All that morning he had preached to a crowd of lifeless flesh, but then when Ruby walked into the room he was immediately filled with this strange, uncomfortable feeling. He was nervous for the first time in decades. He couldn't remember the last time one single man had done that to him. As he continued to preach that morning he watched Ruby in the back drinking his coffee, and the more he talked the less he thought Ruby believed him. It made him question himself, and no resident at the Home had ever done that. He still didn't know why he asked Ruby about the Coming of the Lord. It was irrelevant to their relationship at that point and seemed somewhat juvenile in retrospect, but he did it anyway and Ruby answered it exactly as he expected. Later, he had a great dream. He saw the Coming of the Lord, and Ruby was there looking mystical and far off as ever. It was then and there he knew there was something special about Ruby, something that ran much deeper than the blood under his polyester shirt, something more abstract than life could ever afford itself to understand. The reverend wasn't a brilliant man, but he knew when something was right. He also knew that John Carter was full of shit.

The reverend stood out in the yard under the Cloud and pondered all this, and somewhere between John Carter the idiot and Ruby the Messiah he had a great epiphany. " 'And there was darkness over all the land.' "

He was quoting Luke, chapter 23, verse 44. He was taking it all out of context, of course, but he had done that many times before with great proficiency. It worked then and it worked now.

The reverend stood for a moment considering these instruments and implications in biblical proportions, putting puzzles together improvisationally like some jacked-up sax player, pulling it all out of sorts then putting it back together, brilliantly searching for the one thing that would tear it wide-open. Was there anything to it? Was it the cocaine? Early stages of senility? The Cloud? What?

He dropped his eyes from the Cloud and by accident saw

the Cross—the steel construction that, to this point, had been altogether ignored as anything important. The reverend stared at it, the Cloud behind it providing a mystical backdrop. It stood perfectly out of place. A symbol of the times, of the new millennium. It was biblical, not just a novelty act off some interstate highway in West Virginia. No, it had purpose and the reverend was close to finding it. He walked over and placed his hands on it and felt an insurgence of energy run through his body. He contemplated Revelation, particularly the twentieth chapter pertaining to the *thousand years*. A thousand years had just ended some year-and-a-half ago. There had not been talks of Armageddon for some time now. No Rapture. No nothing. It was old news now. People had moved on to bigger and better things. There was a new president to contend with and he was a jackal to watch. "A thousand years," the Reverend mumbled to himself, his hands still on the Cross. "When it's over . . . Satan will be released from his prison."

What thousand years? The reverend asked himself. The first thousand after the death of Christ, the second? Or was it the many thousands before that?

This was the part of religion that confounded him, and if truth be known, he rarely sweated the technicalities. Why, when one could easily make it up? He had learned early on in his ministry that the core of religion was based upon faith and that faith could handle inference from time to time as long as it was based upon faith. And in this, he made it a point to be faithful.

But he wanted this one. He wanted the pieces to fit—more than just making them fit by banging out the edges and rounding them off. He wanted the most complex of corners to drop into place. He needed facts though, more facts than he had. But luckily under the present conditions—with the cocaine and all—the facts could tolerate a little twisting.

As he worked this out, things began to add up, at least in his mind. And as he got in his car and drove off down through the Brookwood Apartments, stopping at Lisa's apartment and getting out, he had convinced himself whole-heartedly that there was going to be a sacrifice.

People from all over began showing up at the Home shortly after the story made its complete revolution throughout the town and after everyone had a chance to decide what they thought of it. Radicals such as the Reverend Frederick Holmes and his deacons were among the first, along with the Reverend Alfonso

King. As the establishers and maintainers of the social morale they felt not only an obligation but also a right to have their presence known and felt during these most tested of times. But the waters upon which they tread were rough and oftentimes misunderstood. They turned harmless situations into global catastrophes, using words like machetes on people who could care less about some reincarnated Jesus in a nursing home. The staff at the Home took the brunt of these assaults, being described by the Reverend Frederick Holmes and his deacons as the *housers of the heathen* and the *bankers of bad money*. The Reverend Frederick Holmes himself came out to the Home—something he had never done, not even upon the request of a dying congregate—and petitioned Rita Hymer to have this Jesus business stopped.

"It's not that easy," Rita tried to explain.

"I don't care, and the people of this town don't care. I want this madness to stop. No more Jesus talk. No more story. It's over."

As the reverend spoke Rita went into a lackadaisical trance and thought how awfully odd and enjoyable it would be to stand up on the desk and piss on the reverend. Just stand up there, pull the old skirt up and panties down and let it fly.

This was very much uncharacteristic of Rita and she felt rather dirty afterwards. She was a wife and a mother and feared God. And the reverend, although impressive and morally persuasive, did not look anything like a urinal. Ultimately, she blamed it on the Cloud and moved on.

After the reverends and deacons and the First Baptist Church's choir instructor, came others: thrill seekers and otherwise moral jockeys in search of the one who called himself the Messiah. They came in droves expecting a front row seat to the Rapture. And they came one by one during visiting hours, posing as family members lost but now found. They came as cripples—physically and mentally—looking for that long-shot quick fix, getting as far as the nurses' station before getting turned back. One in particular, a Mr. Carlos Rubino, made it all the way to John Carter's room and spent some thirty minutes or so speaking with him. He told John Carter about what was going on and about Neena Moore from *The Globe* coming to do the interview. John Carter seemed very pleased and relayed many messages to him. Elnora found Carlos Rubino kneeling at the foot of John Carter's bed praying. She had Julius escort him out.

People came and stared into windows until curtains were

drawn; they sat out in the yard and pondered over the Cross. They sat on Ruby's bench and stared down into the heart of the Brookwood Apartments and wondered how anyone could live there. They came to the Home because they had heard the tabloid magazine, *The Globe,* was going to be there and most had read it more than they had the Bible. They wanted to see Neena Moore, the writer and photographer who captured so eloquently the 457-pound Buddha from Russellville, Arkansas. They wanted to be a part of something big, bigger than the town would ever allow them to be. They wanted the lights, the camera, the immortality of a beautiful picture. They were rebels and rednecks and the otherwise forgotten threads of the American fabric, but they knew a good thing when they heard it, and this sounded very much like something Jerry Springer would dance for.

When Julius escorted Carlos Rubino out of the Home, Carlos joined the Crowd in the parking lot in front of the Cross and told them of the man who called himself Jesus. He told them of his wild curly hair and of the restraints that held him tight to the bed. He told them of the prophetic things he had heard, and they listened and absorbed it intently. "It was beautiful scripture," Carlos Rubino said. "The most beautiful kind. He may just be the Messiah. Who knows."

The restraints proved a positive for John Carter, although he knew not how; the Crowd began to consider him a martyr. Small, nonviolent protests erupted in the parking lot with demands for John Carter's release. Rita Hymer responded by locking the double doors leading into the lobby and calling the Chatham County Police Department, who responded in kind by sending out one sheriff's car with one ill-prepared deputy sheriff. The deputy pulled up and got out of his car then joined Rita and the others in the lobby.

"Can't you tell them to leave?" said Rita.

"Sure," he said, "but it seems like a rather peaceful demonstration so far, wouldn't you say? Let's watch it for a while. Maybe, just maybe, they'll leave on their own."

So they watched. And as they watched, the Crowd got bigger and bigger. Congregations of mixed ethnicity, of mixed economical and social irrelevance joined together in the yard and around the Cross, some because of what they had heard and others because they had seen the Crowd and needed to be a part of something. For those that didn't quite understand what was going on, they were referred to Mr. Carlos Rubino—

another man of the hour, the man who stood before the new Messiah and received his message. Carlos told them everything, and in return they went off and told others. A great transfer of knowledge was established, and it grew and grew rapidly over mere hours until it held as much menacing force as the Cloud itself.

Inside the Home among the residents there was a relative homeostasis. Most never went outside and rarely ever looked out the window. Their contentment lay in three square, structured meals and one long, prolonged derangement of sleep, with the occasional television to round it all off. The majority of the residents had never even heard of John Carter—it was common knowledge around the Home and among the elderly that senility and confusion often ran rampant like cockroaches down an empty hall. Auditory dysfunction was also common, leaving most of the residents hearing nothing but an empty, continuous hum.

Ruby went uninformed as well. It was the book that captured the all of his attention. He had for the first time in his life successfully detached himself enough from the rest of the world in order to start his book; and not only had he started it but was well on his way to finishing it. Not even the Cloud at this point was able to destroy what he had created.

The staff, on the other hand, were all too aware of what was going on outside. They adapted their behavior slowly but surely in response to John Carter and the Cloud, and as with the opposing opinions of the two most prominent reverends in town, they too had theirs. But unlike the Reverends who could only get to John Carter on short ineffectual occasions, they were exposed to him constantly. Most of them believed he was full of shit and treated him as such. They believed he was confused and symptomatic of his disease. They played along with what he said, some saying in return, "Yes, Lord," or "Oh, yes, Great One."

John Carter did not know the difference. He was only being who he thought he was.

There were others who gave him the benefit of the doubt. They treated him with much more respect than most, although to say they treated him as the Messiah would be taking it too far. Basically, they treated him as a human being and a man, which was more of a moral reflection on themselves than on the situation. Those rare ones made sure that he was properly fed and cleaned and that the restraints were never too tight. They kept the mad balance alive, oftentimes feeling sorry for the man who, in actuality, deserved no sympathy at all.

John Carter was tied down for a reason. In every Home he had ever been in the staff found some reason to tie him down. From harassing the staff and residents to mutilating himself, he always seemed to do something out of the ordinary that required the straps. He was even found responsible for causing somewhat of a riot at the last Home he resided in. He was transferred to the Sunbridge Psychiatric and Rehabilitation Center because of it.

The story goes that he systematically turned the residents against the staff by filling their already delusional heads full of wild conspiracy theories. He then went about the task of actually making the theories come true. The one that started the riot involved mashed potatoes and the pharmaceutical sedative Risperdal. It was postulated by John Carter to a select few residents that the nursing staff, along with the kitchen staff, were putting Risperdal in the mashed potatoes so that the residents would be too drowsy after lunch to cause any problems while the nursing staff watched their daytime soaps.

He then told them chilling stories of nurses gone mad, took them to the nurses' station, and made them go around back and look into the break room. Sure enough, the soaps were on. It was hard evidence, and it made a lot of people who had nothing better to do get absolutely livid. And when the Risperdal capsules showed up in their potatoes—the ones John Carter had so malevolently stashed away in his cheeks each and every time a nurse brought one to him—he was the first to say, "Look, they slipped up and forgot to destroy the evidence."

He repeated this once every week for four weeks until he had successfully unleashed the beast. The geriatric residents, who had lived a lifetime getting stepped on here and there until completely dehumanized and mortally wounded by old age, were incensed to the point that they took over the Home. They held a nursing student hostage in the activity room for two days until the state and local authorities forced their way in, freeing the nursing student—who eventually dropped out of school—and arresting five elderly gentlemen on charges of kidnapping.

John Carter wasn't one of them. During the whole uproar he was nowhere to be found: not in his bed, not in his room, not in the Home itself. They found him five days later at a Motel 6. He was completely off his medication and completely lunified. The state transferred him to a psychiatric facility where he spent five months baking and then transferred him once again to the Sunbridge Psychiatric and Rehabilitation Center in Siler City. He was a somewhat young man in his mid-fifties who, unlike Ruby, did not suffer from a devastating string of bad luck, but was born with the string attached, unraveling at a young age from a psychotic disorder which made him unsafe to be around. The state captured him early; with no family or ties whatsoever, they treated him as a homeless vagrant who was better off institutionalized. They would let him out every few years only to see him back in some emergency room somewhere up or down the East Coast. When he was out, he was traveling; when he was in, he was a menace—a traveling menace whose life's ambition was clear, at least to himself: from a very young age he was Jesus.

But doesn't everyone want to be Jesus—with or without knowing? It's only the majority that has figured out through natural selection or some life-changing event that they're not: usually a car accident of the highest order—head-ons and the inevitable, unmovable tree. A gunshot to the heart can do it too. And of course old age, the saddest of all rejections. How terrible to live a whole life shrouded with this grandiose misconception of mortality—not believing it has anything to do with just being, speaking words that pertain only to the welfare of the self, reading words in the same manner, surrounding oneself only with those that understand, in the same fashion, the rules for that self's survival, creating a universe in the mind that is free and unobstructively open to ponder the higher questions of life: the *who*, *what*, and *when* of the cosmic tongue. The questions only a heavenly being can answer. A God. A Messiah.

The old man knows no answers anymore. They were taken from him at the door along with his pants and watch—irrelevant timekeeper. The old man is stripped of his answers; they are given to the young to be mutilated and molested, changed slightly for the times then sewn to jackets and worn proudly through the young streets. The old man is left to watch—no more questions, too confused for questions. It's best just to sleep it off, leave life to the young or to whoever wants it.

John Carter was Jesus then. He wanted it, convincing himself and a handful of others that he was. There was a yard full of well-wishers to prove it. A house full of dissonance and insubordination. There was John Carter in his bed chanting Blake. There was Charles Apple beside him repeating whatever he said. The staff, the halls—the empty, smelly halls—baskets full of urine-soaked linen and urine-soaked wheelchairs. There were Ruby and Thomas C. McNeil together writing and watching, paying attention to nothing but themselves and the wall, absorbed and unabsorbed collectively.

Ruby heard the commotion earlier in the day but figured it was John Carter or some other resident flying off the handle. It was late evening when he finally stopped typing. He missed supper but knew the lobby doors would be open until ten and that Lisa would be home and he could eat with her. In the lobby he saw a large crowd of staff and a deputy sheriff. They were all standing around with their hands in their pants staring out one of the many windows in the lobby. Ruby decided to bypass them and go for the door. It was locked. "Not tonight, Mr. Riggs," Priscilla Franz said. Priscilla was an evening shift nurse, slightly younger than Lisa. She had not been at the Home long. A new nurse with a fresh, new face.

"What's the big deal?" Ruby asked, staring out at the Crowd in the yard.

Priscilla did not answer. Neither did her cohorts Tiwanda Young and Cheryl Lucia. They stood pressed up against the glass, excited like high school cheerleaders, smiles full of chaos.

"It has something to do with that Jesus fella you got in here," the deputy sheriff said in a low, muffled voice that demanded secrecy.

"Damn fool," Ruby said.

"Yep. It looks as if he's gettin' what he wants."

"I suppose," said Ruby.

Ruby left the lobby and went to the dining room. It was empty and dark. Ruby made his way through the round tables to the serving line. He went around it into the kitchen area. Near the back of the kitchen was a door and he opened it. It led to the outside. He placed a serving spoon at its foot and closed it till the spoon wedged the door open about an inch. He then skirted off the loading dock into the night.

From around the corner he peered at the Crowd in the front yard and parking lot. Hundreds of faces foreign to Ruby, milling around in one unique ball of orderly chaos, mostly silent, bunched up here and there speaking in low, serious tones. Almost directly in the middle of the Crowd and the parking lot was the Cross. It stuck out like a radio tower off a distant hill. Ruby had to adjust himself and take a second look. It confused him and made him understand what he had, to this point, taken for granted.

Ruby followed the darkness around to the edge of the yard then blended in with the Crowd in the parking lot. As he made his way through he could hear bits and pieces of conversations. They were centered around John Carter and the Cross; the Cloud also came up. Ruby looked back at the Cross, then to the Crowd, and then through the windows into the lobby. He could see Priscilla Franz and the other nurses still standing about, along with the deputy sheriff. Were they expecting trouble? Surely not, Ruby thought. "All this for a lunatic?"

"What the hell is going on up there?" Lisa asked as Ruby let himself into the apartment.

"John Carter again. And there's a Cross now."

"A Cross?"

"Yeah, in the middle of the parking lot. Hundreds of people around it. Maybe they'll crucify him. Give him what he wants."

"Surely not," Lisa said.

Ruby laughed, "No. Do you have anything to eat?"

Lisa fixed Ruby some spaghetti, and Ruby told her the complete story, as much as he knew, of the tabloid newspaper and John Carter. "Who knows about the Cross," he said. "There's a deputy sheriff up there right now in the lobby. He's clueless."

"None of this would be happening if it wasn't for that goddamn Cloud," Lisa said. "It has fucked everything up."

Ruby ate his spaghetti and thought about his book and how, only an hour or so ago while typing, he had come to the realization that if it wasn't for the Cloud he probably wouldn't be typing; it had become the perfect distraction from everything, even the Home and his wife. He was doing now what he had wanted to do his whole life and yet felt guilty for not being more a part of the fiasco that was taking over the Home. It was turning out to be one of the strangest events he'd ever been associated with, yet he was willingly and uncharacteristically missing it all.

There was nothing he could do or wanted to do. As a writer he knew the window of opportunity was always half-closed, never half-open, and that the inspiration to get it done came in strange packages, often at strange times. There was never a formula to keep the juices flowing. It was always: run with the ball when you got it.

There was a clear and objective picture now, and Ruby had only to sit down behind the word processor for the words to come. They came so easy that Ruby even thought about other things while he wrote. It felt like cheating at first until he got used to it; then it felt like genius. He started thinking about what he was going to do when the book was finished. His editor's husband worked at Algonquin Books and had, over a company Christmas party, expressed interest in Ruby's writing. He told Ruby that his columns read a lot like short stories and he had thought how interesting it would be to print a collection of them in book form. A sort of *Spoon River Anthology* of Wilmington. He also expressed interest when Ruby told him about his book and told Ruby to call him before talking to anyone else after he finished it. The next day Ruby was hung-over and considered the conversation alcohol-induced. It was only now, well into the later part of its completion with the ending in focus like some estranged sniper, that Ruby found the editor's invitation curious and not that far off from reality.

THE BIG FRESH

Ramell Chapel found the spoon and the door off the back of the loading dock propped open. He then went back to the Crowd and told Carlos Rubino. "You did the right thing, Ramell," Carlos said, which Ramell had obviously thought through: it was Carlos who knew where John Carter was and it was Carlos who had received his gospel, and it was Carlos who should go back in.

Carlos Rubino called council with some of the more prominent members of the Crowd, including Robert Leblanc who ran the Siler City Country Club. He was a right-winged Marxist by night who believed solely in the chaotic evolution of everything. He wasn't religious, but he was a fanatic; and when he heard about the Jesus at the Home, he told his wife not to wait up for him.

Others in council included James Morton, owner and proprietor of the Gold 'n' Pawn on Riley Street in Historic Siler City, and Arthur Tysor, who was branch manager at the Central Carolina Bank on Raleigh Street. Both, like Robert Leblanc, were fanatics in one respect or other.

Carlos Rubino brought to them the news of the loading dock door being open. Robert Leblanc immediately spoke up . . .

"What!" said Carlos Rubino, who was, among the whole of the council, the more sensible, moderate minded.

"Yes," said James Morton. "Until we know for sure."

"No! No!" Carlos Rubino said. "Nothing like that."

"You've missed the point," said Robert Leblanc, exerting his five inches and seventy extra pounds he had over Carlos Rubino to make his point. "They already got him tied down."

"He's right," said Arthur Tysor. "Cops at the door. Doors locked. This thing is big."

Carlos was stumped. The council had spoken, yet what they spoke of was unheard-of and illegal. He stepped back from the Crowd and looked over at the Home and at the deputy sheriff and the nurses who had been in the lobby for hours. It is true, he thought to himself, and secretly it would be nice to have some more time to speak with the one who called himself Jesus.

"How?" Carlos asked.

"Easy," Robert Leblanc said. He then unfolded an impromptu plan to the council that had the intricacies of a well-oiled machine.

THE BIG FRESH

Ruby awakened around eleven-thirty that night. He was naked and Lisa was naked beside him. They had made love and fallen asleep. He sat up on the side of the bed and put his clothes on then walked out into the mugginess of the night. From the apartment steps he could see the blackened sky and below it, farther up the hill, the Crowd. They were milling around and Ruby contemplated the Coming of the Lord and how chaotic it would be. He walked slowly up the hill and sunk into the Crowd then emerged out the other side around the corner. He turned and watched the Crowd for a few minutes then ascended the steps up to the loading dock. When he reached the door he noticed that the serving spoon had been moved. He gave the door a pull and a push but it was locked. "Damn."

It was unfortunate, for he had ideas of writing all night. Instead, he went back through the Crowd, looking into the lobby to see if it was clear—it wasn't. The same deputy sheriff stood guard. Ruby thought of going up to the doors and asking in but that wouldn't be good. He decided to go back to Lisa's and spend the night.

It was a peaceful walk down the hill through the heart of the Brookwood Apartments. There were dim streetlights hidden among young bushy oaks and they created the illusion of walking through space. Ruby enjoyed it so much that he got Lisa out of bed and they went walking down the hill and out of the Brookwood Apartments. They went across Raleigh Street into the small community park. There was no one around and they lazily made their way through the slides and rides, talking of each other and of the Crowd and Cloud and eventually John Carter. They spoke of all three with a malignancy that mimicked cancer. It had become that way with the whole town, a collective switching of the subconscious, like Pearl Harbor or the invention of television. There was no escaping it now that the small town had been raped by it for so long. Too much energy built up under one roof and not enough to do with it. It was as if a lid had been placed over the town and the temperature turned up to medium-hot and the cook left town, forgot about the stew, never came back to stir it or sip it or add water. It was futile. Things had to happen quickly but they weren't. It was a small town, true, and things generally moved slowly, but it was too slow, even the retired recipients on Social Security couldn't find enough to do with their time. It was as if the Cloud was apocalyptic and there was a clock in it and on it, facing down toward the town; and it had no hands, only an alarm and no one knew when it was going to go off—or if it was going to go off at all. It was the most confusing thing they had ever witnessed; everyone said so. There was an agreement on that.

Ruby and Lisa left the park and walked across the street to the Piggly Wiggly. "That's a strange name for a grocery store," Ruby said. "It always has been. It makes me think that maybe pork chops have feelings too. I've never bought pork chops at the Piggly Wiggly."

They stood at the window and stared in and randomly spoke of boxes of cereal and pork chops. A sheriff's car pulled up behind them and flashed a spotlight onto their backs. They turned around and squinted as the driver's side window slowly came down. "Lisa?" the driver said.

"Hey, Tim," Lisa said.

"Making sure you weren't trying to break in."

"I do like to do my shopping at night," Lisa said.

Ruby stood beside Lisa feeling somewhat awkward, not wanting to say anything, not having anything to say. Off in the distance, coming across the tracks out of the heart of Historic Siler City were two sheriff's cars; they had their blue lights flashing, one behind the other, accelerating speed as they passed. "Looks like trouble," Lisa said, staring as they took a right into the Brookwood Apartments.

"Sunditch," the deputy said, referring to the Home. "Someone missing, again."

Ruby tightened up at hearing this. So did Lisa.

"No," said Lisa.

"Yeah. Nothing new about that. Always someone missing, walking off into the woods, dying. Senile old men."

The deputy looked at Ruby then back to Lisa and smiled. "Tell your father I said hello."

"I will," Lisa said.

The deputy pulled off slowly then accelerated when he hit the highway, quickly taking a right into the Brookwood Apartments.

"You're in trouble," she said.

"It's fine," Ruby said.

"What will they do? Or can they do anything?"

"I don't know," Ruby said, thinking back to when Geraldine Griffin had found him at the convenience store—when the possibilities of leaving seemed all too real. He hadn't thought about it in so long that it became more fiction than real, something only senile old men did.

It was impossible for him to consider what might happen now that he had presumably gone missing. Why not just walk on back, explain what had happened? Tell them about Lisa. "Can you move in with me?" Lisa said.

"Sure," Ruby said.

"No, I'm serious. Leave the Home and come live with me. We're perfect together."

Ruby couldn't deny that, but the logistical ramifications were unheard of. His mind wouldn't even let him consider it. His mind had been all about the book for so long that everything seemed distant and numb, even the want and need to go home seemed detached. It was not that he didn't want to go home; it was just that he wanted to finish his book first.

"Don't you think?" she said.

"I do. Let's get out of here before Tim finds out who I am."

They took a wooded path behind the Piggly Wiggly that came up behind the Brookwood Apartments. It was dark and new and it made them both feel alive. When they got home they made love and fell asleep.

The blue lights flashed for hours up at the Home. The Crowd stood around anxious and unabashedly curious, staring at them. They were hypnotic and gave everyone a feeling of importance—as with the Cross and John Carter. The Crowd was more than glad to be witness to it all.

Inside the Home, there were questions being asked and residents awakened for the same questions to be asked again. "Have you seen this man?"

"No," was the collective answer.

"Do you know this man?"

"No," repeated again and again.

"What is your name?"

"I don't know."

Up and down the hall, in and out of bathrooms and closets, under beds, turning lights on in every room and leaving them on, lighting the Home up like Christmas. Brown-suited, flashlight-wielding soldiers with forty-fives strapped to their hips, rounding up geriatrics left and right, upsetting the general population's mood that took many milligrams of narcotics and sedatives to achieve. "Is this necessary?" asked Daisy Moore, pressing down on her stomach as if trying to drop the baby right there on the floor.

"None of this is necessary," one of the deputies replied. "It all seems rather useless to me too, but that's the system for you. Got to love it."

Charles Apple sat on the side of his bed, feet on the floor, smiling as the deputies ran through the room slowly and methodically.

"And you didn't see anything?" a deputy asked Charles Apple.

"Charles Apple didn't see anything," he said, smiling.

They searched the woods around the Home for another hour then one by one got into their cars, turned off their blues lights, and ascended down the hill into the Brookwood Apartments then disappeared.

As the night progressed, they were called back to the Home once more, found nothing, and left.

THE BIG FRESH

Ruby awakened early the next morning feeling strange. He couldn't explain it. It just felt different. It had something to do with what happened during the night, but he had a plan to fix all that. He had thought of it before falling asleep. But it was as if something else had happened. Something he could not recall.

He went into the kitchen and got himself a glass of water then went into the living room and turned the television on—that alone was different. The news was on, and that's what he wanted. After a brief segment of commentary they cut to the weather showing state and local—local being Raleigh, but Siler City would be mentioned in the final role call. After a few minutes it scrolled by: *Partly Cloudy to Sunny, highs 98.*

Ruby was about to turn the television off when he heard something very strange. He fumbled with the remote until he found the volume button then turned it up . . . "a peaceful demonstration turns violent after a resident from a psychiatric facility in Siler City goes missing."

The anchorman, Jim Payne cut in, "For more let's go to Deborah Collins who is standing by in Siler City. Deborah."

Ruby could not believe it, and it was rather unbelievable. The anchorwoman Deborah Collins was standing in front of the Home—more precisely, she was standing in front of a lobby window that had a relatively good size hole in it. She looked clean and polished, smiling like she had nothing to smile about. The hole looked as if a rock made it. It was jagged and open and revealed nothing about the Home. "Jim," Deborah Collins said, "a twist to this already amazing story: a second resident of the Sunbridge Psychiatric and Rehabilitation Center is now confirmed missing. Let me tell you what I now know. Some time after midnight last night the Siler City Sheriff's Department was notified by this very facility here that one of its residents was missing. No names have been given by the facility itself but we have found out through other sources that the alleged missing resident is a one Mr. John Carter. What we know now is that Mr. Carter came to the Sunbridge Psychiatric and Rehabilitation Center about two weeks ago. It is said that he is delusional and a possible harm to himself and others."

"Deborah, do you have any information on the other missing resident?" Jim Payne asked.

"I do. We have just found out that his name is Mr. Ruben

Franklin Riggs. He has been a resident here for some time now. The officials here aren't ruling out any foul play at this time. As I reported earlier, there has been a demonstration going on for about a day now. Demonstrators say it isn't a demonstration but more support for the one resident, Mr. John Carter, who is missing."

"Deborah, is the Crowd saying anything about the missing residents?" Jim asked.

"Yes, they found out about the same time the Sheriff's Department did. They believe the Home has something to do with the disappearances. They don't know what. I spoke with one man and he was referring to John Carter as Christ, Reborn. Now, I do know that the tabloid magazine *The Globe* is coming down to do a story on this man."

"Wow!" said Cindy Morgan, anchorwoman sitting beside Jim.

"Yes, indeed," said Jim Payne. "Is the Crowd saying anything about the other resident? Do they believe they are together or . . ."

"They know nothing about him, Jim, but as far as I can tell they do suspect the two are connected somehow."

"Amazing story!" Jim said.

"Jim and Cindy," Deborah interrupted. "One more thing. If I can get the camera to swing up this way I want to show you something."

At that moment the camera swung hard right then up, out over the tree line exposing a beautiful shot of the Cloud.

"You see this Cloud?" Deborah asked. The camera held on it for a few seconds then dropped back onto her. "It has been here, people are telling me, for over two weeks now. Some have gone as far as to say that it showed up the same day John Carter did. And that's not all." The camera swung around to its left showing the Crowd and the Cross.

"This Cross showed up a couple of days ago. No one knows where it came from or why it's here."

"Amazing," Jim Payne said.

"Yes. When are they expecting *The Globe*, Deborah?" Cindy asked.

"They aren't saying, but I'd be willing to speculate anytime now. The Crowd is only getting bigger out here, and there's no telling what to expect."

"Well, stay on it and we'll be getting back to you shortly," Jim said.

Ruby turned the television off and hung his head. What a mess the day was turning out to be and he still felt the same strange feeling he woke up with. It was like skipping school for the first time or getting really wasted and crawling around on the floor delusional.

He went outside and stood on the deck and looked up the hill. He could see the WRAL Channel 5 van parked in the circle drive, a large antenna sprouting from its roof, connected and corresponding to the world. Ruby made some strange faces to himself, mimicking the collective response to all that Deborah Collins had said. Faces of lunacy and fanaticism. There was no need for a plan now. It was all a question of when.

Ruby went back inside and crawled in bed with Lisa. She was awake and had heard most of what the news had to say. "What are we going to do?" she asked, pulling up beside Ruby under his arm.

"I'm not sure."

There was an awful air of desperation and silence; then Lisa jumped to her knees. "Let's get out of here!" she said.

"And go where?"

"Anywhere. There's nothing for me here anymore and you never did like it. Let's go to Wilmington. You said you wanted to go back."

Ruby thought about this and became excited. She was right. Nothing left. They could find a place to live on the Intracoastal Waterway. She would love it. He could teach her how to sail and fish and he could finish the book and sell it then write another. It would be the same. He didn't need the Cloud or John Carter to finish it. Besides, things were different now. Now he was part of the fiasco, no better than John Carter. He'd have to finish the book elsewhere anyway. "You sure?" he asked her.

"I'm sure," she said. "What the hell."

"I need to get some things," Ruby said.

"That's fine, we'll get 'em on the way out."

"It's not that easy," he said.

"What do you mean?" Lisa asked, thinking the Home was like a Holiday Inn—check out at 11.

"They don't let you come and go as you please like that. If they see me walking out with my things they will try to hold me. Things like that usually end in violence."

"Really?"

"Yes."

Ruby went on to tell Lisa some of the things he had seen in the

Home—restraints and sedatives, et cetera, and how they took the life out of a warm body. Lisa was utterly amazed. "You can't go back," she pleaded.

"It's not as bad as that," Ruby said. "We just need to be careful. I'll find a way back in and get my book and a few other things then leave."

Lisa was happy. For the first time in years she had a purpose and it felt good.

"I need to do a few things myself," she said.

It was ten-thirty in the morning, late in the day at the Home. Ruby needed more time though; he needed for the Crowd to reorganize and grow, get crazy, and do something distracting.

He and Lisa got up and took a shower then fixed breakfast and ate slowly. They had all day to do what would take fifteen minutes. They wanted to do it right.

Carlos Rubino showed up at the Home around noon. He was shell-shocked and weary. He had not slept all night. His clothes were ragged and the glasses he had on the night before were gone and his eyes were puffy and everyone who saw him could tell he wasn't seeing quite as well as before. The Crowd had grown considerably since the early morning hours—no small thanks to Deborah Collins and her WRAL Channel 5 news crew, who were still on location waiting for the big scoop. It was wide open now with other news crews en route.

Carlos Rubino stumbled through the Crowd and out the other side and went up to the double doors and banged on them desperately with a fist. "Off limits," Deputy Frank Wright said.

"No, you must— " Carlos pleaded.

Deputy Frank Wright stepped forward and banged the butt of his billy stick on the glass then with it pointed toward the Crowd.

"No," Carlos said. "It's John Carter."

Deputy Frank Wright immediately recognized what Carlos was trying to say and opened the door. Carlos fell through the door almost hitting the floor before Frank Wright caught him. He dragged Carlos over to a bench and sat him down.

"He . . . he's not the Messiah," Carlos said, mumbling through his dog-tired teeth.

"What are you saying, man?" Frank Wright said.

"John Carter is not the Messiah. He's mean and filthy and we shouldn't have taken him."

"You took him?"

"Yes. Yes. And I told them we should bring him back, but they wouldn't listen. They still believe. They want to make it work. They want to prove something. I don't know what. I don't know . . ."

Deputy Frank Wright straightened up and looked at Carlos Rubino and wondered what the hell he was talking about. He unfortunately hadn't been completely briefed on the situation. He left Carlos and walked over to Rita Hymer's office and interrupted her on the phone and asked her to come into the lobby, which she politely did. Before Frank Wright could turn around, Carlos was out the front doors standing in front of the Crowd.

"Your Messiah is a fake!" he yelled three times before collecting the attention of the entire Crowd.

"He is a fake and you should know this. He is a very indecent man with filthy manners. He urinates on himself and laughs about it. He speaks like the devil yet proclaims he is Christ. He is the Antichrist. The devil himself."

Frank Wright and Rita ran out behind Carlos and stopped; then Rita went back inside for help. Frank Wright ran to his car and radioed the department. Carlos continued to talk. The Crowd shrunk in around him and asked where John Carter was. "He is at the Country Club," Carlos answered, "and no one can get to him. They won't give him up. I pleaded with them, but it's no use. They said they would hurt me if I left, but I had to. That man is not Christ. Oh, Father in heaven, forgive me for I have sinned badly."

Rita returned with Julius and Elnora, and when Frank Wright joined them they grabbed Carlos Rubino by the shoulders and dragged him into the Home then locked the doors. After Carlos calmed down, he told Frank Wright everything and Frank Wright took detailed notes of what he said: the people, the times, the location. It all went down. Shortly after finishing, two sheriffs' cars pulled up. They joined Frank Wright in the lobby, took his notes, and then one took Carlos and handcuffed him and escorted him out. The Crowd was orderly but they shrunk around Carlos and the officer. Some yelled obscenities, others asked if it was true. "Yes. Yes!" Carlos cried as his body was forced into the back seat of a sheriff's car. The deputy went around the car and got into the driver's seat then hit the sirens and lights. The Crowd responded by parting and the car drove off. The Cloud stayed. The Crowd stayed. Rita and the others inside the Home stayed.

THE GERMAN CONNECTION

He was one of the first to get off the train and under his right arm he carried a package the size of an ordinary birdcage, covered in black cloth. Josef saw him from a distance and immediately assumed he was the man Werner spoke of.

He was a relatively young man, handsome with chiseled features; he had a straight back and stood strong and assuring on the plank and stared off at the vassals and uniforms that lined out across the Institution. Josef lost his concentration completely while thinking about the package under his right arm. It was Werner's fault, and he would most surely let him know later.

As the vassals began piling off the train Josef found himself in a very awkward position—for it was not only his duty but a given right that he oversee the unloading of the train, yet the anticipation of not knowing what the gentleman had in store for him was just too much. He eventually decided that all good things were worth waiting for and that a trainload of vassals was a very important thing to tend to. He began the job of sorting while at the same time watching as the man made his way off the plank and into the heart of the Institution.

It was an hour or so later that Werner stood at Josef's feet. "Father Marcus Ramos is here!" Werner said, yelling over the engine of the locomotive.

"Father Ramos?" Josef yelled.

"Yes!"

"From Istanbul?"

"Yes!"

Josef continued his work with inaccuracy, sending the sick left and the others right.

"Damn it, Werner!" Josef yelled. "You're always a little off, aren't you? Can't you see I'm busy?"

"I thought—"

"Of course," Josef said. "Put him in my office and leave me alone."

Werner grinned and backed off. It was a *slit your throat* kind of grin, one Josef had seen many times before. It was a statement not a threat and that's why Werner was still alive. Josef pulled himself back into his work and forgot about it.

After the last vassal unloaded off the train and was directed by Josef where to go, Josef gingerly made his way back to the Block. Inside, activity proceeded as usual with vassals lining the walls naked and otherwise stripped of their humanity. Werner was overseeing a liver dissection. Carl and Herta were amputating legs and Horst was in the process of castrating a male vassal. It was his duty and all the other physicians' duty to make sure after the Great Experiment of the war was over that there would be no more vassals to experiment on. It was a form of self-destruction but one the Führer demanded.

Josef walked over to Werner and pulled him off to the side. "Is the man in my office?"

"Yes, Josef," Werner said, "as you asked."

"Did you see what he was carrying?"

"No," Werner said.

"Good."

Josef walked off and left Werner to his business. In Josef's office the gentleman sat facing the opposing wall, legs crossed and hands over his knees. The package sat on Josef's desk covered in the black cloth.

From behind, Josef quickly assessed the man to be a salesman: black wool suit, perfectly shined shoes, black hair greased down to the skull. Josef was immediately intimidated by the man's immaculate appearance, even after a train ride for God knows how many days from Istanbul. The man reminded Josef of himself, and that was something he hadn't seen in a long while, especially at the Institution.

"What is your business in Istanbul?" Josef asked, startling the young man. He stood up and turned around to greet Josef with a smile and a slight nod of the head as Josef entered the room.

"None at all," the man said.

Josef placed his riding crop on the bookcase behind his desk, then worked off his white gloves and his coat, and then took a seat behind the desk. "My assistant told me your telegraph said you were coming from Istanbul."

"Your assistant is right and I did say that, but it is not true."

The man looked behind him, out the open door at all that was going on. "You have a prolific business here," he said, smiling somewhat uncomfortably.

"It is the war that created the demand," Josef said.

"True," said the man. "But it is you that created this."

There was a moment of silence as the two gauged each other's position in this new relationship, then the man spoke out frankly, "I have heard all about you, Josef. What you do and how you do it and I must say that I am rather sickened by all of it."

Josef sat back and listened and contemplated homicide.

"You are known throughout this land as a merciless physician, an experimenter of life, and an angel of death. You have no religion and no god will claim you. You are the devil himself," the man said.

Josef stared down at the vale-draped package then back to the man.

"You are an innovator though, as much as I want to deny it," the man said, "and I have heard that you have unraveled, or are very close to unraveling the very fabrics of the science of life. What this means I am not completely sure, but it is the reason why I am here."

"You are a very brave man," Josef said, "for speaking with such liberties in my home. I could easily have you dismantled right now. I assure you that all you have heard about me is true, and knowing that, you should be fearing for your life." Josef leaned forward, placing his elbows on the desk and intertwining his fingers. "Is that clear?"

"Very. But you must understand also that I am protected by some very powerful people and such actions, albeit aesthetically rewarding initially, would ultimately result in your own death."

Josef leaned back in his chair.

"I am not here to debate the moralistic issues surrounding your work. I am here rather to petition your services in another such related matter. One that unfortunately requires extremity in measures not unlike what you are used to." The man leaned forward and extended his hand. "My name is Father Marcus Ramos, and I am from the Vatican."

"Father?"

"Yes."

"You don't look like a priest."

"Nor you a physician," Father Ramos said. "I'll agree that this is rather awkward, but these are astringent times in which we live. I did not choose to be here; it was chosen for me. As with you, we are both a product of our times, Josef, and being as such, we must produce accordingly."

"Yes," Josef said.

"You must understand I am not here under the full cooperation of my people. They would not hear of such collaborations. They are older and subsequently wiser, yet applied wisdom is not always the preferable route of insight. What I have seen cannot and will not compare to their deliberations. So, understand what I tell you today can only remain with you. Anything else will be unacceptable."

"You have certainly got my attention, Father," Josef said. "Tell me, what is it you have to say?"

Father Ramos stood up and walked over to shut the door then returned to his seat. He pulled a package of cigarettes from his breast pocket, offered one to Josef, which he accepted, lit them both then sat back down. "In 1782, the Vatican acquired information that led them to believe that a very sacred burial ground had been discovered. Specifically, a tomb in Ephesus, Turkey. It was believed that this tomb held the remains of the Virgin Mary. Upon conferring with other authorities, the Vatican sent Father Anthony Marcelino and some archaeologists to Turkey. Father Marcelino was gone for six months. When he returned, he had in his possession a vessel. The Virgin Mary was not found."

Josef let out a weak laugh then apologized. "Please, continue."

"They say Father Anthony Marcelino was in shock when he returned. He did not speak of the vessel or of the strange inscriptions and hieroglyphics on it. He delivered it to the Vatican then retired to his quarters.

"Many great minds set about the task of deciphering what was written on the vessel," Father Ramos paused, hesitating. "You must understand how spiritual these people are. The last thing they wanted was to violate a sacred artifact, and the fact that Father Marcelino was out of sorts made them proceed with even more caution.

"They never came to a consensus about it," Father Ramos said. "Argument over the dissension led many to believe that whatever it was, was evil. It was finally agreed upon to let Herbert Theodore Maxwell from London study it. He was the leading voice at the time on biblical artifacts—very respected and very well known to the Vatican.

"He studied the piece for three months before returning it with an answer. What he had to say disturbed and angered many people."

Father Ramos paused and fumbled for another cigarette, offering one to Josef, who accepted and lit them both. "What did Maxwell say?" Josef asked, speaking through a cloud of smoke.

Father Ramos looked Josef in the eyes, took a great inhalation of smoke, and then exhaled. "He said the inscriptions and hieroglyphics suggested that the vessel housed the Messiah's seminal organs."

There was a moment of silence and Josef looked at Father Ramos perplexed. "Is that possible?" he asked.

"I think so. And so did Father Marcelino. He was the only other person, besides Maxwell, who could have possibly interpreted what was on that vessel, yet he came back from Turkey with nothing to say. But when Maxwell gave his conclusions, Father Marcelino took the vessel and hid it then killed himself."

"If he was so disturbed by it why didn't he just leave it in Turkey?" Josef asked.

"There was no way he could have. The tomb had been violated. At that point he could do nothing but bring it home."

"Why not hide it from the very beginning?" Josef said. "Why show it to anyone?"

"Who knows; maybe he thought he was wrong."

"Is it possible, though?" Josef asked. "I mean . . . really?"

"Possible that the vessel houses the Messiah's seminal organs?" Father Ramos asked.

"Yes," Josef said.

"It is," Father Ramos said, "if you take into consideration the fact that the Gospel itself is split on what actually happened to Jesus after he died. The *Epistula Apostolorum* says that he was taken from the Cross along with two thieves and buried at *The Place of the Skull.* The first to come upon him there were Sarah, Martha, and Mary Magdalene. Yet, the Gospel of John says that Nicodemus was the first to come to Jesus by night."

"That doesn't explain anything," Josef said.

"Exactly!" said Father Ramos. "It doesn't. That's why it's possible."

"I suppose."

"Please bear with me," Father Ramos said. "The Gospel of Mark says that Joseph of Arimathea went to Pontius Pilate after the death of Christ and asked for the body. Pilate gave it to him. It is said that he took the body, wrapped it in linen, and placed it in a tomb." Father Ramos took a breath and looked at Josef. Josef looked somewhat confused still. "This is where it happened," Father Ramos said. "This makes it real."

"And you believe this?" Josef asked.

"I would not be here if I didn't," Father Ramos said.

"So this Joseph of Arimathea castrated Jesus?"

"Joseph was a rich man," Father Ramos said. "He and his family owned tin mines in Cornwall, England. Tin is the primary ingredient for bronze. And he was very well versed in Greek and Phoenician culture and had alchemical skills. He was also on the counsel that tried and found Jesus guilty, yet he believed in Jesus and he believed in the coming of the Lord."

"Why didn't he stop it?" Josef asked.

"Because he knew he couldn't. He knew Jesus had gone too far by going into Jerusalem on Passover. He could do nothing but go along with the rest of the counsel or possibly be found guilty himself of collaboration."

"So he took the body?" Josef said.

"He took it along with the chalice used during the Last Supper. He castrated the body, prepared it with spices and wrapped it, and placed it in the tomb. He took the seminal organs and the chalice to Cornwall, prepared the organs for preservation, placed them in the chalice, and then sealed it."

"Then placed it in the tomb in Turkey?"

"No," Father Ramos said, "mythology takes over here. I would guess that he hid it somewhere in Glastonbury. How it got to Ephesus, I do not know. I do know that for some time now it has been suspected that the Virgin Mary's tomb was in Ephesus. That would at least account for Father Marcelino's being there."

"Why?" Josef asked.

"Why move it to Ephesus?"

"No, why do all this?" Josef said.

"To rise again," Father Ramos said. "Joseph of Arimathea was a visionary—not unlike yourself. He couldn't save Jesus from the Cross but he could preserve that which one day could make him live again. He was a well-traveled man versed in many ancient cultures. He knew the body was a vehicle for the soul and that it was the soul that continued on after death, not the body. It's hard to say if he believed Jesus would rise in three days. Now, when it actually happened it probably destroyed him, but to call it a spiritual occurrence? No. It was fanatical, instituted, most likely, by his own disciples."

"Yes," Josef said, "that is possible."

"Of course it is. The knowledge that you have now wasn't there then, but there was a vision. It was Joseph's vision that allowed him to do what he did: to preserve the organs until there was sufficient knowledge. That is why I am here. You, Josef, have the knowledge and ability. You, far more than any other man. I do not agree with your tactics but admire your tact. And as history has always shown us, greatness comes not always from great things."

Josef contemplated all that Father Ramos said and was rather intrigued on both a cosmic and childish level. He felt as if he had just heard his Führer speak, standing high on his podium, rocking back and forth on his heels, hands in the air, words comprehensible and real.

What Father Ramos was asking was unheard of and morally against what his Führer had told him. Maybe? He was confused. There were things said by Father Ramos that made sense, though. Tangible sense. And there were opportunities, political and private, that had him guessing.

Father Ramos was not aware at the time that Josef had not been successful at genetically altering anything. The fact was, albeit hidden, Josef had not accomplished much in the way of creating a Master Race. He had sterilized a few thousand vassals which would do a little toward preserving the complexion of his own race, but otherwise nothing major.

Faced with this great opportunity to do something, Josef—for the first time since coming to the Institution—felt inferior and unsure of himself. And that made him feel dirty, which in turn made him want to wash his hands. Which he did.

When he returned he sat down and asked for a cigarette. Father Ramos kindly obliged.

"So Father Marcelino hid the chalice then killed himself?" Josef asked.

"Yes. He hid the chalice then killed himself. He left a note which said: *Let no mortal man ever be endowed with such powers*."

"And you don't believe that?"

"I believe that Father Marcelino saw only what he could and I do not fault him for that. Joseph of Arimathea saw what he wanted."

"Unrestrained?" Josef said.

"Yes but with the ability to know."

"To know what?"

"That even limits are limitless," Father Ramos said. "That time not only heals but it makes things happen. He knew that what he thought in his head would someday come to fruition if only he prepared.

"Giovanni Battista de Rossi discovered the vessel some sixty or seventy years later buried in the catacombs under the Vatican. The Vatican quickly confiscated it from de Rossi; they studied it and concluded that it held no spiritual or biblical importance and dismissed it as fraudulent. It spent the last fifty years on a bookshelf in Father Paul Sebastian's office."

"How did you acquire it?"

"One afternoon I commented to Father Sabastian about how peculiar the chalice was and he proceeded to tell me its story. He spoke of Father Marcelino and the tomb as if a fairy tale. I was immediately intrigued and went about the task of researching. I found nothing to verify its existence before Father Marcelino, and the tomb in Ephesus was nonexistent. But then I studied the Gospel. And I was convinced. I petitioned Father Sabastian for the vessel and he was more than kind to lend it to me. I have not opened it for fear of destroying something I do not understand." He paused and smiled. "I have come here today to ask for your help."

Josef could think of nothing to say. Ideologies conflicted, yet he was intrigued by the prospects. His emotions went rabid. "So," he said weakly, "what exactly is it that you want?"

Father Ramos leaned forward in his seat and reached for the black cloth over the package then slipped it gracefully off. Encased in a finely constructed brass and glass carrier was the bronzed vessel, complete with inscriptions and hieroglyphics. "A child of Christ," Father Ramos said. "If at all possible."

PART 2

All our attitudes, moral, practical, or emotional, as well as religious, are due to the objects of our consciousness, the things which we believe to exist, whether really or ideally, along with ourselves. Such objects may be present to our senses, or they may be present only to our thought. In either case they elicit from us a reaction.

~William James

THE ISLAM CONNECTION

Jayln did not know what her boys were doing the day they took off for Siler City in her brand new station wagon Volvo with a small vial's worth of liquid LSD hidden away in the console. She had been disconnected from them since the incident at the Home and nothing had gone right for her or her family since. The devastation of losing her job took her physically and mentally out of the game. Only her family could understand the importance of the situation. She was middle-aged—early forties—had spent most of her adult life at home with her two sons, Jamal and Ahmed. They had the disadvantage of growing up in a war-torn Pakistan, but early on Jayln and her husband Icma moved themselves and their sons to America. She stayed at home while Icma worked and that's how life went until her oldest son, Jamal, started high school. Then she had an epiphany of the grand sort; she told her husband that things had changed and that she needed, spiritually and mentally, to do something with her life. Contrary to his belief, he went along with what she wanted and asked humbly where her devotion lay. She picked the first thing that came to mind—the usual and usually wrong answer of caring for the sick. Yes, she wanted most of all to become a nurse. Icma supported that. Besides, it wasn't all that crazy of an idea.

That fall she started school at a local community college and was immediately and completely humiliated. She was older and different from the rest of the class. Her values set somewhere off in those spiritual clouds of religion while everyone around her dealt in idolatry and style. She stuck with it though and made it through the first semester barely passing her electives. She cried a lot and complained, her family being the outlet for her frustration. She made it miraculously through another semester then into nursing school. The first time she tried to make a bed properly a corner of the bedspread hit the floor and her instructor failed her. She had to wait a week before doing the practicum again. It was an agonizing week, but one she did nonetheless with her eyes clear upon the objective at hand. She redid the practicum and dropped the bedspread on the floor again, but this time her instructor was looking out a dreamy, fall window and saw nothing but leaves gathering on a cold ground.

It weighed heavy on Jayln's conscience and it took everything she had not to confess the crime. The guilt passed after a few weeks but would always play sadly upon what she thought of herself and her ability to perform the job.

It took almost four years for Jayln to complete a two-year degree. She drove her family crazy in that time and promised she would never put them through it again. Upon graduation, she walked proudly across the platform stage in the middle of Carolina Central Community College, collecting in her hands that piece of paper that means everything and nothing at all, then went about the task of studying for the boards. Two months later she passed.

She first saw the name Sunbridge Psychiatric and Rehabilitation Center in the *Raleigh News and Observer*. It read: *Nurse needed for demanding and challenging day shift position in nursing home setting in beautiful Siler City.*

Jayln stared at the listing. "Where is Siler City?" she asked herself.

She later found out that it was an hour or so west of Raleigh down Highway 64. She called for an application, received it two days later, filled it out, and sent it in—then waited. Three days later she received the call. "Can you come in this afternoon?" Rita Hymer asked her.

"Sure, I think . . . uh . . . yes. Yes, I can. "

"Good."

Jayln was so nervous she forgot that her car, which had been worn-out going back and forth to school, had just bit the dust—it waited silently in the backyard for a $400 clutch job. She called Icma at work in tears. He calmed her down and told her he would be home shortly and then she could take his car. "Thank you," she said. "Thank you."

Jayln made a fool of herself at the interview. Rita's first impression was that the woman in front of her was unstable and had been a homemaker too long to know even remotely the simplest rules of the game. She was sincere though and that counted for something. Rita said she would let her know in a couple of days and that was it.

For those two days Jayln made life a living hell for her family. She was unbearable to be around. After two days, there was no call. Nothing. Jayln calmed herself. After three, there was nothing. Then four and five. Jayln went limp. She stayed in bed for over forty-eight hours, messed in her pajamas once, and forced Icma to the couch. On day eight Rita called and asked

Jayln if she was still interested in the job. Jayln was so weak she could barely squeeze out the word *yes*, but she did and Rita congratulated her.

Icma was so proud of his wife that he took her out that day and signed loan papers for a brand new Volvo station wagon—a Swedish beauty. The next day she drove proudly to work, feeling more American than ever.

Losing that job put Jayln back into that old familiar place of rejection. She felt it; her family felt it too. She slept long hours and did not prepare the meals anymore. She took up smoking and completely alienated Icma from her loins. She woke up at odd hours—sometimes late at night, other times early in the morning, never when it was convenient—always waking someone else up with her mournful, ghost-like ramblings. She made it extremely hard for her family to understand her and even harder to be around.

She was up watching the news the morning Deborah Collins did her live remote from outside the Sunbridge Psychiatric and Rehabilitation Center. It made her cry to hear the name Sunbridge again. All the old feelings came rushing back. Then she heard Deborah Collins say Ruby's name in full—Ruben Franklin Riggs. "Missing?" Jayln said to her herself.

She took a moment to comprehend what Deborah had said then began laughing hysterically. Was it true, she thought. Yes. "Ruby is gone!"

Jamal and Ahmed were in the kitchen reading up on how to make grits when they heard the muffled cry come from the living room and then Ruby's name yelled over and over. They did not know what was wrong with their mother but it sounded as if she was getting progressively worse. They looked at each other and shook their heads. "When," asked Ahmed, "will all this stop?"

"Soon," said Jamal as he measured out a healthy tablespoon of grits and dropped it in a pot of boiling water.

Jamal had already acquired the LSD from a reliable source who assured him it would scramble anyone for at least twelve hours—more if the dosage was right. Hearing his mother yelling at the television was the catalyst he needed to begin what Iman Bainomie called the *Equalization of Destiny*, which was the right and duty of everyone to correct all wrongs done to them. And it was Iman Bainomie who told Jamal that punishment for such wrongdoing should be to the full extent of the crime done. Jamal took that to mean that every man's destiny was equal and if not, should be made such. He felt that Ruby had destroyed his mother's destiny by somehow feeding her those pills, and in return he would destroy Ruby's in the same manner.

It was his own idea to feed Ruby the acid and let him trip for a while. Earlier that year he had read Thomas Wolfe's *Electric Kool-Aid Acid Test* and was fascinated with the characters. They seemed unreal and cartoon-like and very sad. Their lives seemed empty and uneventful. He compared their test with acid to a walk through hell. It was exactly what Ruby deserved.

Jamal and Ahmed ate their grits in silence that morning, listening to their mother in the living room. That afternoon the boys took the Volvo into town and listened to Iman Bainomie speak at the Raleigh Islamic Center. It was the inspiration Jamal needed. Afterward he spoke with Iman Bainomie at great length about the *Equalization of Destiny*. "Whatever you do, do it with good intent," Iman Bainomie told Jamal.

Jamal and Ahmed left the Raleigh Islamic Center and traveled west on Interstate 40 then exited onto Highway 64. A sign informed them that it was 28 miles to Siler City.

Iman Bainomie wrapped up his business early at the center and drove across town to see if he could console Jayln in any way.

THE BIG FRESH

Deputy Frank Wright was driving home when the call went out: possible kidnapping at the Country Club. Up ahead on the left he could see the Country Club sign and it was as arrogant as ever, standing there in a poor man's town all out of place. "Fuck!" Frank said, ramming the palms of his hands into the steering wheel, not wanting anything but a shower and a bed.

He had been up all night and all morning, pulling guard duty in the lobby of the Home. He reeked of that weird institutional smell; he was dog-tired and on the verge of hallucinating. He didn't want to answer the call, but he had an obligation to the people he worked for and to the town that cut his check and paid his bills. He slowed his cruiser to a crawl then made a left into the Country Club. "I'm too goddamned nice," he said to himself then responded to dispatch.

It was a beautiful drive through the back nine of the golf course that led up to the Country Club: the oversized houses, the green glistening lakes full of chemicals and God-knows-what. It was a drive Frank had made many times in his two-year career on the force. Never, though, had he been so delusional. Everything seemed to dance with a klezmer-like rhythm with the black Cloud hanging over him like sourdough bread. Frank licked his lips and imagined himself biting into a heavenly sandwich. It tasted good. He took another bite. This one with everything in it: a house, a fairway, and a lake. It was warm and full of goodness. Frank smiled and wiped his mouth with the sleeve of his shirt.

Some hundred yards away from the clubhouse, Robert Leblanc spotted Frank's cruiser coming slowly and not so directly up the drive. He grabbed a 30/30 rifle, broke out a window with its butt, and fired off a round into the cruiser's radiator. A tuft of white steam rolled from under its hood.

Frank saw this but was not shaken by it, nor was he shaken from his dream. He considered it part of the package. He stopped the cruiser, popped the hood latch, and got out and walked around to the front. While bending over staring at the radiator feeling the heat from the engine, he heard what he thought was a firecracker explode somewhere off behind him and he immediately felt a warm, stinging sensation radiate down his back and arms simultaneously then into his head. He became nauseated then dizzy. He turned and saw nothing out of the ordinary then fell to the ground.

"What the hell did you do that for?" James Morton yelled, looking over Robert Leblanc's shoulder, seeing Frank Wright motionless on the ground, the hood of the cruiser up.

"I was aiming for the headlight," Robert said.

"Well, shit man. You missed!"

"Shut up, James," Robert said.

"I ain't going down for this," James Morton said.

"If I go down, you go down," Robert said. "Just remember, it's your gun."

"Shit!" James Morton said, grabbing his head and twirling around. It was his gun, and every gun in the clubhouse had come from his Gold 'n' Pawn. It seemed like a good idea at the time. A little firepower never hurt anyone when it came to negotiating.

"What's going on?" Arthur Tysor shouted, having heard the shots.

"Robert killed Frank Wright," James Morton yelled, pacing back and forth in front of the window like some nervous junky.

Arthur Tysor walked over to the window and looked out. "What—"

"It's not—" Robert Leblanc pleaded.

"What the hell were you thinking?"

Robert Leblanc backed away from the window and calmly walked across the room then back. It was a large room full of rich things and rich ideas. He went to the window and looked out then repeated the motion once more.

"Where is John Carter?" he asked.

"He's in the lounge with Ramell," Arthur Tysor said.

"Good," Robert said. "We're going to need to go get Frank before anyone else drives up."

"What do you mean?" James Morton asked.

Robert took a deep breath and spun his eyes to the ceiling to show his frustration. "We're going to walk out there," he said, pointing with the butt of his rifle out the window to where Frank lay, "pick him up, and bring him back here."

"You're crazy!" James Morton yelled. "I ain't doing it. You shot him; you deal with it."

Robert Leblanc raised his rifle to James Morton's neck. "You're right," he said. "Now, how about you and Arthur go out there and pick Frank up and bring him back here."

James Morton looked at Arthur. Arthur shook his head slightly. "Sure," James said, raising his arms up enough to show

Robert that he submitted. "If that's what you want."

James and Arthur left the clubhouse while Robert watched them from the window as they descended upon Frank and the cruiser. When they reached Frank they leaned down and grabbed him by the shoulders and legs and raised him some six inches off the ground. They looked back at the clubhouse and saw Robert smiling from out of the broken window, and then dropped Frank simultaneously and started running in opposite directions.

"Cowards!" Robert yelled, extending his rifle out the window and firing off two rounds in the direction James Morton was running.

James Morton fell to the ground then got up, looked himself over and found nothing out of the ordinary, and took off running again. Robert Leblanc dropped his rifle and went out to the cruiser, grabbed Frank by the shoulders, and dragged him into the clubhouse.

John Carter was all alone in the lounge when Robert Leblanc pulled Frank Wright's body in. Ramell Chapel had heard the initial shot and the ensuing argument and found little reason to stick around for more. Robert pulled Frank's body up alongside John Carter then dropped him.

"Heal this man!" Robert Leblanc said.

John Carter was snoozing gingerly but aroused just as Robert Leblanc stopped talking. "What can I do for you, good man?" he said, smiling somewhat lazily up at Robert Leblanc.

"I want you to heal this man," Robert said.

John Carter looked down at Frank Wright who was motionless, a small amount of blood covered the right upper corner of his shirt. "You want me to heal a cop?" John Carter said, laughing slightly with an air of mockery about him.

"Yes!" Robert Leblanc said, irritated at John Carter's lack of empathy for the situation.

John Carter stopped laughing and stared over at Robert Leblanc. "Fifty bucks," he said.

"What?"

John Carter stood up and slowly raised his arms over his head then stretched out his back. "Yes," he said, "to heal a cop I'll definitely need fifty bucks."

"That's crazy," Robert Leblanc yelled.

"I'm Jesus, for Christ's sake," John Carter said, "what did you expect?"

"Yeah. Yeah . . . shit!" Robert Leblanc said, losing his cool by the minute.

He took out his wallet and thumbed through it then pulled out fifty dollars and handed it to John Carter. John Carter sniffed it and smiled then folded it over and put it in the breast pocket of his gown. "I'll need some water," he said.

"Sure."

Robert went off and returned with a goblet full of water. John Carter bent down over Frank Wright and placed his right hand on his forehead and began mumbling a few inaudible words that amounted to nothing. He then took the water and poured it over Frank Wright's head.

Nothing happened. Robert Leblanc was dumbfounded. He wanted instant gratification, the miracle of all miracles.

"You're not doing it right," Robert Leblanc said nervously.

John Carter cut him a look of resentment.

"Well," Robert said, "nothing's happening."

"Of course, nothing's happening," John Carter said. "He's a cop."

"What does that matter?"

"It matters a lot," John Carter said. "Cops have tough skin."

"What!" Robert Leblanc yelled. "Are you serious?"

"It's a fact. They're born with this extra-thick layer of skin. It's like pigskin. That's why they're called pigs."

John Carter grabbed Frank Wright's arm and gave his skin a pinch with the tips of his fingers. "A strange evolutionary mutation," he said, "possibly extraterrestrial. There's no helping this guy."

"You're not Jesus," Robert Leblanc said. "I should kill you right now."

"Sure I am," John Carter said. "Have a little faith."

The faint sounds of sirens could be heard out front, off in the distance. Robert Leblanc panicked and then ran for the door. When he got there he stopped and turned around, ran back to John Carter, and took the fifty bucks from his breast pocket. "You ain't no Jesus," he said then ran outside and hopped on a golf cart and took off across the ninth fairway.

John Carter went to the door and leaned out. "You ain't seen nothing, you sorry motherfucker! You going to burn in hell for taking my money!"

John Carter watched Robert Leblanc disappear over a distant hill then walked back over to Frank Wright. The sirens had closed in and were now sitting outside the clubhouse. John Carter took the goblet and filled it with water then emptied it out on Frank's face. Nothing happened. He knelt down and placed his right hand on his forehead and mumbled a few more inaudible words. Nothing. John Carter was dumbfounded. He took his hand off Frank's forehead then smacked him one good time across the face. Frank sat up, eyes bulging with this look of sleepy confusion. "It's okay," John Carter said, grabbing his shoulders in reassurance. "You've been saved."

Frank Wright stood up and looked at his right shoulder. It was bloodied but not bad. He raised his arm up and examined his fingers. They were all there and they worked. "What the hell happened?" he asked, staring at John Carter who was half-naked in a hospital gown, his hair gray and tangled, his face a sculptuous mold of madness.

"A miracle," he said. "Nothing but a miracle."

A half-dozen sheriff's deputies busted through the door. John Carter remained kneeling and Frank Wright stood half-awake with a superficial bullet wound to his right shoulder. No explanation could be given.

THE BIG FRESH

More news crews pulled up at the Home shortly after Deborah Collins' remote news report went out. They brought their own vans with their own antennas to transmit to their own part of the world.

The Crowd outside the Home expanded as well, spilling into the streets in front of and around the Brookwood Apartments. There were deputy sheriffs scattered all about contemplating silently to themselves the use of tear gas or rubber bullets, neither of which they had ever used in real life. They had been directed by their chief-in-command to maintain some semblance of order—under all circumstances. Whatever that meant.

Family members began showing up around noon banging on the doors demanding their loved ones be released immediately. This put Rita in a fix. She had to call doctors and then insurance companies. The insurance companies put her on hold and when they finally did talk with her they said nothing she wanted to hear. She had to call the doctors back and tell them that the insurance companies wouldn't pay if treatment was discontinued without any reason other than for a Cloud, a Crowd, a Cross, and one crazy Jesus.

Doctor Aaron Vokes was at the Home for his weekly clinic visits when the madness began. Dr. Vokes was somewhat eccentric—an old-timer with young blood who, for the majority of his practice, felt more compelled to work with livestock than people. Local farmers called him about their cattle twice as much as they did about their aging mothers. It worked out for the best that way, for some of his bedside manners and techniques were best suited for the pasture.

He overheard a phone conversation Rita was having with another doctor. Rita was almost in tears. He took the phone from her hand and told Rita to take a break. "Listen, Mark, you need to be nice," he said to the doctor on the phone. "She didn't want to call you in the first place. No one does. It's a country fact that you're an asshole and you're lucky to be practicing medicine. She's doing her job. You do yours."

Dr. Vokes handed the phone back to Rita who was now on the verge of hysteria. There was no one on the line. "He hung up," she said.

"Just as well," Dr. Vokes said. "Let the people go if they want to. Deal with it tomorrow."

He was right, but it was hard to say if she could honestly consider a day that seemed so unfeasible and so faraway at this point. He was working the percentages; she was working the trenches. Things looked a whole lot different from the trenches. You get marred in the trenches; you get mud in the eyes and thoughts get clouded—not unlike the Cloud. There was a good chance for rain the first day the Cloud rolled in. Everyone bet on it. Everyone lost. It was a sucker's bet now, one that was useless. Looking back the Cloud provided only a whimsical folly of a chance. A chance in hell.

Rita had to bet on something though, so she went with Dr. Vokes and his nonchalant position. "Let 'em go," she instructed Elnora and the other nurse. "We'll deal with it tomorrow."

No questions asked. No answers to be given if there were. It was that simple. Too bad everything couldn't be that way.

Rita's home-away-from-home was quickly becoming an empty house and she could hear them now down there at the home office in Charleston, South Carolina, eating their shrimp and grits, speaking as if it was her that ate into their profit margins. She refused to hear it.

"Rita?" Elnora said, sticking her head around the corner into her office. "Mrs. Monroe's family is here to take her home."

"Tell them that Mrs. Monroe fell out of bed this morning and cracked her head open. Tell them she's in a coma."

Elnora cut a curious grin and waited for another answer.

"Let her go," Rita finally said. "Let 'em all go."

Rita left her office and went out into the lobby to see if anything had changed. It hadn't. She leaned forward and looked up through the glass at the Cloud and spaced out on the idea of photosynthesis for the soul. She needed a vacation. She wasn't eating and her skin was pale. Out in the yard and on the street were hundreds of faces, all empty and open to suggestion. "Get a life," Rita said to herself, thinking of the irony implied.

She could see the Reverend Alfonso King's blue Mercedes making its way slowly up the drive. Where was John Carter? Where was Ruby? News crews everywhere for no good reason at all. It's all a mistake. Jesus Christ. "We need locusts," Rita said. "And some lamb's blood."

"That's not funny," said Deputy Kirk Merchant, who had taken Frank Wright's place and was now standing guard in the lobby.

"You don't see me laughing, do you?" Rita asked in return.

She turned her attention to the reverend who had his window

down with one hand out of it and the other on the horn; he was trying to get the Crowd to let him through. Very much out of character, the Crowd did not respond favorably. They began beating on the hood and rocking the car back and forth. The reverend rolled up his window. He made it to the circle drive and the Crowd broke away and let him roll to a peaceful stop. He got out of his car and adjusted his suit, said a few words in argument to the Crowd, then walked toward the Home.

"Let him in," Rita said to Deputy Kirk Merchant, who obliged promptly.

"What in God's name," the reverend came in yelling, "are you trying to accomplish here?"

"Back off, preacher man," Rita said. "If you can move them, then do it. If not—"

"Where is Ruben?" the reverend asked.

"Gone."

"Is he dead? Is he in the woods somewhere? Did he take a taxi out of town? What?"

"I don't know," Rita said.

"That strange guy, John Carter, he's gone too, isn't he?" asked the reverend.

"Yes," Rita said.

"It ain't right," the reverend said. "Something ain't right."

He adjusted his pants then retired to the restroom.

Through the Crowd came another car. It was long and black and full of suits. It did not slow down for the Crowd. The Crowd sensed this and moved quickly to the side to accommodate it. The car entered the circle drive and pulled to a stop behind the Reverend King's blue Mercedes. The Reverend Frederick Holmes and four of his deacons stepped out. They were suited-down and immaculately groomed. The reverend himself, being short and stocky, resembled a retired Russian officer.

"Let them in," Rita said.

The doors opened and the reverend and his deacons entered.

"Mr. Merchant," the reverend said, "how's the wife?"

"Good. Two months away from another kid," he said.

"What is that, three?"

"Four," Kirk Merchant answered proudly.

"For such a young man," the reverend said. "I'd not be surprised if you make it to ten or twelve before retiring. For a man like myself, who has given up the breeding, it's like watching it snow."

Kirk Merchant laughed a silly laugh then composed himself. Rita was across the lobby ignoring the fact that the Reverend Frederick Holmes and his deacons were there.

"Mrs. Hymer," the reverend said, drawing Rita away from the glass. "Your Home is in shambles. I am rather disappointed."

"You're not the first," she answered.

"I wanted you to know that I contacted your employers in Charleston and told them exactly what was going on up here."

"Preacher!" Rita yelled in disbelief.

"Wait! Wait!" the reverend said, catching Rita by the proverbial throat before she exploded. "You must listen and understand before you try to speak. They assured me that they did not approve of any of this business you got going on up here. I'll tell you again. Let it go. Let it go. Let it go."

Rita rolled her eyes out the glass, over the Crowd and Cloud, past the Cross, and down into the Brookwood Apartments. "It's gone," she said in one exhaustive breath.

"Don't fool with me, woman," the Reverend Holmes said.

The Reverend Alfonso King came out of the restroom; he was jacked-up on the good stuff. He saw the Reverend Frederick Holmes standing in the lobby with his deacons next to Rita. "Back off," he yelled, walking over and standing between the two.

"Don't you have a cable show to tape?" the Reverend Holmes said laughing.

It was common knowledge on the gossip circuit that Reverend Holmes thought little of Reverend King and even less of his cheaply produced cable access show.

"Don't you have a home to wreck?" the Reverend Alfonso King said, stepping toward Reverend Holmes as if to throw a punch.

All four deacons stepped forward at once. "That's okay, boys," the Reverend Holmes said. "His boat is sinking."

The Reverend King was high and he wanted to smack down Reverend Holmes. It had been a long time in the making, ever since Reverend Holmes pulled his convoy into town about a year ago. Reverend King felt that Reverend Holmes's Bible-belted, Southern Baptist ways didn't fit then, and they surely didn't fit now. If that wasn't bad enough, he was also a Mason, high-ranking, which made him elusive and untouchable. That always made Reverend King laugh because it reminded him of when he was young playing cowboys and Indians, creating secret organizations comparable to the KGB.

Reverend Holmes and his deacons walked back into the Home while Reverend King stayed out front with Rita. "I don't know what's wrong with that man," the Reverend King said to Rita, consoling her.

"He's an asshole," Rita said. "Excuse my language, but he is."

"No, you're right," the reverend said. "He is an asshole."

They both had a good laugh then watched the Crowd shift and swell in the afternoon. Deputy Kirk Merchant stood in front of the double doors with his hands behind his back. His hat sat low on his forehead giving him a slick, defensible look. He was a young man with three kids and one on the way. He needed it.

The Reverend King was watching the Crowd when another car pulled slowly through it. It was a rental car—that much he knew; it split the Crowd in half. But it wasn't the car that caught the reverend's eye, nor was it the Crowd splitting like the Red Sea; it was what he saw on the other side that intrigued him the most. Standing on the front deck, about halfway down into the heart of the Brookwood Apartments were two figures. One he barely recognized by her long hair and slender body as Lisa, but it was the other that confounded him. A blurred vision of an older man, taller than Lisa, and slender too. The reverend adjusted himself for a second look then excused himself. Deputy Kirk Merchant unlocked the doors and the reverend took off through the Crowd, down the drive into the Brookwood Apartments.

THE BIG FRESH

Ruby was drinking a cup of cold coffee and Lisa was having herself a cigarette when they saw the reverend. "This isn't good," Lisa said, putting out her cigarette.

"No, it's not," Ruby answered.

The reverend walked fast with questionable purpose. Ruby and Lisa went inside the apartment and locked the door. "Hide in the bathroom," Lisa said.

"He knows I'm here," Ruby said.

"How about the closet?"

"It doesn't matter," Ruby said. "He knows."

Ruby thought about the situation then went to the kitchen and opened the back door. There were still no steps. The reverend made it to the front door and turned the knob vigorously, multiple times, then fumbled through his pocket and pulled out a set of keys. Ruby heard him insert one into the doorknob. He looked at Lisa with confusion. "He has a key?"

Lisa made a girlish face by dropping her eyebrows and grinning slightly with closed lips. She was looking for approval, but Ruby had none to give her. As the front door swung open Ruby jumped out the back. While airborne he considered all he would say and do once he hit the ground. Once he did though, his left leg sunk into a stump hole and he fell face first. There was an initial sensation of pain then he felt the leaves—they were warm and odorous and had a strange air of decay about them. Ruby closed his eyes and contemplated three months of traction in some off-the-wall hospital. The only up side would be the morphine, yet that too had its drawbacks.

When he rolled over and looked up, he saw Lisa staring down, and behind her stood the reverend.

"What were you thinking, man?" the reverend yelled.

"Are you okay?" asked Lisa.

Ruby contemplated broken bones again then pulled his leg out of the stump hole. It worked just fine. "I'm okay," he said then stretched out his legs on the old summer leaves.

"That was stupid," the reverend said. "You could have hurt yourself."

Ruby lay on the ground and watched as Lisa and the reverend stared down at him. He felt like a divine dish—caught and cleaned and ready for ingestion.

"Get up, man, before someone sees you," the reverend said.

Lisa ducked back inside and came out with a small utility ladder. She lowered it till it was about two feet off the ground then dropped it. Ruby got up and brushed himself off. Around the corner and up the hill he heard a great roar go out. "They're getting hungry," he said.

"They tried to flip my car," the reverend responded.

After composing himself, Ruby set up the ladder and then crawled back inside the apartment. The reverend was pouring himself a glass of Coke when he got in.

"Tell me what's going on here," the reverend said, taking a sip of his drink and sitting down at the kitchen table.

"Nothing," Lisa said.

"And you want me to believe that?" the reverend said.

There was silence.

"Ruby, here, goes missing," the reverend said, "and I find him on your front porch. Then he jumps out your back door? Come on."

Lisa could not speak. She stood there motionless, staring down at the reverend.

"She was just helping me out," Ruby said. "We thought you would turn me in."

"Turn you in?" said the reverend.

The reverend took another drink and thought about the situation then broke out laughing. "You thought I would turn you in?"

"I have no idea," Ruby said.

The reverend took another drink while laughing and almost choked. He then set the drink on the table and grabbed Lisa by the arm and pulled her to his knee. She giggled quite girlishly and went along with what the reverend was doing. She put her arm around his neck and gave him a kiss on the cheek.

Ruby was confounded by these actions but tried desperately not to show it. He went to the refrigerator and pulled out a Miller Lite, opened it, and took a strong drink.

"Cops are everywhere," the reverend said. "I'm not so sure they're after you, though. It's the Crowd, it's putting everybody on edge."

"Maybe it's the Cross," Ruby said.

"I think it's the Cloud," Lisa said. "It's like the moon—a full moon—messing up everything."

The reverend laughed again. "The Cloud is beautiful. It makes a summer day not so boring."

"Speak for yourself," Lisa said.

"Are you going back?" the reverend asked Ruby.

"For a few things," Ruby said. "Then I'm leaving."

The reverend cut a strange face. "Where are you going?"

"Home," Ruby said.

"Where is home?"

"Wilmington."

The reverend thought about what Ruby said and about John Carter and the news crews. "I think that's a good idea with everything going on here. Lisa will take you."

Lisa looked at Ruby and smiled. "That's a good idea," she said. "I need to get out from under this Cloud for a while myself."

Ruby took another drink and smiled. The reverend motioned for Lisa to get off his knee then he stood up. "Whatever you need, I'll get."

"You don't have to do that," Ruby said. "Really."

"I think it's better this way," the reverend said. "You go up there now and all hell is going to break loose."

"He's right," Lisa said. "No reason to chance it now."

Ruby considered it. "You're right."

"So, what do you need?"

Ruby told him he needed the manuscript, the word processor, his wallet, a pair of pants, and a shirt.

"Just leave the word processor," Lisa said. "It's old."

"No. I need it to finish the book," Ruby said.

"They're a dime a dozen at the Gold 'n' Pawn," the reverend said.

"I need this one," Ruby said.

"Sure. No problem," the reverend said. "I'll be back in a few minutes."

The reverend gave Lisa a hug then left.

"I need to run uptown before we leave," Lisa said, "and get some money out of the bank. You want to come?"

"I think I'll stay here and wait for the reverend."

"Sure?"

"Yeah, I'm sure," Ruby said. "I'll be here when you get back."

Lisa grabbed her keys and a hat and gave Ruby a kiss. "He has a key to your house?" Ruby asked again.

"What?" Lisa said surprised. Then catching herself, she added, "Oh yeah. Why not? I have a key to his. He *is* my father for Christ's sake. Do you need anything?"

Ruby smiled. "Maybe a six pack for the road."

Lisa kissed him again; then he walked her to the door and watched as she got into her car and drove off. He was in a very spiritual mood now, giddy like a schoolgirl. He was young and in love, or rather, in love and feeling young. It was Lisa's energy that did it, and it transferred easily over to him when they were together. And he made sure that he never took too much so as not to drain her or push her away. He even gave some of his to her even when she didn't need it—only to prove that he cared and that the street ran both ways and that he would go both ways for her.

He went back inside and got his beer and then went out on the deck, fearless now with love and allies. He checked his legs again to make sure he didn't injure himself in the fall. His right shin was scraped but nothing else. A scrape was good and the stinging made him feel alive. He had nerves of steel and they were throbbing.

Up the hill he could see the Crowd and the Cross and the news vans parked along the outer stretches of the circle drive. It all happened way too fast and it was surreal, bordering on the edge of uncertainty with the ability to go either way at any time. Deep down though, Ruby felt as if it would end like most things: with a little bang and a puff of smoke, a pseudo-climax that fizzles out at the most inopportune of times, leaving everyone with this dissatisfying taste of emptiness in their mouths.

It was the Cloud that captured most of Ruby's attention as he stared up through the electrical wires and oak trees—a massive display of lazy energy frozen in the landscape like park benches and telephone poles, a beautiful beast of uncertainty. The Reverend King was right, Ruby thought, it is beautiful in its own manifested way and it certainly does break up the monotony of the summer.

Ruby drank his beer and dreamed out loud of spending the rest of the summer on or around the beach with the breeze and that feeling of standing on the edge. And he thought how nice it was going to be to have Lisa there with him, an uncertain flower herself, wallowing and wading in the newness of it all.

Ruby finished his beer and went to the refrigerator for another, the last one, and took it to the front deck and drank it slowly. He had not drunk that much in months and it felt good, the way he wanted to feel, and he wanted to make it last. He stared up the hill at the news vans and their phallic antennas probing the Cloud softly, and at the Cross. He could barely make out the top of it, but he knew it was working its own magic. How strange everything had become, seemingly overnight without any prediction. No one saw it coming. How could they? Why would they? It was more of an illusion anyway. A tumor on the town—and such malignancies are best kept out of the hands of fortunetellers.

Ruby sat on the doorjamb and drank slowly and waited for the reverend. Random cars passed to his left and right, and each time Ruby would lower his head slightly so as not to be recognized. Cops came in and out almost routinely. There was an ambulance that entered then left again with its lights and sirens flashing. There was a red Volvo station wagon that pulled up to the back of the Crowd, stopped, then backed slowly down the drive.

The Hispanic children were out in the streets playing as if nothing had ever happened, as if the Cloud was now a part of their cowboy-and-Indian game show. They shot holes in it every time they fired their sticks at it, and the Cloud bled silently just for them.

Always the silence, Ruby thought, standing back staring at the new beast. The town completely foreign yet familiar, like Vietnam—just to say it conjured up ideas of insanity. To walk the jungle or the street, it was the same thing. It all depended on who you were walking with and if there was murder in mind. Ruby considered Vietnam, when it happened and now, and regretted the day he ever gave Kay the right to persuade him not to go. She was thinking of herself of course, and he was thinking of himself. He understood that, but after it was all over he always felt guilty when the subject came up, as if the country might have done better if he was there.

"*Mother, can't you give me some advice*," Ruby sang in a low scratchy voice. "*For what to do when I cry. Father, can't you give me some advice. For what to do when I die.*"

There was another ambulance, its lights and sirens flashing and crackling. Behind it were two sheriff's cars. They too had their lights and sirens on. Ruby watched as they made it steadily through the Crowd into the circle drive. He stood and finished his beer and thought about the reverend. He should have been back by now.

Ruby went into the living room and turned on the television. For ten minutes he watched as Rachel tried to explain to Keith—in a soap opera—why she loved Brett even though she was carrying Keith's child. Ruby flipped a few channels and got relatively the same mess. He turned it off and went back out on the deck. The ambulance was in the circle drive just sitting there with its lights flashing; the sheriff's cars were behind it. "Where the hell is he?" Ruby asked himself.

Ruby went inside and turned the television back on. He left it on this time and went to the bedroom and picked through Lisa's many hats. He found a black toboggan and stretched it over his head then went to the bathroom to see that it made him look like an old hipster, lean with an air of mystery. Jack Kerouac reincarnated.

On the way out through the living room Ruby glanced at the television and saw Deborah Collins once again standing in front of the Sunbridge Psychiatric and Rehabilitation Center. Ruby grabbed for the remote control and turned it up. " . . . can't say at this point," Deborah Collins said. "They found a dozen or so firearms on the premises. They are not saying much about the deputy who was shot. It is known that he was the first on the scene and the only one injured. One of the missing residents was found in the clubhouse. He was not injured. An ambulance has just now brought him back to the facility. We're hoping to catch a glimpse of him any time now."

"Are you still seeing a large number of onlookers at this point?" Larry Fox, afternoon anchorman for WRAL Channel 5, said.

"Even more, Larry. And what's so fascinating, talking with some of them, is that they're not really sure why they're here."

"I'm not sure either," Ruby said.

"Other strange developments here at the facility—a prominent member of the religious sect has been detained inside for questioning after an alleged robbery. I am not sure—"

"Son of a bitch!" Ruby yelled, flicking off the television, thinking for a second, then turning it back on, flipping to the People's Channel with some strange hope of finding the reverend sitting there in his blue heaven taping his television show. It was a long shot—one that didn't pan out. There was nothing on the People's Channel. Nothing but a blue screen with an advertisement scrolling by: *Eat Lunch at Brownie Lue's.*

Ruby left the front door open as he took off down the steps across the grassless yard onto the pavement. He was disguised in Lisa's toboggan, yet he felt vulnerable and open as if he had already been stabbed and was bleeding. There was nothing he could do now but walk and hope that somewhere between him and the Crowd and the door to the Home he would think of something better than what he had in mind. He knew the reverend couldn't take the wrap for something he didn't do. That was a fact. He also knew there was a chance he could get caught like John Carter. That was a chance he had to take.

At first he walked by a few people here and there, stragglers of the machine, then more and more until it was standing room only, like some glorious rock concert. Ruby squeezed through, listening to fragments of conversations as he went. The topic of the day seemed to be immortality. "What do these well-wishers know of immortality?" Ruby asked himself and then asked it of himself and decided to drop the question for fear of coming up with the answer.

He worked his way past the Cross and the Sunbridge Psychiatric and Rehabilitation sign with its orange sun and came to rest two or three rows back from the front of the Crowd—the front being the circle drive and a fluorescent orange strip of plastic that read *Do Not Enter.* It stretched from the corner of the Home across the circle drive to the woodland on the other side of the news vans. Ruby saw all this and immediately realized he had misjudged the complexity of the situation.

The ambulance was parked just on the other side of the rope with its lights flashing; the ambulance attendants stood behind it speaking with a couple of deputies. There was laughter in their talk and they seemed very relaxed. Ruby could see Rita and Elnora and Julius standing inside the lobby looking out. Neena Moore was also there standing beside Elnora with her Pentax ME super 35mm camera with zoom lens dangling like a grenade from around her neck. She had taken a plane to the Raleigh/Durham International Airport then rented a car from there. She had a leisurely drive down Highway 64, reminiscing all the while of old lovers and such. She was going to stop by her parents' house before coming to the Home but rounded the hill from Pittsboro and saw the enormous Cloud dangling like sourdough bread off in the distance and knew she should get to the Home as quick as possible. When she arrived she saw the Crowd and the Cross and barely made it through because of the cops and news crews. She got out of her rented car and immediately started snapping pictures. Most of the Crowd ignored her, but some of them knew her parents and recognized her. The news spread like small pox, infecting even the vaguest of vagabonds in the Crowd. Neena was eventually forced inside the Home behind locked doors.

She seemed content though, as Ruby looked at her, firing off a few shots from her camera here and there, standing and talking with Elnora Brown like two cheerleaders during a third quarter football game. Ruby wanted to be closer but feared getting caught. He wanted to see the reverend, but he couldn't. The Crowd swelled forward then sank back, repeating its action over and over. It was one living, breathing machine and Ruby was a part of it now. He could do nothing but inhale and exhale with it.

"What's the hat for?" a young woman beside him asked. She was curious and bored.

"Cancer," Ruby answered.

"Where?"

"In the brain and down the back," Ruby said. "All over."

"You still got your hair."

"It's a wig."

The woman smiled then disappeared into the Crowd.

Ruby laughed. "Afflictions are good for something," he told himself, pulling the toboggan farther down onto his head.

There was an older gentleman in front of Ruby who was standing on his toes to see over the Crowd. Ruby leaned forward and asked him what was going on. "That Jesus fella is in the ambulance there and they're 'bout to bring him out," the old man said.

"Is that a fact?"

"Yeah, and they say he shot Frank Wright in the heart. Didn't kill 'im though."

"What about Reverend King?" Ruby asked. "I hear he's in trouble."

"Oh yeah, they caught him digging through somebody's stuff in there. Had the man's wallet in his pocket. Found drugs on him too."

"No shit?" Ruby said.

"Shit yeah," the old man said. "That one alone will get 'im a good eight months."

"Shit."

"Oh yeah."

Ruby contemplated eight months. Eight months alone in prison. Eight months alone in prison, being a preacher with a cocaine habit—nothing good could ever come of that.

At some point the back doors of the ambulance swung open and John Carter emerged. He stood erect and tall with a big goofy grin etched across his face. He seemed unscathed by the excessive show of enthusiasm for his return. Two deputies stepped forward to assist the attendant; one was Kirk Merchant.

As the attendant reached for John Carter's shoulder the clipboard that was under his arm slipped out. Kirk Merchant, out of pure reflex, leaned over to catch it. As he did, John Carter slipped the .45 from his holster and wielded it toward the sky, letting off one gigantic explosion that sent everyone to the ground, face down. One collective scream of fear went out, then silence. Everyone froze then slowly regained themselves, stumbling cautiously to their feet.

John Carter stepped forward with the .45 dangling precariously above his head. The deputies pulled theirs and aimed. They intensely studied their target, and no betting man would have ever given John Carter a chance in hell. Ruby felt the tension. It was out of control. Rita ran out of the Home and stopped some ten feet behind John Carter. "Mr. Carter!" she yelled. "This is not appropriate. Put the gun down now!"

John Carter did not acknowledge her at first. Instead he walked toward the Crowd in the vicinity of the Cross. The Crowd swelled back.

"Oh, Holy Mother of Mary!" he said, staring out at the beautiful rhapsody of a Cross for the first time. His eyes glassed over.

"Put the gun down!" a deputy yelled from behind a news van. Deborah Collins was behind him with a microphone; she was obviously shaken but still transmitting.

John Carter did not listen. He didn't have to. For the first time at least since Ruby had known him, he was in control—or so it would seem. He walked to the Cross and placed his left hand upon it and closed his eyes. There was a climactic gasp from the Crowd as it swelled forward.

John Carter took his hand off the Cross and walked around it to the other side, placing his back up against it facing the Crowd. Then he stretched out. The Crowd gasped. There was a period when nothing happened; when the Crowd, the cops, John Carter, everybody and everything simply froze, as if joining the Cloud in some strange dark way for a moment of silence. It was peaceful yet puzzling, especially to Ruby whose agenda was wrapped vicariously up in the fiasco. He did not have time; nor did he particularly care to give anymore up to the strangeness of the moment.

Ruby thought of this while surveying the scene and determined that if he could safely make it to the loading dock on the back side of the Home, it would most likely, at this time of day, be unlocked. He sank back into the Crowd and began working his way around.

The reverend was inside and had unfortunately been apprehended while trying to get Ruby's things. It was the wallet that pegged him as a thief. And when they searched him and found the small portion of cocaine wrapped tightly in a baggy hidden away in his own wallet, the cops assumed right then that the reverend's habit had forced him into a life of petty theft and that it was best to stop it now rather than to wait till it was completely out of control. They had him cuffed and were on the way out when they heard the shot.

Elnora and Neena caught the last of the reverend's escapades, with Neena snapping a few unauthorized shots for her story—which was unfolding like a glorious fairy tale. She and Elnora stood in the lobby staring out the large panes of glass—right beside the one with the gaping hole in it—taking pictures here and there, wishing secretly that John Carter would break off completely so that the story would have its fatalistic climax. Elnora particularly wanted it, to show Neena that her old hometown wasn't as boring as she herself actually made it out to be. Neena wanted something to happen, but she wasn't completely betting the bank on it. History showed her that not all stories ended in romantic disaster. It was her job to make it up, and with every picture she took there were a thousand words she was going to add to it.

Under the Cloud was the Crowd, and all in it had their eyes upon John Carter. It was what they had waited for. They had become part of the moment now for sure, not just another face in the crowd; they had purpose, and even more than purpose they had direction. It was do or die, a life-threatening situation which transforms one into a spiritual being of some sort. It was the removal from the same old day-to-day dead flesh that excited them the most and it was John Carter that transformed them. They had been prepared and were now ready for anything and it did not matter at this point what—for the pot was set to boil and whatever happened was sure to be blown directly out of proportion. It was a recipe for the Apocalypse, and John Carter played it to its full potential—not even a stray bullet could move them now.

John Carter stood poised, his head leaned back rubbing against the .45 raised to the Cloud. The deputies stood off with not enough information from their high command to know or understand completely what they should be doing. They all felt collectively reassured though that as long as the old man didn't fire the gun again they wouldn't have to fire theirs.

John Carter opened his eyes and stared out into the Crowd. He lifted his head off the Cross and stared out at them more intensely, as if realizing for the first time the Crowd existed. He stepped away from the Cross. "What do we have here?" he said, expecting no answer and getting none. "A witness to the slaughter?"

He looked up at the Cloud then back down, twirling a complete circle—almost falling—before coming to a stop. The cops held fast with their guns drawn. Rita went back inside the Home. Neena Moore reloaded her camera then stepped outside. The Reverend Frederick Holmes, his son Julius, and his four deacons pulled up behind the glass in the lobby. "What the hell is this?" the reverend said, mortified.

Elnora silently chanted Buddha.

John Carter regained his bearing and waddled forward till he was about five feet away from the Crowd then began spitting off scripture like it was Sunday morning. "Fallen is Babylon the great!" he yelled.

A great gasp went out across the Crowd. "She has become a home for demons and a haunt for evil spirits. A haunt for every unclean and detestable bird."

There was a great quietness in the yard. Ruby sensed this. He moved farther to the back and worked himself slowly around.

"Why are you here?" John Carter yelled, walking back and forth in front of the Crowd. "Are you looking for salvation?"

"We've come to see the man that calls himself Jesus!" A lone voice yelled from the back.

"Yes," said another.

"Ah, the eternal struggle." John Carter said. "You people have been looking for something ever since the day you were born. You have cowered and stolen your way to greatness with no soul in your shirts to concern yourself with. Heathens! Adulterers! Fornicators and Masturbators! You sicken me with your smell. You wouldn't know Jesus if he spit in your face. 'Let me tell you about heartache and the loss of God. I'll tell you about the hopeless night, the meager food my soul forgot. I'll tell you about the maiden with wrought iron soul.' "

These words frightened the Crowd immensely. One, because they were not well versed—not even rudimentarily—in the verses of Revelations; and two, only a handful had ever heard of The Doors, yet none knew the words to "The Wasp."

" 'The Negroes in the forest, brightly feathered, and they are saying: Forget the night! Live with us in forests of azure. Out here on the perimeter there are no stars,' " John Carter said then raised his other hand till both were giving praise to the Cloud. Everyone in the Crowd stared up at it. " 'Out here we is stoned—immaculate.' "

John Carter's hands remained in the air. The .45 stiff and straight. "You want Jesus, do you?"

John Carter lowered the .45 down about halfway until it was parallel with the Crowd and ran it over the tops of their heads to the right then stopped. "Ruben!" he yelled.

Ruby considered the thoughts of running when he heard this but froze instead. When he looked over at John Carter he saw the .45 pointing directly at him. "Shit," he said to himself in a whisper then straightened his back and turned to face John Carter.

"Come over here!" John Carter yelled, directing Ruby with the .45.

Ruby considered what John Carter was doing as a joke, finding no validation, no value whatsoever in it. But the .45 was real and no matter how insane John Carter seemed, he had already proven that he could make it work.

The Crowd opened up generously in front of Ruby, and he walked out and stood in front of John Carter. "Do you know why you're here?" John Carter asked.

"No," Ruby said.

"You have no clue, do you?"

Ruby shook his head, feeling somewhat silly not knowing how to react to the question.

"Take off your shirt," John Carter said.

"What?"

"Take it off, and the toboggan too. You look silly."

Ruby took off the toboggan then slowly undid the buttons of his shirt and slipped it off. Over his heart was a nice-sized hickey that Lisa had placed on him the day before. On his right upper chest was the tattoo. John Carter walked over and looked at it then removed his gown and stood butt-naked in the parking lot in front of Ruby. They stared at each other for some time then John Carter showed Ruby his tattoo. It was on his right upper chest as well—a faded circle with an indiscriminate marking inside of it. The circle was the same dimensions as Ruby's. Ruby took note of that.

"Do you know why you're here?" John Carter asked again.

"No," Ruby said then leaned over and spoke softly into John

Carter's ear: "Look, I'm on my way out of here. If you just give me a few minutes to get my things, I'll be gone. You won't have to worry about me anymore."

John Carter laughed. "After all the years it took to find you," he said still laughing. "You're not going anywhere."

Ruby lowered his head and rubbed his eyes. His head was hurting—too much to think about and not enough time to do anything about it. John Carter faced the Crowd. "Your Rapture is coming," he said, swinging the .45 around, pointing it at Ruby. Ruby's head began to hurt more. Flashes of light strobed frantically. He closed his eyes, but it was no use.

The Reverend Alfonso King was watching from inside the lobby. He was handcuffed and there was a deputy beside him. He broke free from the deputy and made it out the door. No one followed. "Stop!" the reverend yelled as he ran full force toward John Carter. John Carter swung the .45 around and fired one shot. The reverend fell to the ground. Ruby ran over to him and turned him over on his back. The reverend's eyes were open and glassy, pupils tightly constricted as if he had been doing some heavy cocaine. "Reverend!" Ruby yelled, shaking him by the shoulders.

The reverend smiled slightly to let Ruby know he was all right. "He missed," the reverend whispered. "Get out of here."

Ruby stood up and ran for the lobby. Another shot went off, shattering a large section of glass in front of him. Everyone inside the lobby dropped to their bellies.

Ruby stopped running and turned slowly toward John Carter. John Carter swung the .45 around and pointed it at Ruby. Ruby's head pounded harder and the flashes of light were blinding. At some point it became too much and Ruby raised his hands high above his head to signify his surrender. At the same moment a large thunderous crack of lightning came from the Cloud. It was spiritual and mythical all the same and took everyone quietly by surprise. Then the Crowd let out a gasp as another crack of lightning shot out across the sky. John Carter looked up at the Cloud then walked over to Ruby and placed the .45 to his chest. In panic, Ruby extended his arms out farther. Another bolt of lightning struck out horizontally across the sky, followed by a loud rumbling thunder. "You don't know me, do you?" John Carter said.

"No," Ruby said with his eyes closed and his hands raised to the Cloud.

Ruby opened his eyes and there was a loud thunder and

lightning. The Crowd inhaled and exhaled as one, and the deputies stood frozen in their actions. The reverend got up from the ground and stared up at the Cloud. Neena Moore hovered like a technological vulture snapping shots every few seconds, reloading like an expert machine-gunner with her bag of tools on her shoulder. Ruby stood in front of John Carter, his head pounding, not knowing what was going on. He lowered his left arm and placed the palm of his hand on John Carter's forehead. There was another crack of lightning along with thunder then it began to rain hard with a never-before-seen fury. John Carter dropped the .45 and went to his knees, kneeling before Ruby. Ruby fell to the ground beside him and had a grand mal seizure. The grandest of them all.

Neena Moore stood outside under the shelter of the circle drive and snapped her shots, frame after frame. The most intense shot being the one of Ruby with his hands in the air with John Carter kneeling before him and the Cloud off in the background with a strict bolt of lightning frozen to its belly.

She contemplated greatness as she snapped it, seeing Jesus Christ and the Anti-Christ simultaneously. She saw the Crowd reacting all too expectantly as the thunder and lightning called forth the rain. They raised their hands with Ruby and closed their eyes and felt the relieving coolness of the rain as it pelted their faces. They laughed and cried and mixed emotions generously and epidemically; they were confused yet overjoyed. They felt as if a miracle had just taken place—but what's the miracle in a summer shower?

Neena lowered her camera and gazed out in wonderment. Elnora came out from the lobby and stood beside her. "Oh perfect Buddha!" she said in a raised voice competing with the falling rain, which fell in an almost continuous sheet. "I didn't expect that."

Neena reached into her bag and pulled out another roll of film. "This is big."

They stood out there in it—deputies, reporters, and cameramen stood behind and beside them. Cameras rolled, but no one spoke. Deborah Collins sat in her van staring out as if she had committed some unforgivable crime. Her hair was wet and her make-up had run down onto her shirt. She was in no condition to tell the world what just happened. Neena reloaded and snapped a picture of her. Deborah saw her but did not react. She just stared at Ruby and at the rain. The deputies eventually regained their dutifully upheld composure and ran out and seized John Carter. Neena took pictures of that as well.

THE ISLAM CONNECTION

Jamal was horrified at what he saw. He had not expected such an event, especially coming from the man who had drugged his mother into unemployment and subsequent insanity. His mentor, Iman Bainomie, did not mention anything about it nor did he mention the possibility. Neither did his mother. "What does it mean?" his younger brother Ahmed asked, cowering beside him, rain pelting them both.

Jamal did not answer.

"Are we in trouble?" Ahmed asked.

Jamal did not answer. He stared at Ruby, as much as he could, as Ruby lay on the ground jerking incomprehensibly, the seizure working out his every muscle. Jamal then ran forward and grabbed Ruby by the arm. "I'm sorry," he yelled. "I didn't know."

Ruby did not answer.

"I have done something terribly wrong," Jamal continued.

Behind them the deputies wrestled with John Carter. One saw Jamal and rushed toward him. They both hit the ground. "Stop!" Jamal yelled.

The deputy wrestled him down then pulled out a set of handcuffs. Ahmed ran forward and pushed the deputy off. The deputy landed on his back. "You little punk!" he yelled, scrambling to his feet.

Jamal and Ahmed backed off. "You don't understand!" Jamal yelled. "We've—"

Another deputy came up behind them, but they saw him and ran. "It's in the sweet tea!" Jamal yelled as he and his brother disappeared in the Crowd. "I swear I didn't know!"

The deputies stopped and stared at each other. "What did he say about sweet tea?" the one asked.

"Who knows," said the other.

THE SOUTHERN BAPTIST CONNECTION

After taking out all of her money and closing her account at the Better Bank and Trust, Lisa stopped by the Fast Way for cigarettes and beer. The parking lot was empty and there was only a clerk inside the store. He was on the phone. Lisa smiled at him and he smiled; then she went to the back of the store where the cooler was and pulled out a six-pack of Miller Lite. All the way to the register she thought of how beautiful a drive out of town and to the coast it was going to be, sipping beer and listening to the radio or just talking with Ruby about all they were going to do when they got to Wilmington. Nothing else mattered anymore. She had completely given in to the idea of being someone and somewhere else. She thought of going back to school and becoming a teacher or radiologist, anything, someone with a title behind her name. That seemed an important thing to do for the majority of the world, why not? With Ruby, everything seemed possible. Premature or not. Besides, she was in love.

She sat the beer on the counter and smiled at the attendant, who smiled back. His name was Steve—at least that's what his badge said. "Will that be all?" Steve asked.

"A pack of Marlboro Lights. Soft pack," Lisa said.

The attendant reached over his head and pulled down a carton of Marlboro Lights, opened it, and pulled out a pack.

"How's your father doing?" Steve asked.

"He's fine," Lisa answered. "Thanks."

It wasn't at all out of the ordinary for a complete stranger to be asking about her father. It happened all the time. Sometimes in inappropriate places, like in the back seat of her car with her legs shoved over her head with some dog in heat crawling over her. No, it wasn't unusual; her father was a powerful, prominent man in the community. "Strange things happening, aren't they?" Steve said.

Lisa looked outside at what the dullness the Cloud had created then back to Steve who was still holding her cigarettes.

"Don't you think it's all for a reason?" Steve asked, tapping the cigarette packet on the counter to a beat Lisa was not familiar with. "I mean, isn't everything for a reason? Everything being related, that is. You know, worlds have been destroyed for less."

Steve looked as if he had drunk too much coffee during the morning. He had nervous energy that spit through his frail body. His teeth were crooked and stained a yellowish-brown, and Lisa immediately lost interest in the cigarettes. "What's your problem?" she said.

Steve backed off and cut a glance out the window—Lisa had no idea he had just spoken with Christopher Riley and was now in the process of stalling her. "None here. Just being polite," he said. "Don't you like small talk?"

"Well, forget the cigarettes, just ring up the beer."

There was a moment and Steve froze in it then slowly reacted. "Sure thing."

He rang up the beer and Lisa paid. He reached for a bag, but Lisa stopped him. "No, thanks," she said.

"What does your father think about all this?" Steve asked. "Can't he do something?"

"Sure," Lisa said. "He's doing something right now."

"Good," Steve said. "Good man."

Outside, she took a deep breath and shook off what Steve had given her. She got in her car and backed out. Just before entering the highway she yielded for the oncoming traffic. It was one vehicle. One large four-wheel-drive vehicle with chrome bumpers and running lights. It reminded Lisa of Christopher Riley's truck and subsequently reminded her of him. And she thought of him for that moment.

As she watched and waited, she saw the truck swerve over into the oncoming lane and when it was fifty or so feet away she saw Christopher Riley in the driver's seat, hunched down with that dirty ball cap on his head. She initially tried to put her car in reverse, but it was useless; the nerves had taken over and they were sloppy, fumbling with all thumbs. She pressed the gas, then the brakes, then fumbled some more until she found reverse, then gassed it—with Christopher Riley and his big truck close in front of her.

She wasn't looking where she was going. It didn't matter. The only thing that concerned her was what was in front of her. She shot across the parking lot then into the side of the Fast Way. Her car dug deep into the building, coming to rest inside behind the counter. Steve the attendant scrunched up along the back wall, cowering there like an imbecile. Lisa got out and shook off the dust and was immediately pissed off when she saw her car. She could see Christopher's chrome bumper staring at her and that made her even madder. And Christopher was just sitting there. She walked around the counter and out the front door. "Get the hell out!" she yelled.

Christopher had his door open before she could finish her words. He met her halfway and she swung her fist and connected on the right side of his forehead, sending him to the ground. He immediately got up and took a swing at her but missed. She connected again and before he knew it she had connected again. Steve came out and tried to grab her around the waist, but she was too wound up and slippery. She threw him off and continued at Christopher. "You bastard!" she yelled.

"You fucking whore, you!" Christopher yelled then slung a fist that caught Lisa on the jaw.

The first bolt of lightning cracked across the blackened sky somewhere around this time. It stopped all three of them for the moment. Steve smiled. Christopher looked up in amazement. Lisa thought of Ruby then landed another fist to Christopher's jaw. When it began to rain Christopher couldn't see the meaning behind what he was doing anymore. He jumped in his truck and in haste popped the clutch, which sent the truck lunging forward. The driver's side mirror, which was as big and as chromed-up as the front bumper, caught Lisa on the forehead and dropped her to the ground. Christopher Riley freaked out and drove off scrambling mad across the parking lot. Steve ran over to Lisa and checked for a pulse. He couldn't find one and freaked out himself. He left her there in the parking lot—in the rain—and went inside to call for help.

When the paramedics arrived they found Lisa still in the parking lot—unconscious, but with a strong pulse. Steve was relieved. As they loaded her into the back of the ambulance, he watched. And when they pulled off he called Christopher Riley on his mobile phone to tell him that he was one lucky son of a bitch and to never ask for another favor again.

THE BIG FRESH

When Ruby awakened in his room it was quiet. Deathly quiet. The quiet before a storm. Ruby was on his back, and he could vaguely make out the patterns along the crest of the ceiling. His shoulders were sore and his head swam with the emptiness of a drained swimming pool. He turned over onto his side and stared at Thomas C. McNeil, who was on his back staring over at Ruby.

"What the hell are you looking at?" Thomas said.

Ruby picked his head up off the pillow and gave Thomas another look. "What did you say?" Ruby asked in an almost dazed withdrawal.

"Why don't you bring that pretty face over here and let me give you something to really look at," Thomas C. McNeil said.

Thomas did not move, but he spoke wildly like a drunken Irishmen, slurring his R's and tripping his Y's.

"You can talk?" Ruby said.

"You thought I couldn't?"

"No."

"Of course you did," Thomas said. "That's why you never would shut up. Always something dramatic to say. Banging on that typewriter all hours of the night."

"My fault," Ruby said, "I—"

"When I was young I had a brother like you," Thomas said, interrupting Ruby. "Always forgetting the world was around him. Wanted to change everything. Never could accept that things were just as they were for a reason. He was learned too. Eventually he boxed himself in. Collapsed. Had that famous nervous breakdown, like Nietzsche—the poor bastard."

Ruby sat up on the side of the bed. His head was light and swimmy, and he felt as if he were coming off a long, sustained drunk. The events of the afternoon were trapped within those drunken walls. It was Lisa that first came to mind, then the reverend.

"You're a piece of work," Ruby said. He walked over to the window. It was raining. Ruby vaguely remembered the rain or anything else for that matter—one of the side effects of a good seizure.

"I want you to take that goddamn picture off the wall," Thomas said. "Damn woman, she was ugly when she was alive and even uglier dead."

When Ruby turned away from the window he saw Julius in the doorway. He was tall and clumsy-looking, overweight in a jolly way around the midsection. "Any coffee?" Ruby asked.

Julius didn't say anything at first. He just stood there staring into the room as if emulating Ruby's previous catatonic, depressive state. Julius was high though. Higher than his son-of-a-preacher-man self had ever been. He, unlike most clergymen's offspring, strayed little from the straight and narrow. Be it a fear of God or a fear of his father, Julius kept his nose clean and his eyes and mind straight ahead. But he, more than any of the rest at the Home—except for a few residents—took the spiked tea the Amir boys concocted rather personally. One could say that it came at the wrong time in his life while others would argue much differently. Julius graduated high school the same year Lisa did, and like Lisa he had not the prowess academically to sever the stealthy arms of the paternal religious sect. The Reverend Frederick Holmes did not like it much when his one and only son dropped out of the University of North Carolina at Chapel Hill and started work as a nurse's assistant at the Sunbridge Psychiatric and Rehabilitation Center. Not even the idea of bringing comfort to the sick brought comfort to the man who held three degrees himself—not counting his Masonic Supreme Leader degree which, in itself, accounted for more than anything Julius could ever hope to achieve—so his father reminded him.

Julius was thinking of all this when the LSD came knocking upon his conscience. He was helping Mrs. Greathouse, a resident at the Home, with her disposable undergarments when it came in. He had Greathouse on her side when her cheeks began to giggle and speak. It was Arabic, but he understood every word. Her ass revealed to him his father's plan, the great and large of it all. If not wholly then partially whole—enough to take the Lord's name in vain twice, like a machine gun.

Mrs. Greathouse asked to be powdered, but Julius was lucky to get the diaper on straight. He ran out to the lobby in hopes of catching his father, but he had already left.

"You all right?" Elnora asked him.

"Not at all," he said.

"Me neither." Her Buddha had temporarily vanished.

Julius wasn't sure, but he somehow felt that Ruby was involved in whatever was going on inside his head. He did in fact make it rain. That much Julius knew.

Standing in the doorway seeing Ruby, it was if a great puzzle had fallen out of his mind into his hands, with each piece working its way into order. Was it the hallucinogenic? Was it Lipton? The Cloud? The Crowd? The Cross? The overdue rain?

"What's wrong?" Ruby asked.

"Everything," Julius said.

Julius was shaking when he stepped into the room and leaned his oversized, out-of-shape body onto Ruby's. "We're friends," he said, "right?"

"Of course we are," Ruby said.

"Here's the deal," he said, covertly and seriously. "My father is the king of the world, or so it seems, and something . . . something is going on. Crazy, I know. Something always going on. He has plans though. Real big plans. Something. Something big. Something holy. A holy revolution, I think."

"Sure," Ruby said, acknowledging that Julius was all out of the sorts and out of his realm, bordering on incoherence. "You okay?"

"No, I'm not."

Julius stepped back and grabbed Ruby's shoulders as if he were falling, making Ruby look him in the eyes. "You made it rain," he said, crying out in the revelation of it all.

"What are you talking about?" Ruby said, holding Julius up.

"The rain," Julius said, pointing out the window. "You made it rain. You did. You really did."

"The rain made it rain," Ruby replied. "That's all."

Julius pulled closer. "Can't you accept that some things are bigger than this world? That there possibly is a Heaven and Hell out there and that good and evil really do exist?"

Ruby did not answer.

"He's a Mason," Julius said. "You know that, don't you? You know what that means?"

"Who?" Ruby said.

"My father."

Ruby did not know. The fact is he had only vaguely, in passing, heard of the Stonemasons. There was a lodge in Wilmington; he had seen it before but knew of no one who actually went to it. He thought of it as a party shack where middle-aged and retired men went to shake off the cold once in a while.

He knew nothing of the Stonemason's history—that they originated out of England some three centuries back, that they compose one of the largest fraternities in the world, elusive and denominational. A boys' club with symbols and songs and a

Grand Wizard who stands out like God Himself. Accused of everything from being the Ku Klux Klan to the organizers and swindlers behind the Publisher's Clearing House Sweepstakes. The Masons could have shot Kennedy and publicly announced it and Ruby wouldn't have known.

"What are you saying?" Ruby asked.

"I'm saying . . . " Julius said, slipping back into his head trying to shake off the LSD. It ran a complete circle around his brain, and then stopped to catch its breath. Julius laughed. "I do not know."

THE NIRVANA CONNECTION

Neena Moore drank the sweet tea that Jamal and Ahmed had so graciously laced with lysergic acid. She—like Rita, Elnora, Julius, and a couple of dozen more, including deputy sheriffs and news crews who, in the course of a busy day of roping and reporting, had stumbled across the Sunbridge Psychiatric and Rehabilitation Center's dining hall and subsequently the tea—was now in the process of transforming one twisted morning into one even more twisted afternoon.

The effects were subtle at first, like the ramblings of a slow-moving train, clicking and clacking through the subconscious like a whisper—not too faint to go unrecognized but not too obvious to distract either. Neena picked up on it quick. She broke away from the crowd in the lobby who, in her mind, had started acting rather diplomatic and sanitary about the state of things; she made her way back into the heart of the Sunbridge Psychiatric and Rehabilitation Center to where John Carter was.

She was buzzing when she entered his room—slightly, of course, just enough to give her that distorted, inquisitive attention she needed. She saw Charles Apple in the corner sitting on his bed and smiled. Charles Apple smiled back. "Can I use this chair?" she asked, pointing to the chair that sat at the head of his bed beside the nightstand.

"Charles Apple can use this chair," he said.

Neena's mind was beginning to buzz faster. She thought Charles Apple said he wanted to eat the chair. "Sure you do," Neena said, smiling awkwardly. Charles Apple smiled awkwardly back.

Neena took the chair and placed it beside John Carter's bed.

"Come to suck my cock?" John Carter said.

"Sure," Neena said, sitting down in the chair adjusting herself like a sterilized surgeon on a smoke break.

"Do you mind?" she said, holding up a small tape recorder so John Carter could see it.

"Oh yes," John Carter said, "the great recording session. What will she find? God? A cock? A ride through Central Park?"

"I want you to tell me about Ruby," Neena said.

"The rainmaker, Ruben Riggs," John Carter said. "What do

you need to know? What?"

He had his head off the pillow surveying down his body. "You want to know his birth name?"

"Sure," said Neena.

"It's Christopher. He was born in Poland. Uhhh . . . nineteen hundred and forty-four, maybe. Kidnapped by Catholic nuns with machine guns, so they say. Smuggled off to London then St. Louis, Missouri then Alexandria, Virginia then to Wilmington, North Carolina."

He raised his head again and looked down the length of his body. It was like looking down two long mountainous highways. "Can you loosen these straps?"

Neena looked at his feet and saw the leathers wrapped around his ankles. It was industrial leather, the kind found on boots and backs of horses. She had been tied down herself once before—her first month in New York by a man who worked at the paper. He was in advertising and sales. Shy and unpleasant at the office, at home he drank a lot and listened to heavy metal music. Neena had fallen for him only because of a technical glitch in her self-esteem—the city made her feel lonely and somewhat vulnerable to the diseases of the mind. She wanted to use him as a quick fix, a sort of appetizer before the main New York course. But straight off their first date she found herself on his bed playing some Batman and Robin game she thought he had just made up. The leathers were already in place though and they fit perfectly around her chubby wrists.

"What's this?" she asked as he strapped her in.

"The same game," he said.

"Why would Batman tie up Robin? Aren't they on the same side of good and justice?"

"They are," he replied. "It's just that Batman is a closet homosexual and it's time for Robin to know how he feels about him."

Neena was angry at first, but the sex turned out to be rather relaxing, even under the circumstances. She faked it the rest of the night then slapped him when he finally untied her.

"Don't ever do that again," she had said with a somewhat laughing grin on her face.

"Listen, girl!" John Carter said. "Pay attention!"

Neena focused on the leather straps then moved her eyes to his toes. He wriggled them and traces of light with a multitude of color ran from them like rows of headlights down an interstate highway. Neena shook her head and smiled. The LSD shook its head and smiled too.

"You want me to untie you so you can tie me up, right?" Neena said.

"What?" John Carter replied, dumbfounded by Neena's airy disposition. "No. No. No. Just untie me, woman!"

Neena spaced out again and John Carter dropped his head in disgust.

Others around the Home who had tasted of the sweet tea were feeling the effects of it too. The majority of the residents who remained found themselves in awkward and unfamiliar situations. They laughed and cried simultaneously. They looked at their decaying bodies with a strange, new exuberance. They took off walking in all directions, exploring old territory with a childlike wonderment.

Rita, Elnora, Julius, and other workers also felt the effects of the lysergic acid. They felt it but could put nothing concrete together. They assumed that what they were feeling was directly related to the rain, which was directly related to the Cloud, the Crowd, the Cross, the cops, the news crews, and the all around messed up day itself.

Of all the staff, Rita probably slipped the furthest the fastest down that totem of tripping. At some point, she went to her office and called her husband and told him she wasn't coming home. "I'm in love with Jesus," she said, "and will be his disciple any day."

"That's good," her husband said, thinking of the many times Rita had called him to say she would be staying late. "I too love Jesus and will be his disciple."

Rita let out a mighty yell of discontent. Her husband laughed.

"Good-bye, my love," she said then hung up the phone.

She placed a call to the Sunbridge Psychiatric and Rehabilitation Center's main office in Charleston, South Carolina, and informed them that she had quit and went on to tell the person on the other end of the line what she really thought of the Sunbridge Psychiatric and Rehabilitation Center.

"You can't do that," the personnel director said.

"It's already been done," Rita informed him.

"You'll never work for us again if you quit like this," he said.

"That's why I did it," she said while hanging up the phone.

THE SOUTHERN BAPTIST CONNECTION

Two religious factions parted way that rainy afternoon. Two of the same house. Both schooled teachers. Both on considerably different paths. The Reverend Alfonso King, seemingly the rebel evangelist of Siler City, was escorted away from the Home with an almost immediate and irrevocable tarnishment to his ministry. The other, the astute Reverend Frederick Holmes, watched the entire transgression from the dry aspects of the lobby with his deacons standing beside him. It was he who first acknowledged his regrets to the Reverend King as they escorted the reverend by.

"What will you do now?" the Reverend Frederick Holmes asked, smiling like some Russian cosmonaut just off the space station Mir.

The Reverend Alfonso King could not say a word. Logistically he was trapped with the cat out of the bag. No one would ever get another chance to know how sincere a man he actually was.

One southern religion—an evangelical Protestant denomination—with two men and a half dozen crude and unusual ideas floating around. There was one church burning and one standing tall across the street from the Sheriff's Department. Reverend King did not know that his church was burning. Reverend Holmes did. The boys on the back row had struck again.

Reverend King had tripped and spilled his cards, and he had none up his sleeves. Do-or-die time had passed and what was left reminded him a lot of his first few days in the military when no one particularly knew what to do with him and no one seemed particularly curious to figure it out. So they hurried him along through the system making him feel rather unimportant along the way; then without warning they froze him where he stood and ordered him to stand there, no questions asked. *Hurry up and wait* was their motto, and a silly one at that. The sheriff's deputy hurried the reverend into the Sheriff's Department then into a cell then left him with nothing but time to think about everything he ever tried to forget.

It was a sad situation for the Reverend Alfonso King, but the

Reverend Frederick Holmes was in no position to be spilling out sentimentalities, especially over a man he had never particularly cared for in the first place. On top of the plans he had already composed for himself and his people, the Reverend Frederick Holmes composed a few more, which were done directly in response to the events of the rainy afternoon. He and his deacons left abruptly after the Reverend King was escorted out. They drove down through the Brookwood Apartments and out onto Raleigh Street toward the historic downtown Siler City. From the comforts of their car they saw the old brick buildings off in the near-distance with a dash of smoke rising over them, breaking out through the rain. "We are the purveyors of morality," the reverend said.

"Amen," said the deacons.

"Purveyors of the clean fabric that must be re-sewn in order to be re-worn."

"Amen."

It was a ride full of amens through the historic downtown Siler City—one after the other as if they were covering something up. Embarking and barking farther, past soaked crowds standing on street corners—leaderless and mad, rabid in their wetness. They drove past the Sheriff's Department and their own church, sitting there like some watchdog atop its doghouse. They drove past the Dry Dock Seafood Restaurant, whose parking lot was full of parked cars with headlights on high beam and shirtless teenagers sitting and standing on shirtless hoods. They drove past them not remarking—on to the front door of the Wren Memorial Library where the reverend got out.

The reverend walked through the library, not saying a word to Gloria Swinton at the front desk as he passed, and went directly to the back where the People's Channel was located. There was a cooking show being filmed live. Edward Brohams acknowledged the reverend's interruption but signaled for David Moore, the cameraman, to keep rolling—which he did. Lady Etna was on the small, makeshift stage with a small, makeshift, functional kitchen in front of her. She was halfway through the process of making coleslaw—to add vinegar or not was the question she posed to her audience.

The reverend was in no state to concern himself with the science of cabbage and mayonnaise and whether or not vinegar made it better. "Get off the stage, Etna," he said, stepping through the few chairs set up for the few who came to watch the show.

"Excuse me, Reverend Holmes?" Lady Etna said, dropping her tablespoon of apple cider vinegar into the large bowl of coleslaw. "This really is inappropriate."

The reverend stepped up on stage. "Turn it off," he yelled, waving to David Moore and Edward Brohams. Edward signaled to David and with a flick of a switch, television screens that were tuned into Lady Etna's cooking show went blue.

"What is all this?" Edward Brohams said.

The four deacons came into the studio and joined the reverend on stage.

"Who runs the show here?" the reverend asked.

David Moore looked at Edward Brohams and Edward Brohams looked over at the reverend then back at David. They had not been privy to the happenings outside and were now completely confused.

THE BIG FRESH

Ruby stood at the nurses' station with a perplexed look upon his face. On the other side sat Dr. Vokes with his right sock and shoe off, his right leg crossed over his left, massaging the ball of his foot and acrobatically clipping his nails with a pair of surgical scissors. The best Ruby could tell, he was also talking to himself in a lackadaisical Sunday afternoon kind of way. Ruby had tried once to get his attention and was unsuccessful, left the desk, walked down the hall to the dining room and got himself some coffee and returned. His head still had that funniness about it, reminiscent of a hangover.

"Can't say that I have," Dr. Vokes said to himself. "Sure. Sure. Common practice in the world. Yes it is . . ."

Ruby felt unsure if he should disturb the doctor or not. It was that reason why he gave the doctor so much time to himself. It was believed by many that waking someone while sleepwalking could be detrimental and Ruby did not know how much of that same theory applied to this particular situation.

After a moment the doctor looked up at Ruby gingerly and with a quieted smile spoke. "They make you or break you," he said, referring to his feet. "Had the jungle rot once. Gave me a complete new outlook on things. You looking for some religion?"This made Ruby think of the reverend, of the paraphernalia he had in his pocket when the cops arrested him. "Have you seen the Reverend King?" Ruby asked.

Dr. Vokes slowly and methodically replaced his sock and shoe before answering. "No religion here," he said, "just a bunch of eclectic geriatrics with a habit and a few drug pushers to help 'em out."

Ruby remembered the rain now, and John Carter and the gun.

Dr. Vokes began to speak liberally. "Have you ever seen the movie *Apocalypse Now*?" he asked.

"No," Ruby answered, although he had, years ago. It didn't matter because the doctor wasn't listening.

"No," he said, "I mean really watched it. Like, not stoned, but removed, floating?"

"No," Ruby said.

"Then you know how weak Brandon actually was. He was too nervous for the jungle, almost urban in his ramblings. Coppola let him do that, you know. For two million dollars he let him ramble like a bicycle down a dirt road. Now, Hopper—that was real. He was all over it."

Elnora came down the hall and went behind the desk and into the medicine room. Charlie Robinson, a resident at the Home, was close behind in a wheelchair. He had just had his left leg removed a month or so back. The right one was already off—poorly controlled diabetes. Charlie was a drunk whenever he could get the juice. He resembled William S. Burroughs in the face—sunken and distorted. He wheeled up behind the desk and parked himself beside the doctor.

Elnora came out from the medicine room with a syringe and needle. The needle was unsheathed. Her eyes were wild and glassy, staring at the bead of clear fluid that hung like a raindrop from the bevel of the needle. "Magic," she said.

"Clearly," Dr. Vokes replied.

"Morphine?" asked Charlie.

"Yes," said Elnora.

"Class II opioid," said the doctor not knowing either way. "China would have taken over the world if it hadn't been for its addiction to opium. And we would have won Vietnam—if wars were meant to be won or lost."

Ruby asked Elnora if she had seen the reverend. She did not answer. Her mind was notably fixed on the task at hand. She shook off the bead of morphine then lowered it down to Dr. Vokes's arm.

"Hey, what's up?" Charlie said. Elnora and the doctor laughed.

"Where do you want it?" Elnora said.

"I'd like it in my vein, but you're probably going to put it in my ass."

"Put it in his vein," Dr. Vokes said.

"Is that an order?" Elnora said.

"Yes," Dr. Vokes said. "I order you to put that morphine into that man's arm. Expedite."

Charlie Robinson dropped his left arm on command, exposing the antecubital and Elnora stepped forward. She gave his arm a thump with her index finger then sank the tip of the needle under the skin and advanced it till a flash of blood appeared in the chamber. She then sank the plunger, evacuating all the morphine into Charlie Robinson's arm. "How now you brown cow," Dr. Vokes said laughing as Charlie's face went expressionless.

Elnora removed the needle and disposed of it, then

maneuvered Charlie's wheelchair out from behind the nurses' desk. She gave him a push and the chair went gliding gracefully off, coming to rest some twenty feet down the hall.

"What the hell was that about?" Ruby asked himself, expecting no answer to be given, realizing it was a question best left unanswered.

Outside in the lobby stood four deputies, one being Kirk Merchant himself. They stood in a circle in front of the double door, taking turns sniffing the barrel of Kirk Merchant's .45. Four men of law, schooled and entrusted by the county to uphold it, taking turns breathing in the fine sulfuric residue left behind from John Carter's rampage. They all took their turns; then they took out their own guns and gave them a sniff, comparing the difference. They were all high on the good stuff: life, their jobs, the sweet tea they had with lunch.

Ruby entered the lobby expecting bedlam. Instead, he caught the last of the gun sniffing. He walked up to the four deputies and inquired about the reverend's whereabouts.

"You going to send a lightning bolt down on me if I don't tell you?" one of the deputies said.

Ruby did not understand the hassle. He had missed the correlation that everyone else seemed to pick up on so easily. He was completely unaware that everyone in and around the Home, including half the town by now, associated the two events—the raising of his hands and the rain—as being one in the same. As related as brother and sister. It was hot. It was muggy. It was a small town on the verge of nuclear fission. There was nothing better to do.

"Yes," Ruby said, irritated and hung over.

A laugh broke out amongst the four. "Get back to your room, Jesus," one of the deputies said.

This confused Ruby even more. He made a lunge for the door, but Kirk Merchant pulled up fast in front of him, expelling his pistol from its holster and drawing it up clean and fast to Ruby's nose. "Recognize this?" he said.

Ruby did. And yet somehow he felt more confident with John Carter behind it. Kirk seemed too hostile and open to suggestion, somewhat juvenile with his cohorts in company.

Ruby backed off. "Sure thing," he said, raising his hands in submission. All four of the deputies looked at each other then looked outside, not sure if they should be expecting a lightning bolt.

Ruby exited the lobby backwards, made it back to the nurses' station, and found Dr. Vokes and Elnora engaged in a trivial conversation about euthanasia. Down the hall he could see some of the residents out and about, bumping around, some shirtless, others without bottoms, their hair wild and tameless. Nothing seemed unusual about what they were doing.

Ruby went to the dining hall. A few residents remained hunched over, slopping slowly through their mashed potatoes. There were cooks and cleaners in the back, and they danced around their work to the almost symphonic rattles and rings of their hardware. Ruby slipped through them and out the back door without detection. Once outside he made his way around the corner into the rain with little concern about the Crowd—he had been in it before, had ridden its wave, and was neither frightened nor defensive because of it. But when he rounded the corner, he was stopped by the sheer amazement of what he saw. The Crowd stood large, wet, and motionless, with a military dress-right-dress look about it. Rain fell hard. Bolts of lightning stretched infinitely and erratically across the sky. It was five, six o'clock—maybe later. A summer evening, yet almost completely dark. There was no escaping the brilliance of the mood created. But for the Crowd to stand there in it, absorbing it up like a sponge? Ruby couldn't put it together.

He walked slowly out in front of them toward the Cross. There was an opening near the middle of the Crowd and he went for it. The Crowd acknowledged him by opening up, as if on automatic pilot. Ruby was taken back by this action and proceeded on through the opening slowly, staring back and forth at the multitude of faces that flanked off to his left and right. Faces with no emotion, blank, not staring at Ruby but staring at something about him, an idea. He felt as if there was some respect to be had in their stares, as if he had done something and missed it himself. He had seen it before, before important games, championship games with the national anthem ringing out across the field and into the stands, creating this universally simultaneous feeling of adoration and oneness.

Maybe, Ruby thought, but it was raining far beyond cats and dogs, with lightning and a giant lightning rod of a Cross snuggled up amongst them like a rudimentary convection oven waiting to happen.

Ruby walked slowly through the stares of the Crowd, thinking of the reverend and of Lisa and how strange the day had been. No one in the Crowd spoke, and as Ruby stepped out the other side the Crowd closed in on itself, turning carefully toward Ruby like a precise, choreographed machine. He himself turned and walked backwards for a few steps, wanting so much to ask the Crowd what the deal was, wanting to ask them about the reverend and if they had anything better to do. If anyone had anything better to do? If there was anything left to do? Or left undone?

He answered all his questions like a politician then turned away from the Crowd and made his way down the hill to Lisa's apartment. The front door was open. Left open. He remembered now. It was left open by a man in search of a reverend.

THE MASONIC CONNECTION

The rain danced over and onto the town like a mad peddler of songs, criminal in its instincts, indiscriminate and lawless. Those in the Crowd outside the Sunbridge Psychiatric and Rehabilitation Center felt it; those in the streets, along street corners and parking lots, felt it too.

It produced a driving madness far greater than that of the Cloud. Nevertheless it was an extension of the Cloud, an appendage that wrapped and wallowed its way into the most indeterminate corners: corners of the city, of the mind, of worlds yet to be discovered. Outside, it was like this: driven, being driven like nails into fingers. Upon rooftops it could be heard constantly rapping, tapping away, attempting to open up and violate.

It was there, in the homes of those who refused, as of yet, to venture out, that men and women and children of all ages wrapped themselves in timbers and passed time the only way they knew how: they watched television. It kept a restless mind occupied—kept it numb and dumb and virtually incapacitated. It was just what the government ordered.

Staring into a blue television screen, everyone waited for that suspended cross, glowing and gold like a metallic sun, and those words: MAKING THE CONNECTION to show up mysteriously below it. And then the music: uuna chucka uno cha, sounding like some seventies rip off from *Sanford and Son*. And then for the Reverend Alfonso King to show his bright, bloated face, smiling in a dear reverence that acquitted all. The beloved Reverend Alfonso King, still beloved by those who had not heard of his transgressions and by the few who did not care. It was time for the Reverend Alfonso King's Power Hour of Prayer Show.

When the blue screen faded—after no floating cross, no MAKING THE CONNECTION, no chucka uno cha—there was no Reverend Alfonso King either. Instead, situated in the small auditorium in the back of the Wren Memorial Library, sat the Reverend Frederick Holmes behind the desk draped in blue cloth. Behind the reverend, standing close and confidential, were his four well-dressed deacons. The reverend sat straight and proud and when the belated cue came down from David

Moore to begin, he did.

It was a dissertation of sorts, spoken technically and professionally but absorbed almost immediately by most into that clumsy realm of disinterest—almost automatically—as if planned, as if part of some ancient recipe of natural selection that only a few have the ability to comprehend. The words the Reverend Holmes spoke were nothing like what the people watching were used to. They had spent too many hours listening to the simple-minded Reverend King.

The Reverend Holmes continued to speak, though, in his formidable nomenclature. Children who would have been interested in hearing what the Reverend Alfonso King had to say were now dropping out, sailing off to bedrooms and bathrooms, to other corners of interest. Women too found the Reverend Holmes unromantic—not that the Reverend King was, but at least he was funny and funny went a long way to a small-town housewife.

The Reverend Holmes was on a mission though, dictated by some higher order, lecturing incoherently in foreign languages unheard of by common man, not meant for the untrained ears of normality. No, unlike the Reverend King, Reverend Holmes was after something far greater than the mere *connection* with common man. He did not concern himself with popularity or popular culture. He was beyond that, speaking in codes, firing off with machine gun rapidity. He first turned the women and children away with his dryness, then came the men. One by one they turned their simple heads. Some feeling inferior to the reverend's brilliant display of intellect; others superior, placing the reverend on some juvenile rung alongside spelling bee contestants and honor roll students. Eventually all who were left watching him were all who Reverend Holmes wanted. Almost inherently, he knew. As if trained to know. It was then and there that he put out the call. A *call of the wild* of sorts to all his Masonic brethren listening and watching. It was time. For what? For whatever the Masons wanted. Or more precisely, for whatever the Masonic Brothers of Columbus Lodge No. 102 wanted.

THE BIG FRESH

Ruby walked into Lisa's apartment almost instinctually as the blue screen on the television flashed off and the Reverend Frederick Holmes began speaking. Ruby understood more than most in the town, and that's what kept him there. Up to the point when the reverend divulged the whereabouts of the other reverend. It was then that all the reverend had to say turned to babble.

Ruby found the telephone book. It was in the bathroom, opened and turned over on its face. Lisa had been looking up resorts. Beach resorts. It made Ruby smile. The thoughts of Lisa and him at the beach together made him smile.

He put the call into the Sheriff's Department.

"Say that again," the voice on the other end said. It was a bad connection. Blame it on the weather.

"The Reverend Alfonso King," Ruby said.

"Yeah, what about him?"

"Is he there?"

"What?"

"Is he there and if so can I speak with him?"

There was a crack, then silence, then a deep sigh of frustration from the voice on the other end. "No," he said then hung up.

"That bastard!" Ruby said.

He called back and got a busy signal.

He waited a minute and called back.

"Listen," Ruby said, "I know the Reverend King is there and I know he has a right to phone calls. Now if you don't want me to call my cousin, who is a Boston district attorney, then I better hear his voice in the next few minutes."

Ruby was irritated and pissed off. His escape had not gone as planned up to this point and he was looking to correct that. Even if that meant telling the front desk clerk at the Sheriff's Department that he had a cousin who was a Boston district attorney.

The man on the other end took another deep sigh, told Ruby to wait, and then placed him on hold. Muzak started up, the likes Ruby wasn't familiar with. Not bad, though. It gave him time to think and a backdrop to bounce his thoughts off of. He would need to get the reverend first; then, possibly, the reverend could help him locate Lisa. Something in that order. If order was to be had.

There was a crack in the music then the same grumpy man. "Two minutes," he said.

A moment later the Reverend King was spluttering salutations as if standing in front of a church after services. "Reverend," Ruby said, "It's me, Ruby."

"You dear angel," the reverend said. "Maker of miracles. Evangelical beauty. I knew. First time I saw you. I knew."

Ruby ignored his rambles and focused on his plan. "I'm going to come get you."

"Righteous be thy name. Christ has risen again."

"We need to find Lisa. She hasn't come back, yet."

There was a crack in the line, then a crack in the reverend's voice, a sob, and a whimper.

"She's been hurt," the reverend said.

"What?"

"She's been hurt," the reverend said again. "She's at the hospital."

Ruby lowered his head and closed his eyes to help absorb all that he was hearing. It helped but made him realize that his plans, that Lisa's plans, had taken a devastating blow. One he was not fully able to comprehend.

"I've got to go, Ruby," the reverend said.

"I'm still coming to get you."

The reverend took a proud swallow and wanted to say everything he had ever thought of saying but didn't in just one short and glorious sentence. The clerk had his hands on the phone before he could think of it. Ruby heard the struggle. In the background, just before disconnection, he heard the reverend yell: "Ruby, you are great!"

The television screen was blue. The gravelly hiss of the rain could be heard from inside the apartment and it gave everything a desperate, lonely feel. Ruby hung up the phone. He found one message on the answering machine. It was Christopher Riley. His voice was strained and worried. "I didn't mean to do it," he said. "It was an accident, Lisa. You know me. I love you and I want to make this thing work."

Ruby considered homicide, ridding the world of one more useless punk. He was a punk himself at one time and understood the limitless angles that all punks worked off of. Whatever happened to Lisa, Christopher Riley was involved.

Ruby went back up the hill to the Home. The Crowd parted for him and he went up the steps to the loading dock, through the back door—which was unlocked—and through the kitchen. Dr. Vokes was still at the nurses' station when he passed, along with Rosa Hurley who looked as if her water would break at any minute. Ruby went back to his room to see if Julius was still there. He wasn't.

"Get the hell out!" Thomas C. McNeil yelled.

"I liked you better as a carrot," Ruby told him and then left.

"It's a dusty microscope that we look at each other through," Dr. Vokes said as Ruby passed by the nurses' station. The doctor was smoking now—a practice that had long been done away with in such places. It put a stamp upon his authority. It made Ruby want to smoke too.

In the lobby, the four deputies remained posted in front of the double doors. Elnora Brown and Neena Moore stood off to the right of them. Neena Moore had her Pentax ME super 35mm slung over her shoulder like a pocket book. When she saw Ruby she went for it like a pistol and got off five quick shots before Ruby could make it across the lobby.

It made him feel like a spectacle. A large, clumsy zoo animal in an invisible cage with thousands of gawking faces staring in.

"You're going to get hurt doing that one day," Ruby said to Neena.

"It's a free world," Neena said, her eyes wild and staring.

"Until we destroy it. Have any of you seen Julius?" Ruby asked.

Elnora laughed. Then Neena.

"Let us just say," Elnora said, "that Julius is in Rita's office getting reprimanded."

Kirk Merchant cut a sharp look at Ruby then lowered his right hand down until it rested on the butt of his .45 and gave Ruby a smile. Ruby smiled back. The other deputies laughed.

Ruby found Julius behind Rita's office door. Rita was wrapped around him like an anaconda, sucking at his neck, hands on his crotch. Julius looked uncomfortable, violated in a schoolboy kind of way. Rita hesitated slightly when the door opened—enough for Julius to pull himself free. Rita made no bones about it. She stood up straight and adjusted her skirt and top, sat down behind her chair, and smiled. "What can I do for you?" she said to Ruby.

"Mr. McNeil is wet," Ruby said, staring over at Julius, who had cowered himself into the corner.

Julius did not move. He stared at Ruby as if he were unfamiliar to him. Traumatized. Another victim of a woman and her hormones gone mad.

"He needs drying and turning," Ruby said, emphasizing drying and turning.

Julius snapped to attention. "Yes. Yes," he said. "Drying and turning. Thomas C. McNeil. Old Clyde needs turning."

Julius rushed passed Ruby and out the door.

"Stay awhile," Rita said to Ruby, as he made a turn for the door. "We need to talk about your future."

"It's fine," Ruby said then left.

Julius had Thomas C. McNeil turned to his side, diaper off, bare ass shining when Ruby walked in the door. "I thought you said he was wet?" Julius said.

"No. No. Leave him alone," Ruby said. "I need the van."

Ruby was referring to the Ford Econoline cargo van that sat out front. It was purple and yellow and had the Sunbridge logo painted on its side. It was used to transport residents back and forth to various places—swimming pools, parks, high school football games on Friday nights. Ruby had always refused to be shuttled around in it. He considered it as bad as, if not worse, than the ambulance itself. "I'd rather take a taxi," he told Elnora the first time she tried to get Ruby on it.

"It is a taxi," Elnora said.

"It's a vehicle for the dead."

Now it seemed his only salvation. Julius told him that if the keys weren't in the ignition then they'd be over the sun visor. "But only authorized personnel can drive it," Julius said, rolling Thomas C. McNeil over on his left side and covering him up.

Ruby looked at Julius funny. "You can't be serious?"

Julius wasn't. He just wanted in on the ride.

"I'll drive," Julius said.

They made it out the back door, through the Crowd, and to the van in record time. The van was situated behind the Channel 5 van. Deborah Collins and her crew were nowhere to be found. They went in through the side door and made their way to the front. After a minute of fumbling, Julius regretfully told Ruby that the keys were nowhere to be found. The van smelled moist and moldy, and the rain pounding on the roof made it all seem alive, if only botanically.

Ruby stared out through the front windshield through the rain. He could see the Crowd and the Cross, and the lobby was lit up like an operating room. Just to the right of the lobby doors, situated in the circle drive, was Reverend King's blue Mercedes.

"What's the odds the reverend left his keys in his car?" Ruby asked.

"Slim to none," Julius said. "But I'll be back."

Julius crawled back through the van and exited the side door. He made his way around the vans and came up behind the reverend's car. He gave the driver's side door a pull and it opened. He got in and shut the door. A few seconds later a puff of cloudy white smoke bellowed out of the tailpipe and the lights came on. Ruby got out of the van as the car lunged forward. The deputies did not concern themselves with any of this. Ruby got into the car. The Crowd opened up and they were gone.

THE MASONIC CONNECTION

The clerk had just hung up the phone and was in the process of taking the Reverend King back to the holding cell when a group of men wearing hosiery over their heads threw open the front doors to the Sheriff's Department and rushed in. All carried shotguns of varying gauges. They were all wet, and the hosiery was wet too, concealing little, if any, of their identity.

"Put 'em up!" yelled one of the men.

The clerk and Reverend King did just that.

"Is that you Rodney?" the clerk asked, staring inquisitively into the hosiery.

The men stopped and stared at each other.

"Damn, Lanard. Why did you have to do that?" Rodney said.

The Reverend King took an extended second look himself.

"Hey, that is Rodney," the reverend said. "And Bradford and Richard and Douglas."

The four men dropped their weapons to their sides.

"What do we do now?" one of them asked.

Rodney shook his head. "Come on."

They exited out the doors and ran across the street and up the steps of the First Baptist Church.

"It doesn't matter," the Reverend Holmes said, staring down at the four wet assailants from the pulpit. "Finish the job."

Rodney informed the reverend that the Reverend King was not in his cell but it appeared as if he were leaving.

"Get him, too," the Reverend Holmes said.

The clerk was returning from the back where all the detainees were kept when the doors swung open again. Four men in cotton toboggans this time, with eyes and mouthpieces cut out, ran in.

"Damn it, Rodney," Lanard said.

"This ain't Rodney," a squelching voice said. "Now get me the keys for that cell in the back and let's go."

Lanard didn't get paid enough to disobey him. He didn't even get paid enough to waste a few minutes negotiating. He grabbed the keys and walked toward the back. Rodney, Douglas, Richard, and Bradford followed.

In the back was one large holding cell. Within that cell sat one Robert Leblanc, one James Morton, one Arthur Tysor, one Carlos Rubino, and one Reverend Alfonso King.

While Lanard opened the cell, Rodney pointed the barrel of his gun at all those he wanted out.

"What about me?" Carlos Rubino said.

"Feel lucky you're still alive," Rodney said.

Robert Leblanc, James Morton, Arthur Tysor, and the Reverend Alfonso King stepped out of the cell. Rodney pushed Lanard in.

"Best you keep this to yourself," Rodney said to Lanard as the door locked.

"Your momma goin' to be sorely upset with you," Lanard said.

Rodney turned back around upon hearing this and pointed the shotgun to Lanard's chest. "My momma won't hear about this, will she?"

Again Lanard didn't get paid enough to argue with the likes of a tobogganed, shotgun-wielding Rodney. "Your secret is safe with me," Lanard said.

"And this ain't Rodney."

"Sure," Lanard said.

On the way out, two more deputies were forced into surrender and detention in the one cell in the back with Lanard and Carlos Rubino. The four gunmen then took the four prisoners across the street, up the steps, and through the front doors of the First Baptist Church.

"Was that Rodney Crutchfield?" one of the deputies asked Lanard Wilson.

"Yes," Lanard said. "Yes it was."

THE BIG FRESH

The windshield wipers sang violently back and forth, scraping off only a portion of what was needed to see. Julius and Ruby sat leaning forward in their seats, Julius driving, hallucinating here and there on the psychedelic landscape.

It was too dark now to see the old brick buildings and factories with the plumes of smoke filtering their way out from random rooftops, but Ruby could imagine them—to believe it was only yesterday that he and Lisa stood in the Piggly Wiggly parking lot staring off at them.

Julius had only been in town about as long as Ruby, though he had the luxury of working his way through it on a daily basis. He felt comfortable in describing to Ruby all that his father and others in the town had described to him about the historic buildings, their transformations throughout the years, and their existing future. Ruby did not mind listening to what Julius had to say. It kept him focused without digging his wheels into one unnecessary rut. In certain situations, Ruby knew that even the best could find themselves mired down in a psychological play of abstract *reasonings* and *what-ifs*. It was best to let Julius do his guided tour bit, so long as the car remained going forward.

From Raleigh Street they made an illegal left onto Second Avenue. They drove slowly, weaving in and out, avoiding what seemed to be a pedestrian parade of half-naked, slapped-neck youths. They strolled freely from one sidewalk to the next, some banging on the hood of the blue Mercedes as they passed. Julius attempted to describe this behavior but eventually gave it up to driving. Such behavior, as Ruby had observed many times after a heated sporting event, needed no explanation.

The streets remained cluttered with pedestrians up to the Sheriff's Department and beyond, as far as Julius and Ruby could see. They pulled the blue Mercedes into the parking lot in front of the Sheriff's Department and got out.

Across the street, the First Baptist Church was lit up like a holy spaceship. Along the street and up the steps stood congregations of men in colorful attire with shotguns and rifles strapped across their shoulders. It reminded Ruby of a Shriner's convention. Not that he had ever been to one himself.

Ruby and Julius went into the Sheriff's Department and found no one at the desk. Dead silence except for the occasional two-way radio squelching off behind the desk.

"This is spooky," Julius said.

"Not as spooky as seeing you and Rita Hymer getting it on."

"Hey. Hey. Not so loud," Julius said, walking about behind the front desk. "That was completely out of my control."

Ruby let out a yell and four voices answered him in unison. They followed the trail of voices to the back and found Carlos Rubino and the three deputies. "Where's the Reverend?" Ruby asked.

Lanard immediately and enthusiastically spoke up.

"Didn't I speak with you on the phone?" Ruby said.

Lanard was pickled. Caught in the same system he helped to create. "Sure," he said in his own defense, "but things were a little busy then."

Lanard divulged to Ruby all he could without endangering his position anymore than it already was. Meanwhile, Julius found the key and let them out.

After making an official statement, Ruby and Julius left. On the way out they overheard Lanard putting out the call to all the other deputies across Siler City. A *call to arms* so to speak. Grown men with prides as fragile as dry ice, with connections to firearms and laws as old as man. To Ruby, Lanard's call was the equivalent of a child running to his mother when the world doesn't work out as he had planned, crying and snotting, spilling his *wheres* and *whats* and *whys* on a soft shoulder. So what if Lanard had a basic right and obligation to inform his deputized brethren, he was only doing his job. The bottom line is this: ain't no one ever liked a cop, not even when he's doing a good job. Cops create unnecessary tensions with their presence and mediocre interpretations of the law. They have attitudes because of this. And they have guns, as big and as brilliant as the smiles upon their faces. At least that's what Ruby thought at the time.

THE MASONIC CONNECTION

The Reverend King was led up the steps of the First Baptist Church. He was a witness, firsthand, to the pagans and pirates that littered the entrance to one of the oldest buildings in historic downtown Siler City. Masked men full of color and clad, strapping rifles and shotguns to their shoulders and backs. An imbecilic group of men yapping and yodeling in the rain about the coming of salvation. They made a hole for the reverend and teased him as Rodney Crutchfield escorted him by the wrist up the steps and into the sanctuary. The reverend tried numerous times to respond to their catcalls, but Rodney wouldn't let him. Every time he tried to get a word out Rodney would pull up on his wrist, creating this sharp pain that muted out all his mind wanted to say.

It was the reverend's observations, made from the back seat of a deputy's cruiser and on the steps of the First Baptist Church, that the beautiful historic town of Siler City was under some sort of siege. Spirits induced to riot. But for what? The reverend considered Ruby's miracle of rain and its potential for creating madness, inadvertently of course, like that of beautiful flesh to a serial killer.

The reverend didn't rule it out, but deep within his dried-out soul he felt the presence of another power or possibly another man. This was more ancient than the towering bricks of the factories downtown, more eluding than Revelation itself. There was good and evil being played like a game of chess, and he could smell it. When he entered into the sanctuary he was momentarily blinded by its beauty, its stained glass art of John the Baptist, its vaulted ceilings that stretched mathematically beyond the eye, the rows of cherry-stained benches, and red velvet carpet as thick and lush as wet asphalt. He adjusted himself, feeling somewhat inferior, thinking of his own humble sanctuary down on Third Street and how it never looked like a church because it was actually a renovated grocery store. And this, this First Baptist Church had always loomed in his subconscious, an entity or something he never could explain. He hid it there, thinking that nothing good should ever have to hide.

Now, with the pagans and pirates, the rain and weapons, that entity loomed before him as one concrete testimony that all wasn't well up on the hill. And as he made it up the aisle with Rodney Crutchfield dragging him by his wrist he saw what his spiritual and prophetic mind believed to be the reason for the season. There was the Reverend Frederick Holmes dressed like the Grand Wizard himself, standing erect, statuesque, with the pride of a granite tombstone. On his head was a hat, cone-shaped with sequins. Around his arms and shoulders, flowing down his back and onto the red velvet carpet, was a robe. It was flamboyantly bright red and orange, sequined in the same pattern as the hat, resembling high school hieroglyphics, that of a goat head, of a pair of eagles joined at the hip, and of the forever *seeing eye*—that of the Illuminati.

He stood just center of the altar staring down at the Reverend King and the entourage that followed, which included Rodney Crutchfield and the three other masked assailants, along with Robert Leblanc, James Morton, and Arthur Tysor. About them in the aisle and among the benches were a few dozen more men, all strapped and shouldered with shotguns and rifles, all with the same flamboyantly bright red-and-orange-sequined hat upon their heads. In New Jersey they would have been homosexual deer hunters, cross-dressers of the deer and doe: The Queer Buck Club. In Siler City they were the Masonic Brothers of Columbus Lodge No. 102. Peaceful men usually on peaceful missions—fish fries and all that good stuff. They were known to be upstanding—opposed to down-standing, which did not exist. They went to church and work and played golf at the Siler City Country Club only when their wives and children did not need them. They drove Buicks and Cadillacs and SUVs of all sizes. They wore tennis shoes on Saturday. They were God-fearing, as opposed to God not-fearing. They were the granite pillars to this brick town. And once a month, Thursday nights, they congregated out on Austin Bridge Road in a cinder block building the size of a good-sized doublewide trailer and donned their flamboyant hats and dress and played cowboy-and-Indians, Mason-style. They were Masons, as opposed to Moose or Elk. They were loyal men who only needed to be called. For what? For whatever a Mason wanted.

The Reverend Holmes stood above them, counting their heads as if counting sheep. A shepherd to his flock. He was where the flamboyant buck stopped. Head of all Masons in Siler City and possibly the tri-state area. Possessing the Order of the Red Cross, a chivalric order, which made him a knight. He was connected to the upper echelon of power. Wined and dined in the presence of the most secretively seductive and influential men of the time. Privy to the most detailed of all plans. Planning himself. Standing up there on the altar, the most flamboyant of deer hunters, eluding and excreting from himself like a glorious ball of flatulent steam that which gives men like the Reverend King the idea that all isn't what it seems up on the hill.

A turning point as it were, historic or not, to be decided as all things are in those years to come with hindsight and headlights shining down with microscopic accuracy. The Reverend King could see it. The Reverend Holmes could see it. Unfortunately, they were both looking at two entirely different things.

"Welcome!" the Reverend Holmes said, extending his arms out to the reverend as if to hug him but not.

The reverend smiled suspiciously not answering, not knowing what to say even if he wanted to. Rodney Crutchfield brought him up to the first step of the altar then pulled him back.

"Mr. Leblanc," the Reverend Holmes said. "Good to see you as well."

The Reverend King looked around to see if anyone else thought the Reverend Holmes was acting a little strange—enlightened and giddy, as if a near-death experience had sent him on a goodwill crusade across his mind. The Reverend King had personally never seen this side of the reverend. To him, the Reverend Holmes was a first-rate asshole, the kind you find in hospitals and supermarkets.

"What happened out there?" the Reverend Holmes asked Robert Leblanc.

"Everything was fine," James Morton said, "up until Robert shot Frank Wright."

"Everything would have been fine if you had done as I said," Robert Leblanc answered. "And I was aiming for his radiator."

"It doesn't matter," the Reverend Holmes said. "We'll get it right this time. Leave Rodney here with me and you take the rest of the boys with you and finish the job."

Robert Leblanc nodded. He, James Morton, Arthur Tysor, and the three masked assailants—Bradford, Richard, and Douglas—left the two reverends and Rodney Crutchfield at the altar and went about the task once more of retrieving John Carter from the Sunbridge Psychiatric and Rehabilitation Center.

"Quite a mess you've made for yourself, reverend," the Reverend Holmes said.

"And what about yourself?" the Reverend King said, his eyes wandering about the room.

"There's no problem here," the Reverend Holmes said. "Look around."

The Reverend Holmes paused and they both took a generous look around the sanctuary. Nothing in it seemed spiritual to the Reverend King. "No," the Reverend Holmes said, "no problem here. Only solutions. I surround myself with solutions and with people who make things happen."

The Reverend King thought about how the flamboyant hats made everyone look like eccentric deer hunters and almost laughed.

"You make things happen, Alfonso, in your own special way," the Reverend Holmes said. "I admire that. I don't like you, but I admire that."

The Reverend Holmes pointed to his right where a few men were setting light to lanterns along the side wall of the church then to the left to where the same was taking place. The Reverend Holmes pulled up the sleeve of his cloak and looked at his watch.

"It's nothing to make it rain," the reverend said, staring at his watch.

At that moment the lights went off in the First Baptist Church and all across Siler City. The Reverend Holmes looked up from his watch smiling. "But now to really make it rain," he said, "that takes some coordination."

THE MASONIC CONNECTION

One large ball of total blackness, the kind only a fetus can recall, enveloped the city. At the same time a brick—a Historic Siler City brick, full of age and wisdom—hit the windshield of the blue Mercedes. Julius swerved in reaction and wound up on the sidewalk.

"Holy!" he yelled, tooling the blue Mercedes back onto the road narrowly missing a band of teenage pedestrians.

"Did you see that?" Julius yelled.

"Of course, I saw it," Ruby said. "Did you see the lights go off?"

Julius looked around. "No."

The town was black and awkwardly out of place with itself. Julius slowed the blue Mercedes down to a crawl and worked it in and out of the crowd that had taken to the streets in droves.

"Lost," Julius said, staring out at the faces that passed by the windshield like smoky aberrations—ghosts in some insane night. They trailed by as if floating, cutting empty, far-off glances through the windshield of the blue Mercedes, then moved on. A symphony of mournfulness, graceful and uninterrupted. Ruby saw the beauty in it but felt safer with the doors locked.

"What do you mean, you're lost?" he asked Julius.

The hospital was dimly lit, set off on an incline. Its generators hummed from below its belly. The hospital was brick and quaint, resembling the rest of the town, and Ruby could only stare at it and imagine what he'd find inside—hoping it wasn't another Sunbridge.

Julius pulled the blue Mercedes to the front of the emergency entrance where three ambulances sat, asses to the wall, lights flashing. "Busy night," Julius said.

"That could be a good thing," Ruby replied.

They took a moment to stare through the large panes of glass that stretched the entirety of the brick wall of the emergency department. There was chaos on the other side, created and uncontrolled, an apparent disaster not unlike the night itself, consumed and consuming more. Ruby felt the pressure. He had been a part of it before, knew what was at stake. He was unsure of Lisa though. It was that unknown variable that kept him focused. He had a plan and Lisa was part of it. That much he knew. Without her, without the catalyst, all would be null.

"Sure you want to do this?" Julius asked, sensing Ruby's ambivalence.

"No choice," Ruby said.

There was a moment and they allowed it: staring out, breathing, getting themselves right in the head, then Julius laughed. Not the nervous, get-the-tension-out kind of laugh but the more hilarious, dumbfounded kind. "What are we doing here?" he asked with LSD running rampant through the virgin forests of his mind.

"You stay here," Ruby said. "And keep the car running."

Ruby slammed the door and made for the Emergency entrance. The doors sensed him coming and opened and Ruby was immediately enveloped in the chaos and noise. He kept focused though and concentrated on the desk where a lone woman was manning three phones with five people standing on the opposite side of the desk staring condescendingly down on her. She had a pen behind her right ear and a computer screen directly in front of her. She was the brainchild of the whole operation. The data collector. The air traffic controller of the whole emergency department, overworked and underpaid. Ruby smiled when she looked at him and she smiled back, ignoring the other five that had been asking questions for half an hour or so. She asked Ruby what he needed and he said "Lisa."

"Lisa, who?" she asked.

It was at this point he realized he had no idea what Lisa's last name was. Never occurred to him to ask. Grade school salutations and et cetera, et cetera, yet he never asked. The clerk smiled at his torment and was unaffected by the noise and demands of the situation.

"You mean Reverend King's daughter?"

"Yes," he replied, "of course. King."

"She's in the intensive care unit," pointing off to her right down a hall. "It's past visiting hours, but they may let you in. It's worth a try."

Ruby thanked the clerk then left. He was immediately stopped by Geraldine Griffin. She had been crying and her face was red and swollen around the eyes. She did not act surprised or angered by Ruby's presence. No, Ruby sensed that maybe she was even relieved to see him. "That son of a bitch finally did it," she said. "I told her. You know I did. You were there."

Ruby nodded his head sympathetically. He looked over Geraldine's shoulder into the open bay across from her and saw the young Hispanic woman from the Pine Knoll Trailer Park. "Maia," Ruby said to himself. He remembered her name and was surprised by that.

She was bloodied and without breath.

Ruby felt his thoughts sink past his heart and he began to cry, almost involuntarily. He stared at Maia but was consumed by Lisa, and he thought of Kay and cried even more. The idea of death and the complete uncertainty of life, the conscience of good and evil, the open festering wound of mortality. All Ruby wanted was peace.

"I'm sorry," he said to Geraldine, who was now crying with Ruby.

"Me too," she said.

Ruby gave her a hug and walked off down the hall. When he reached the intensive care unit he ignored the visitation policy that was bolted to the door and walked in. It was somewhat dimly lit but dark and remarkably quiet. The rooms were arranged in bays like the emergency department, with curtains pulled shut in front of each bay. Ruby went from curtain to curtain, pulling them back. He checked half the unit before a nurse saw him and called him down.

"Are you Jessie, by chance?" Ruby asked her.

"No," the nurse said.

"I'm a friend of Geraldine Griffin," he said. "She's out front in the emergency room. She wanted me to come back and check on a friend of hers, Lisa King."

The nurse did not budge. She was adamant that her visiting policy be adhered to.

"If I can just see her for a minute," Ruby said.

"She's unconscious," the nurse said as if to break Ruby's spirit.

"I don't care," Ruby answered, wanting to cuss her out for being such a bitch.

There was a deep sigh of disapproval; then the woman directed Ruby toward the back of the unit to the last bay. She pulled the curtain back slightly and there was Lisa—eyes closed, supine, hair as straight as ever, beautiful, a large bruise upon her forehead. She lay there with her eyes closed, no sign of any bodily malfunctions other than the bruise. "Two minutes," the nurse said then walked off.

Ruby pulled the curtains closed and walked over to the bed.

He needed a miracle, a bolt of lightning, some rain. He placed his right hand upon her head and felt her hair. He closed his eyes and thought how wonderful it would be to be God, to have miracles leaking from his fingertips ready to use. He ran his fingers down the side of her face back behind her neck. He could hear the thunder and lightning outside and the faint rumblings of the generators two floors below him. He had reached a precipice in the most unique of journeys. All roads led to Lisa with none traveling on without her. Ruby had told himself during those days of hospitalization after Kay had passed away that he would never depend on someone so much again.

As he held Lisa's head in his hand he wished most of all that he did have the power to make it rain, to change the ill-fated mortal hands of time. It would be too perfect though. That he knew. And nothing had ever been that perfect.

It was then that he felt her head move and a warm hand to his lips telling him not to react vocally or violently to what was about to happen. Lisa sat up in bed slowly with a comfortable grin upon her lips. Ruby could do nothing but watch as she disconnected herself from a variety of tubes and machines and stood up on the side of the bed. She walked over to the curtain and peeked out. "I know a back way out of here," she whispered.

"What?" Ruby said, still amazed at what he was seeing.

"Follow me."

They waited and watched for a minute as the nurse walked among the bays then behind a curtain. They took off out a door opposite the way Ruby came in, down an empty hallway that looked like an abandoned medical ward, down a stairwell, busting out full stride into the lower parking lot. Lisa was almost hysterical when she finally stopped to give Ruby a kiss. "I knew you'd come," she said. "I didn't know what else to do. I thought he was out to kill me. So I faked it. I faked it all. They ran so many tests, flashlights in the eyes, but I just lay there. I knew you'd come."

Ruby kissed her and told her that the car was out front. They jogged across the parking lot and along the edge of the brick building. Lisa was in nothing more than a hospital gown, and Ruby could see her backside and it made him feel giddy.

"My father with you?" she asked as they rounded the corner to the emergency department and saw the blue Mercedes.

"No," Ruby said, out of breath. "I'll explain later." They

piled into the Mercedes; Julius gave Lisa a stoned look of approval, said hello, and then pulled the blue Mercedes onto the highway.

On the way back to the apartment Lisa told Ruby about her confrontation with Christopher Riley and Ruby told her about the reverend. She blamed it all on the Cloud again and Ruby assured her that everything would be fine.

"What are all these people doing?" she asked, referring to the multitude of pedestrians that dotted the highway through the headlights.

"A religious catastrophe," Julius said and then went on to explain how Ruby made it rain and how his father had succumbed to madness in an unexplainable kind of way.

"Watch the road," Ruby said, interrupting purposefully. He didn't think Lisa needed to hear everything, especially when everything didn't add up.

Julius took the hint and they drove the rest of the way in silence, staring out at the chaotic mess that only seemed to get worse. Lisa held onto Ruby and Ruby held onto her.

At the apartment, Julius kept the car running as Ruby escorted Lisa up the steps and inside. "We are still going, aren't we?" she asked.

"Yes," Ruby said, laughing, pulling her close. "But I've got to find the reverend first."

"He's okay, isn't he?"

"I'm sure he is," Ruby said.

They held each other for a few minutes with the thunder and lightning, the rain coming down hard outside, feeling each other's breath, wanting more than ever a prolonged uninterrupted union.

"I've got to go," Ruby said.

"Let me get some clothes on and I'll go with you."

"No," Ruby said, "it's better that you stay here."

Lisa did not argue. She walked off through the dark apartment and came back with a candle, lit it, and placed it on the coffee table. "I'll pack while you're gone."

Ruby smiled. "Just get some rest."

Lisa stripped down out of the wet hospital gown and Ruby left her standing there completely and comfortably naked in the middle of the living room. It was what he saw as he made his way down the steps to the blue Mercedes. "Where do we go from here?" Julius asked as Ruby slid into the passenger seat.

"Tell me about your father," Ruby said.

THE MASONIC CONNECTION

"Have you ever considered," the Reverend Holmes said to the Reverend King, standing confidently in his red and orange, flamboyantly adorned Masonic gown, "that God never was the good guy in this eternal religious struggle of ours? I mean, we know there was a battle and that Lucifer was banished from the heavens, but do we really know that God was the good entity, or is he just saying it? Did good actually win over evil that day? I mean, really?"

"Yes," the Reverend King unabashedly said.

"Of course," said the Reverend Holmes. "You are a man of faith—blind yet reverent."

There was a moment of total awkwardness where each of the reverends let the other float freely in his own thoughts and beliefs without stopping the other. Then the Reverend Holmes let into the Reverend King. "Your God is a fake!"

"What are you saying?" the Reverend King yelled back.

"Oh, give it up. I've watched you carry on. You sicken me. Exploiting and rummaging through your religion like a homeless man through the garbage. You're in it for the money. Admit it."

"No!" the Reverend King said. "You're wrong." Although not completely. The money was relatively good compared to a factory job—and the hours, you couldn't beat the hours. "This is my town," the Reverend King said. "Not yours. You know nothing about me."

"I know your real name isn't Alfonso King," the Reverend Holmes said.

The Reverend King dropped his head upon hearing this. It was true; he had a story.

"I know you drove a truck in the early eighties. Got arrested in Pensacola, Florida for selling stolen VCRs. VCRs you took off your own truck. Did seven months in the Pensacola County Jail for that one. Is that where you found religion? Among the soulless rejects of the penitentiary? Isn't it funny," the Reverend Holmes said, "how a man must first find religion before he can actually have it. As if religion was elusive in some way, as if it didn't want to be found. You probably used religion to justify your own evil ways. Let God tell you it was Satan making you do all those evil things. How convenient. Remember, it was Eve who ate the apple that destroyed the world, not me."

The Reverend King was dumbfounded. He couldn't figure out which way the reverend was going with all this, as if the Reverend Holmes had snapped and was spiraling off incoherently through some unknown cosmic universe of cowboys and Indians. It felt like a trap, yet religion, as the Reverend King knew it, sometimes played itself out as such. He knew one had to be quick to catch the idiosyncrasy of the trade and even quicker to figure it out and have an answer for it.

"So," the Reverend King said. "What are you saying?"

"Look around," the Reverend Holmes said. "This is not your church, and my God is not your God. My God is the great Emancipator of the Spirit. Yours is the Great Oppressor."

"My God is the only God," the Reverend King said.

"And," said the Reverend Holmes, "for Muhammad it was Allah. You're a blind man, Mr. King."

The Reverend Holmes raised his arms and stretched them out as if across the entire room. "This thing," he said, "is bigger than you."

The church doors opened and a dozen more men came in wearing the Masonic uniform, carrying rifles and shotguns. The lanterns flickered and the doors shut.

"Let me tell you a story," the Reverend Holmes said. "During the start of the Second World War my mother, who was Russian, was captured by the Germans in Hungary. She was mistaken for a gypsy or a Jew and sent to Poland to a concentration camp. While there she worked in the officer's kitchen, cooking and washing dishes. It was there that she met a young officer, a doctor. She fell in love with him and he with her and they went on to have a rather unconventional affair.

"Eventually though, something went drastically wrong. There was something not right about the doctor; he used her love in immeasurable ways. Before she knew it she was pregnant and before the war was over she had twins—not identical; on the contrary, they were remarkably different. When the young doctor saw them he was outraged because he felt only one could be his. In anger, he marked them with tattoos. "Before the war was over one child was rescued by two nuns from Rome.

"When the war ended the young doctor fled, taking the other child with him. My mother was liberated shortly after that and married an American GI.

"I learned all this shortly before she died."

The Reverend Holmes broke momentarily, his face showing all the signs of a man in deep reflection. The Reverend King stood somewhat impatiently in front of him not completely understanding where the story was going, wishing so much that he had himself a little bump to help him through it.

"You can imagine how surprised I was to hear this," the Reverend Holmes said. "I was angered yet intrigued. I asked myself, what did this doctor do to my mother?

"I asked myself, who are these twins?"

The Reverend King looked around to see if anyone else was listening. They were all busy dancing around with their shotguns and rifles acting like militant Shriners at a KKK rally.

"I did my research," the Reverend Holmes said. "That's what I did. I put a few calls out to my brothers and waited. Within a week I had standing before me a man who claimed to be a prisoner in the same camp my mother was in. He worked on the medical ward as a janitor.

"He told me that he remembered the doctor. He remembered how possessed the doctor was. He told me of an ancient vessel that was brought in by a Catholic priest. He said that he had overheard the conversations between the priest and the doctor had."

The reverend hesitated for a second then looked at the Reverend King. "Do you know what that man heard?" the Reverend Holmes asked.

"Of course not," the Reverend King said.

"You'll get a kick out of this," the Reverend Holmes said. "The vessel held Jesus's seminal organs."

The Reverend King cut a queer grin in hearing this absurdity. The Reverend Holmes picked up on this and laughed. "Exactly," he said and then gave the reverend time to compose himself.

"But consider the idea," he continued. "The possibility of something so erroneous and vile. It would have to be delicately constructed with variables so mathematical, so human and frail. Anything and everything in this cosmic arena could have destroyed it in mere seconds. If you can fathom that then you understand that what we're actually talking about here is the story of our own existence. The birth of man.

"And when I found Ruben laid up in a hospital bed in Wilmington and I saw that tattoo, just as my mother said, I thanked the Great Creator of the Universe for letting me be the one."

"Ruby?" the Reverend King asked.

"Yes, Ruby is a child of Christ. The first-born."

"Wh—?" the Reverend King stuttered.

"Salvation?" the Reverend Holmes said. "Possibly."

"Ruby," the Reverend King said again proudly.

"But the question is why?" the Reverend Holmes said. "Why do all this in the first place? To save the church? To dissuade science? To give validation to some ancient words and to a religion that has done nothing but confuse its people and start wars? Who knows? Either way, it happened. The doctor made it happen. And my mother made it happen."

"I knew it," the Reverend King said. "I knew something was special about that boy."

The Reverend King's face glowed with pride. Everyone saw it. It ate him up inside—full of respect and adoration and all that stuff that goes along with it. It was, no doubt, his friend Ruby the Reverend Holmes was talking about.

"So," the Reverend King said composing himself. "I suppose you're the other one."

The Reverend Holmes laughed. "Don't be absurd. The other one is tied to a hospital bed over at that nursing home."

"John Carter?" the Reverend King said.

"Yes."

"That foul man?"

"Watch it," the Reverend Holmes said. "Do you know how hard it was to bring those two together?"

"Ruby doesn't know?" the Reverend King asked.

"That's the beauty," the Reverend Holmes said. "He's the son of Christ yet a phantom to his spiritual existence. He could be as adorned as the Queen of England, yet he has no idea. No idea at all.

"Again," the Reverend Holmes continued, "the ironic beauty slaps me in the face. No one would believe it anyway. Think about it. He would be ostracized, excommunicated from this system we have so blindly forged for ourselves. There is no place for him, at least not among the common. He would be an outcast."

"He could be salvation," the Reverend King said proudly.

"What do you know about salvation?" the Reverend Holmes yelled. "Your whole existence is wrapped around one simple parable after another. You live off of blind faith. Seeing what you need to see. Saying what's been said before. You're just like Ruby except you're nothing special. Under that pale wrinkled skin of yours is nothing."

"This is absurd," the Reverend King jolted. "You have no faith or religion."

"On the contrary," the Reverend Holmes said, "I've got faith and religion, far more than you can imagine. I use the same Bible you do to deliver the same message. For my message is your message, yet it's your God that is wrong. He's the wicked seed in this cosmic dance of ours. He is the manipulator and punisher, hiding behind that cloak of almightiness."

Reverend Holmes pointed to the podium where he stood every Sunday to deliver his sermons. "I stand up there and preach my sermon and smile my smile and think how glorious a day it will be when all eyes open to the facts that have been before them all along.

"You're right. Ruby is salvation," the Reverend Holmes said. "But he's my salvation. One ransomed salvation for the Great Creator of the Universe himself. A sacrifice."

There was a moment of awkward silence then the Reverend King broke out into a jovial chuckle. "So let me get this straight," he said. "Your mother had twins. One is Christ's child, which is Ruby; the other, a mad doctor's, which is John Carter? And now you're upset because you want to be special too?"

The Reverend Holmes laughed. "Do you know why you're here?"

"No," the Reverend King replied.

"You're here because I don't like you. Never have. Not since the first day I saw you. But Ruby does. And he'll come for you."

The Reverend King lost it, literally, at that moment—call it a breakdown, call it withdrawal, call it what you want. He attempted to give the Reverend Holmes all the focus his inflamed speech so rightly deserved, but he kept floating back and forth uncontrollably to that area of the mind that allows nothing or nobody to disturb it—the Sunday afternoon abdication of the mind.

It upset the Reverend King greatly, for even he felt the impetus of the moment. It was time for Armageddon, yet he had not the bags nor the baggage to grasp it completely. He became anxious and sweaty, swollen from hands to feet just enough to create a bind below the belt, accompanied by a roll and rumble of the bowel. "So this is it?" he said, bending over slightly to compensate for the heaviness. "This is the Apocalypse."

"What's wrong, man?" the Reverend Holmes said, upset by the graceless way the reverend had turned his great speech into a soliloquy.

The Reverend King stumbled forward, anxious now, swinging like a blind boxer. "Let's get it on!" he yelled. "Come on!"

A handful of Freemasons ran over and stood in front of the Reverend Holmes.

"I've seen the glory of the coming of the Lord," the Reverend King yelled. "Holy Christ. Jesus Almighty. Stand up and fight the devil or be gone!"

He made a be-gone motion with his hands, opened his eyes completely, and then closed them. The Reverend Holmes motioned to his congregates to let him go. The Reverend King stumbled into one Mason after the other, possessed, speaking half-audibly, half-tongued, yelling out over and over, "Let's go! Let's go!" attempting to draw the Reverend Holmes into a fistfight. A Holy War of the sort that he could one day tell his friends about.

It was futile though; the Reverend Holmes had more of a gentleman's plan for how the evening would unfold. He had poise and patience, nerves of wrought iron steel.

The Reverend King on the other hand, was jonesing. He needed a bump worse than he could have ever imagined. He fell back among the pews, rolling over them one over the other before coming to rest on his back, arms and legs stretched out, moaning inaudible incantations. "I need candy," he said right before submitting to the gods of unconsciousness. "Anybody?"

"Take him to the fellowship hall," the Reverend Holmes said. "He's useless."

THE SOUTHERN CONNECTION

Along the front and side of the Sunbridge Psychiatric and Rehabilitation Center, throughout the parking lot and grass, the Crowd stood frozen as if in time, soaked and staring at nothing in particular. The Cross loomed haplessly above them like a set of rabbit ear antennas atop a black and white television set—no one quite sure of the reception or even if the television was plugged in—just standing and staring at nothing in particular, waiting for the world to collapse in on itself.

Kirk Merchant and the three deputies could be seen through the windows in the lobby. They were animated and hilarious to watch; they drank iced tea and poked billysticks into each other's bellies. Back and forth they went, poking and giggling.

There were no more news crews or news vans to be seen. Deborah Collins left right after Ruby. She had seen enough—and for her nothing was nearly as romantic in rain.

Robert Leblanc, James Morton, Arthur Tysor, and the three masked assailants—Bradford, Richard, and Douglas—saw all this as they drove up the hill through the heart of the Brookwood Apartments, headlights off, debating among themselves the most efficient means, if any, of extracting John Carter from the Sunbridge Psychiatric and Rehabilitation Center. After extensive debate it was settled by James Morton and Arthur Tysor that using the door off the loading dock would, in the long run, cause less of a consequential ripple. All this to the chagrin of Robert Leblanc, who advocated driving the Astrostar mini-van through the doors of the front lobby.

"Don't fuck with me!" Robert Leblanc said as Arthur Tysor pulled the van to a stop just behind the dumpsters, which sat across the parking lot from the Sunbridge Psychiatric and Rehabilitation Center.

"Can we do this?" James Morton said, as they piled out of the van with their rifles and shotguns.

"If you had listened to me the first time," Robert Leblanc said.

"Fuck you," Arthur Tysor said. "Fuck you and your rifle."

They cut around the backside of the Crowd along a tree line to the back door and found it shut and locked. Damn. "Did you honestly think it was going to be open?" Robert Leblanc said.

James Morton made a lunge for Robert Leblanc but was stopped by Arthur Tysor. "Cool it," Arthur said. "There's got to be another way."

The three masked assailants stood off behind them not saying a word. The rain fell. The thunder and lightning cracked and rumbled.

"There's only one thing to do," Robert Leblanc said. "Follow me."

He was off the dock and halfway across the parking lot before anyone could stop him. By the time they caught up with him they found themselves standing under the verandah, directly in front of the two doors that led into the lobby of the Sunbridge Psychiatric and Rehabilitation Center. Robert Leblanc tapped the butt of his rifle on the glass and Kirk Merchant dutifully stepped forward to acknowledge him.

"Hello, Kirk," Robert Leblanc said in a loud conversational tone.

"How's it going, Robert?"

"Not bad. Look—" Robert Leblanc said before Kirk Merchant interrupted him.

"Aren't you supposed to be locked up?" Kirk asked.

"I suppose," Robert Leblanc said. "But look, you've got that crazy Jesus fella in there and we need him. Now, we don't mean to get defensive here but we will if we have to. Just hand him over and we'll be gone."

One of the deputies reached for his radio and the three masked assailants nervously raised their rifles and shotguns. James Morton and Arthur Tysor jumped back in surprise. Kirk Merchant reached for his pistol and shots rang out from the barrels of the three masked assailants. Large panes of glass came crashing down. Kirk Merchant and the deputies scattered, along with Robert Leblanc, Arthur Tysor, and James Morton. The three masked assailants—Bradford, Richard, and Douglas—stood their ground, firing off shots automatically. It was too late to renounce. The barrels were hot now and the minds behind those barrels even hotter—some with adrenaline, others with a good mix of adrenaline and lysergic acid. And there were Vietnam flashbacks for Robert Leblanc, Arthur Tysor, and James Morton. It was just like the good ole days.

Glass shattered and fell to the ground with each passing bullet. Each side dug in now behind overturned benches and pillars of Sheetrock, behind planters and one purple van with the Sunbridge Psychiatric and Rehabilitation Center logo down its side. They all had their rifles, pistols, and shotguns raised firing, aimlessly about, ducking, reloading, and firing again. It was a standoff at the Sunbridge Psychiatric and Rehabilitation Center—surely meant to make a big screen somewhere.

The rain fell. The thunder and lightning cracked and rumbled. The Crowd stood firm to their antebellum beliefs. No one inside the Home came out to see what the happenings were all about; they brokered their own minds and came up with new and improved ways of seeing the world. Dr. Vokes meditated through his own jungle and had blood on his hands from a successful episiotomy to prove it. Rosa Hurley lay before him on a brown plastic covered couch with her shoes and scrub bottoms off. Infants in the mortal night. No time to notify the father. Elnora Brown stood behind Rosa, pulling her arms back as if to swing her in a lackadaisical circle. "Push, damn it!" she yelled. "Push!"

Elnora Brown, having never had a child herself, never considered the art of breathing much of an art. She was tripping though, as was Dr. Vokes and Neena Moore, who stood above them snapping away with her Pentax ME super 35mm like some twisted, third-trimester, pornographic photographer, smiling mad through her journalism, destroying the world one fat Buddha at a time. Sounds of bullets—fireworks for the first-born—rang out in the near distance. Rosa Hurley was sober, shocked, and staring.

"Get the water hose," Dr. Vokes said in a calm, trancing voice.

"Water hose?" Rosa Hurley exclaimed.

"What do you need a water hose for?" said Elnora Brown.

"It's stuck," Dr. Vokes said.

Elnora Brown leaned over and looked down at Rosa's crotch. "No it's not," she said.

Dr. Vokes took another look. "Yes, it is," he said pointing.

Two shoulders and one sloppy head stuck out of Rosa Hurley's twat as though they had always been there. Half-in, half-out, the story of a wanna-be ice-skater whose mother never loosened up her cunt long enough for him to put his skates on.

"It's not a fucking cow!" Elnora said, grabbing Rosa's arms again. "Push," she said. "Push, goddamnit!"

"Breathe," yelled Neena over the snapping of her Pentax ME super 35mm. "Breathe."

The rain fell. The bullets fell with it. Robert Leblanc had escaped the madness and was now rounding the circle drive in the Astrostar mini-van; he picked up speed as bullets ripped open the front windshield. He ducked, gassed it, and plowed through the double doors into the lobby, letting the Sheetrock and metal fall where they may. Simultaneously, a 9-pound, 8-ounce baby boy burst free from the loving grip of his mother's cunt to take his first infected breath from a world that was already well on its way to becoming over-populated.

What was more exciting, at least to the altered minds and artists, was the way the placenta then crawled itself out of Rosa Hurley's evacuated womb like some living, breathing organism. And if it wasn't for Walter Rhoe who came in on the tail end of it, Dr. Vokes, Elnora Brown, and Neena Moore would have scooped it up off the couch, wrapped it in a blanket, laid it on Rosa's stomach, and called it a boy.

"Charles Apple need not worry. Charles Apple going to heaven."

"Yes, Charles Apple going to heaven," Charles Apple said.

"Yes, Charles Apple going straight to heaven. Charles Apple do good. Charles Apple do real good."

"Charles Apple want good. No bad. Bad is good. Good is bad."

"Charles Apple untie Jesus. Jesus and Charles Apple go to heaven together. Friends forever."

"Charles Apple friends with Jesus?"

"Yes. And what a friend we have in Jesus."

"Yes. What a friend."

John Carter swung his feet over the side of the bed and placed them on the floor. He stood up slowly, feeling the orthostatic effects of being supine for so long. He was dizzy and somewhat confused—baseline for a geriatric Jesus. He pulled off his gown then the wet diaper that hung like a bag of sand around his waist.

"Charles Apple," he said. "You are a friend and a disciple. Tried and true. Yes, sir. Tried and true. And you'll always be remembered for the good deed you've done."

John Carter adjusted his eyes and stretched out his back. He heard the distant rumblings of a Fourth of July in full effect and became excited. He walked over to Charles Apple and placed his hand upon his head. "From this day forward," he said, "no matter what rooster cocks his crow in the early morning hour, no matter what leper may harness your back and ride you like a pony, you will always be my disciple. Charlie the disciple."

"Charlie Apple is Jesus Christ, too," Charles Apple said.

"Sure you are," John Carter said.

Naked as Rosa Hurley's baby and just as filthy, John Carter left Charles Apple and his room and strolled dyskinetically down the hall past the nurses' station and into the dining room. There, he made his way past the stainless steel Lipton tea canister that had so righteously helped distort the minds of all who drank from it, past the cold cuts and frozen croissants, past the industrialized stoves and sinks and spoons the size of shovels, past dishes and drains and roach-infested paraphernalia to the door. He opened it and stepped out onto the loading dock. He felt the moist warmness of the night and closed his eyes and listened to the rain, the thunder and lightning. Liberated and free, schizophrenic and flying, he walked off the loading dock and around the corner where the Crowd stood like waxed bystanders in an innocent museum. He saw three masked assailants with rifles and shotguns. He saw Arthur Tysor crouched behind the purple van. There was gunfire like miniature bursts of lightning—*Padap, Padap*.

His head was still quite dizzy and schizophrenic as always—worse in the evening and the rain didn't help. He saw the Cross—the beautiful symbol of crucifixion. It stood above everything, at least to John Carter's twisted eye. It was industrialized to fit the times, jagged and harrowing. He walked up to it and laid his hands upon it. "Father," he said, "why did you forsake me? Why?" he said again, backing away from it.

Behind the back of the Home adjacent to the loading dock was a maintenance shed. Inside it was a three-step metal ladder. John Carter found it and took it back out to the parking lot and set it up in front of the Cross. James Morton saw John Carter's naked ass bending over the ladder, balls banging the sides of his legs like a pornographic grandfather clock. "Jesus Christ," James Morton said then called for Robert Leblanc, who was holding his own from the cushioned confines of the Astrostar mini-van.

They regrouped outside and attempted to make a run for John Carter but were unable to get past the deputies' crossfire. James Morton and the others could only watch as John Carter ascended the steps of the ladder to the top of the Cross where he clumsily turned and laid his back up against the metal beam. He then worked his arms over the crossbar to where it looked as if the Cross had him in a full-nelson—which can be translated into one awkward crucifix applied by a wrestler. Robert Leblanc yelled for Arthur Tysor or James Morton. "Anybody!" he yelled. "Get him down off that damn thing."

No one moved. It was a study in learned behavior—not even a young John Wayne would have been able to talk his way into that one.

They watched as John Carter adjusted himself on the Cross, mumbling incoherent biblical phrases of rejection and sacrifice. His footing slipped and he fell to the ground. The Crowd reacted with a collective and fearful moan.

"So," John Carter said, picking himself up slowly off the ground, "you're not dead after all."

He crawled back up the ladder and onto the Cross, adjusting himself even higher than before, hugging it this time.

It was no use though, his cards had been played, full of dumb luck and coincidence. Before he could turn around and take his place a great bolt of lightning reached out and touched the Cross, electrifying it, sending John Carter flying some fifteen or twenty feet, back-first, into the Crowd. Robert Leblanc yelled. Another bolt of lightning hit the Cross. The Crowd took a few collective steps back exposing John Carter. He lay motionless, a tuft of smoke curling from his head. Robert Leblanc yelled again. Then once more. From a distance it sounded like the cackling crow of a rooster.

THE BIG FRESH

"Did you see that?" Julius asked as he and Ruby sat out front of Lisa's apartment contemplating their next move.

Julius sat in the driver's seat with a remarkable grin, one denoting enthusiasm beyond control, pointing his finger like a slap-happy child up the hill to the Sunbridge Psychiatric and Rehabilitation Center, not knowing he had just witnessed the second bolt of lightning hitting the Cross.

"Damn!" Julius yelled. "Did you see that?"

Ruby had, but not the one that counted—the one that took John Carter out.

Down the hill came a vehicle with one headlight. It was an Astrostar mini-van full of dejected assailants. As it picked up speed and passed the blue Mercedes, Robert Leblanc, who was driving at the time, saw Ruby, as did Ruby him. Two complete strangers destined to dance the cosmic dance. Robert Leblanc slammed on the brakes and slung the Astrostar mini-van in reverse.

"What the hell you doing?" James Morton yelled.

"The other guy!" Robert Leblanc yelled. "It's the other guy!"

At that moment two sets of headlights accompanied by two more sets of flashing blue lights rolled gracefully down the hill from the Sunbridge Psychiatric and Rehabilitation Center into the heart of the Brookwood Apartments. Robert Leblanc saw this as he pulled up parallel to the blue Mercedes; he connected eyes with Ruby, looked in his rearview mirror, then at Ruby once more, and then gassed it. Julius looked over at Ruby confused. "What the hell was that about?"

Ruby shook his head. "You got me."

"That was Robert Leblanc driving," Julius said.

"Was that John Carter in the back seat?" Ruby asked.

Julius didn't know. The two cop cars sped past them and fell in behind the van.

"What do you think?" Ruby asked.

"Robert Leblanc is a good friend of my father's. He's also a Mason," Julius said.

Another bolt of lightning struck across the landscape and they could see the faint outline of the Crowd—stationary and somewhat resembling tombstones. Nothing else moved.

Julius fired up the blue Mercedes and took off after the van.

Within the heart of historic downtown Siler City a large body of youth congregated. Perpetuated by acclimation and chaos and by youth itself, they resiliently went about the task of taking apart a town that took 150 good years to put together. Brick by brick, window by window, flesh to steel, no emotional attachment to anything—too young to remember a war, even younger for a class in economics, philosophy, or sociology. An educated man would have called them animals. Shirtless and irreverent, tossing back cans of beer and cigarettes like old veterans. Ages 12 to 21, some younger, some older. Moving in and out of calamity, one block to the next like rabid hockey players. Children of the new night, coming about as close as anyone to putting their hands upon the pulse of what was actually going on. School was out, so it seemed, and it was never to open again. A Molotov cocktail took care of that.

It was like driving through a teenage car wash. Almost like watching it snow. Julius brought the blue Mercedes to a crawl then to a stop. Up ahead they could faintly see the oscillating blue lights of a deputy's car. It too had been surrounded. The Astrostar mini-van and the other deputy's car had taken a less congested side street and were nowhere to be seen.

Outside the car, to all four sides, congregated a crowd of motley proportion. Through the rain and headlights Julius and Ruby were able to see their twisting bare torsos—young men and women, girls, boys—like a ball of wet, propagating snakes. Some crawled bare-chested onto the blue Mercedes; others took pieces of brick and pipe and busted out its headlights. Julius mumbled incoherently. He wanted Ruby to say something, to reassure him that everything was going to be all right, but he didn't.

"Should I gas it?" Julius asked.

"No. But nudge forward a little. Maybe we can break free."

Julius let off the brake and the car rolled forward. This angered the crowd and they began to hit the car harder. Julius and Ruby went some twenty feet before stopping. In front of them the deputy's car rested on its side, blue lights flashing. Inside, Kirk Merchant and another deputy sat juxtaposed shoulder-to-shoulder, .45s drawn, cringing like blind puppies.

Ruby watched the blue lights work their magic, turning and sparkling up the rain like an antiquated Ferris wheel—no pieces of brick or pipe touched them, as if the crowd gained some twisted strength by having them there. Ruby's head began to hurt as it did before his last seizure. It was bad news for him. "Not here," he whispered to himself.

The front windshield cracked open, then the back, and shortly after that came the sides. The noise of the rain and crowd filtered in, sucking Julius and Ruby completely into the moment.

A young man stuck his head in through the front windshield. "Don't worry," he said. "We ain't going to hurt you. We just want to smash up your car."

He had a grin that was irreplaceable. "That's good to know," Ruby said.

The boy said something else as he retracted his head through the glass, but they couldn't understand him. A moment later the blue Mercedes began rocking back and forth, one side to the next, until a great heave put it on its side. A large cheer went up throughout the crowd.

Julius scrambled hysterically to gain some semblance of equilibrium. His trip had taken a bad turn and there were no signs of it getting better.

"Calm down," Ruby said.

"How?" Julius yelled.

Ruby wallowed his legs around until his feet caught traction on Julius's shoulders then pulled himself up through the passenger side window frame. He then worked his feet along the dash until he found a good hold, pushing and pulling himself completely out of the car until he stood erect and irritated, straddling the door frame high above the crowd, soaked and staring down, somewhere on Raleigh Street in the middle of historic downtown Siler City.

"That's him!" someone in the crowd yelled.

THE BIG FRESH

Slowly the erratic madness of the crowd turned into a flowing assembly, pushing up along the frame of the blue Mercedes to get a better look at Ruby.

"Is that really him?" said a young girl, her eyes big and staring.

"Yes," said a boy. "I saw him earlier today. He's the one."

They moved closer. Julius worked himself up and out of the window of the blue Mercedes and came to stand alongside Ruby. "They think you're Jesus," he said. "Look at 'em."

It was true; most had heard of the man who brought thunder and rain from the Cloud and that fact had become so much a part of them all. And the fact that Neena Moore—that local hero of journalism—was in town to do a story of just such a biblical phenomenon made it seem that much more feasible and right that they too should consider the possibility of a living, breathing Jesus.

Why not? And why not in Siler City? The turn of the century. It's written in the Book somewhere, passed on by pastor and auto-mechanic-turned-Sunday-school-teacher every week, every other day; somewhere, someone is turning heads by prophesying the coming of the Lord. The Reverend Alfonso King did it—probably more than anyone else. Babbling, rattling, coughing up fragments of scripture, pasting them together like a jigsaw puzzle with holy spit.

It is common knowledge in Siler City and across the South as well as portions of the North and Midwest that someday the Lord is coming back. It was also believed, mostly by radicals and those of blind faith, that the turn of the new millennium would bring him. The year 2000. Y2K. The apocalyptic Rapture.

Not only had the Reverend Alfonso King subscribed to it, but regional and national figures such as Jerry Falwell and Oral Roberts had given in to the idea that when the clock struck midnight—eastern time, of course—on December 31, 1999, a great awakening would occur. Spirits and angels would descend and take back what was rightfully theirs. And there would be Jesus standing in the clearing smoke in all his holy glory.

"Clean up your kitchens!" the reverends would yell. "The Lord is coming for supper!"

But the new millennium had rolled in and everyone woke up to a bright, cloudless day. There were no meltdowns, no airplanes in the backyard, no Third World rogue nation playing space cowboy on the World Wide Web, and no Jesus sitting in the kitchen sipping on a cup of joe, waiting for the ham and eggs.

It was like waking up to a pseudo-Christmas, not really wanting or asking for anything outright but feeling disappointed just the same when nothing materialized.

Most people went about their business. They let the whole idea and event sort of slip back into their subconsciousness. There was no need to subjugate it to any form of legal action. It was just one of those things.

And out of all this it was the young people who weren't afraid to ask all those questions left unanswered or ignored by the authorities and adults who felt it better to just leave it alone. Their *whens*, *wheres*, and *whys* were based upon the one thing religion hates the most: Science.

It is the classic clash of color and pride, so to speak. Good versus Evil. Science versus Religion. Both prophetically claiming to be right. One wanting to debate; the other wanting to pray. "It's faith," says Religion over and over, holding it up like armor in front of its face.

"Answer the questions then," says Science, frustrated and out of place.

"We don't have to," says Religion. "We have faith."

"Faith, shit," says Science. "Answer the questions."

"No," says Religion.

And, of course, no question ever gets answered when there is so much history riding on it. It was just that attitude that brought everyone out into the street; and it was that unexplained, indefinable faith that sent them into a rage. Not to mention a climactic disaster that was well on the way to destroying the town. It was definitely a strange time to be living in Siler City.

Ruby stood above them—not as a figure of authority, just above them. There was no easy way down from the car and he had not, as of yet, figured it out.

It was a Craftsman fiberglass, six-foot ladder that eventually got him down—some enterprising young rogue who identified Ruby's dilemma, answered by unloading a couple of historic bricks into the glass door of the locally owned Pope's Hardware Store. Morally and ethically, it bothered Ruby none. He and Julius climbed down off the side of the blue Mercedes just the same.

"Are you supposed to be Jesus?" a teenage girl no more than thirteen asked; she was bare-chest and squinting.

"No, I'm not," Ruby said.

"Is this the Rupture?" asked another girl, shirtless too, no more than fifteen, with the tits of a superstar.

"That's Rapture," Julius said.

"Who are you?" the girl asked, turning quietly to Julius.

"Vergil," he said laughing.

No one acknowledged him. "You know . . . Vergil," Julius said again. "Dante's guide through hell."

No one reacted or spoke up.

"I'm Jesus's guide through hell," Julius said louder, irritated now.

There was a moment of nothing and Julius felt inferior. "Forget it," he said.

"Is this the end of the world?" the fifteen-year-old girl asked.

"No," Ruby answered.

"Why are you here then?" she asked.

"Why are you here?"

"Nothing else to do," she said.

"You don't mind the rain?" Ruby asked.

"It's better than waiting for it," she said. "My daddy said I better get used to it because it won't ever stop unless you make it stop."

Ruby laughed at this.

"How about this," he said. "You flip my car back over and I'll make it stop."

"We don't want it to stop," yelled a shirtless boy from the rear.

"We like it," yelled another.

"All right," Ruby said. "If you don't flip my car over I'll stop it."

They weighed their options then some ten young men pushed the blue Mercedes back on its right side.

"Get the cruiser while you're at it," Ruby said.

The boys joined again and brought the cruiser to its feet. Its driver, Kirk Merchant, and the other deputy passenger, were nowhere to be found. Gone. Ejected and fled the scene of the crime.

"It's not always this exciting," the thirteen-year-old, shirtless girl said, her hair matted down straight by the rain.

"Why destroy the town?" Ruby asked.

"Reverend Holmes told Michael Talbert that it wouldn't

destroy the town," the fifteen-year-old girl said, "that it would make it stronger because all these buildings down here are insured, and that local builders and suppliers would get the business and revenue for fixing them."

"Sounds like something he would say," Julius said.

"We've got to go," Ruby said.

"Where you going?" the thirteen-year-old girl asked.

"The First Baptist Church," Julius said looking at Ruby. "That's where you'll find Reverend King. I'm positive."

"Are you going to punish us?" the thirteen-year-old girl asked Ruby.

"No," Ruby said. "But you girls should put a shirt on. Matter of fact, none of you should be out here. I want you all to go home. When I come back I don't want to see anyone out here. Okay?"

"Okay," came a scattered multitude of voices.

Ruby climbed into the blue Mercedes followed by Julius.

"Do you think there's anything to it?" Julius asked as he fumbled for the ignition.

"To what?"

"To you being Jesus?"

Ruby laughed. Julius found the key in the ignition and turned it. The motor turned over a few times then caught. "It would be a kick in the balls if I were," Ruby said.

"Yeah, I suppose," Julius said then moved the blue Mercedes off slowly, no lights now and shards of glass for a windshield.

They drove slowly up two blocks then made a left on Second Avenue. Up ahead in the distance they could see a flood of lights: headlights and battery operated lights and what looked to be firecrackers exploding.

"What do you suppose that is?" Ruby asked.

Julius leaned forward to get a better look then stopped the car. "That's the First Baptist Church," he said.

THE BIG FRESH

Julius pulled the blue Mercedes into an old Exxon station that had been closed down some two decades and recently converted into a flower shop. Up ahead a good hundred yards, they had a full-screen, panoramic view of the ordeal taking place. To the left of Second Avenue was Town Hall, fully lit up with generators and floodlights. A great fortress of brick and mortar, house to the laws of the land, county to state, and state to nation. Beside Town Hall, down a brick pathway past a statue of a local revolutionary named Nathan Pickett—who, according to the placard, single-handedly diverted the British out of Siler City by dressing up as a woman, riding into their camp, and telling them that a horrible, infectious disease was killing everyone in town—sat the Sheriff's Department. It was considerably smaller than Town Hall but possessed in its own way an ideological oneness within the system. Another great fortress of brick and mortar. House to the enforcers of the law of the land, the usual seat belt tickets and DUIs. Sanctioned by the county of Chatham and state of North Carolina and the union of the United States of America to rise up when the aptitude of any given situation warrants—like some rabid banshee—and fight. Fight with months and years of training: self-defense, riot control, firearm proficiency. Fight using all those toys in the basement: M16 rifles, .45-caliber pistols, 12-gauge shotguns, M130 grenade and tear gas launchers and canisters, bulletproof vests, and riot gear, including billy sticks and stun guns. All those toys and nowhere to go. Sitting there, collecting dust, getting bored, waiting for just such the occasion.

In front of the Sheriff's Department stretching up the street past Town Hall, parked parallel down the middle of the street were sixteen cop cruisers—sixteen, sheriff and state trooper alike. Doors open and floodlights on, deputies and troopers crouched behind them with rifles and shotguns, bulletproof vests, and loudspeakers. All this, including the floodlights, was directed and concentrated on one location directly across the street, casting eerie shades and shadows like a family portrait on the First Baptist Church.

There was no movement outside the church. No lights to be seen inside. The great Romanesque columns in front of the church had been riddled with bullets and nearly every giant pane of glass across the front and down the sides had been shot out. Rifles and shotguns hung from windowsills and ledges like ornaments, spitting out flames randomly. A volley of weaponry with a volley in return from across the street. Loudspeakers rang out, "You are surrounded. Drop your weapons and come out!"

A barrage of gunfire responded.

The rain fell. The thunder and lightning cracked and rumbled.

"We've got to do something," Julius said.

"What?" Ruby said, overwhelmed by the shear display of chaos.

"I don't know."

"Do you really think the reverend is in there?" Ruby asked.

"My father?" Julius said.

"No," Ruby said. "The Reverend King."

"Oh," Julius said, thinking about his father. "There's a very good chance, I suppose."

Ruby considered a suicide run for it, provoked mostly by nervous energy that ate at his entire system. He wanted out but not without the reverend, not after what the reverend tried to do for him.

It was as if the whole thing had been taken from a bad Saturday afternoon movie, full of bad actors and bad plots, and with an all around bad feel to it. The struggle was there, laid out for Ruby in black and white. To the left sat the State and to the right the Church. A struggle as old as prostitution itself. A struggle that had started more wars and killed more people than a dozen estranged Hitlers could possibly wish for. This confounded Ruby, for even though the lines had been clearly drawn, it was not all too clear why. What did the Reverend King have to do with it? And what about the Masonic Reverend Holmes?

These questions weighed heavily on Julius as well. It was hard being the son of a preacher man—even harder when that preacher had some twisted idea of divinity and a Master Plan as old and mysterious as the Masons themselves.

The scene was difficult for Julius to take. To sit in the blue Mercedes with every piece of glass cracked or busted out, with LSD running laps around his head like a jockiless horse, creating unnecessary tensions and paranoia, flights and fights through the head like bolts of lightning through historic downtown Siler City. Without a word he jumped out of the blue Mercedes. By the time Ruby absorbed what happened, Julius had run some fifty feet up the sidewalk and cut sharply across the street into a narrow alley between the Smith and Buckner Funeral Home and the Better Bank and Trust.

"Shit," said Ruby in frustration.

He weighed his options then got out of the blue Mercedes and walked carefully across the street and into the narrow alley.

The alley was sheltered and dry and Ruby stopped once he was under it. He looked back at the blue Mercedes and could barely see it through the rain. Sounds of rifles and shotguns, pistols and loudspeakers could be heard just up the street. Overhead, the sounds of thunder and lightning.

The rain had long since flooded out Second Avenue, creating a sort of Venetian illusion. The cops and cop cars sat in the dead middle of it, ignoring it, firing off rounds as automatically as their weapons would allow.

THE MASONIC CONNECTION

The Masonic brothers inside the church felt somewhat indifferent about the situation. Before this all started they were good, down-home men through and through. They worked their jobs and on the last Thursday of every month would dress up and become Masons. Once every two months, usually on a Saturday, they would go out to Robert Leblanc's farm and fire their weapons. It made them feel extremely strong and invincible to do so, as if nothing and no one could ever touch them. Of course this was grandiose thinking, perpetuated mostly by the fact that these men had nothing or nothing better to do with their lives. They had wives and kids, but they needed that little extra something they could call their own, that little extra something that completes the package. That was where the Masons came in. One gigantic knight in shining armor.

But now all that chanting and training and oath-taking meant more than a six pack of beer and a few laughs. Now most of the men just wanted out without hurting or letting anyone down. They fired their rifles and shotguns with an almost inept silence, wishing most sincerely only to be home—that long-forgotten, neglected home.

THE BIG FRESH

Ruby found a door in the alley. It led down a small passage dimly lit by a generator the funeral home kept maintained for just such an occasion. At the end of the narrow passage were three doors: one to the left, one straight ahead, and one to the right. The one straight ahead was open and Ruby took it. He went down a flight of stairs into another dimly lit hall. There, he quietly called out for Julius but received no answer. There he made a promise to himself that he would kick Julius's ass if he ever found him. He then took off walking down the hall.

At the end of the hall was a door. Ruby took it, ascending immediately up a flight of stairs. He opened another door and stepped out onto plush red carpet. Off in the near distance Ruby could hear the rumblings of gunfire. He began walking cautiously toward it. A ways down the hall was a door and upon that door, engraved on a golden nameplate, were the words: *Baptismal Pool.*

Strangely enough, it occurred to Ruby that he had never been baptized, not once, not even by mistake. He took the door, thinking of nothing better to do at the time, and went up a flight of rickety, wooden stairs to a platform. Below, he saw the baptismal pool; it was full of filthy-looking water with green rings around the edges. Behind the pool on the wall was a mural: a brilliant forest scene with a creek and birds. It was an attempt to make people believe they were getting baptized down by the river, possibly by John the Baptist himself.

Out front was the sanctuary. Ruby could see the gunfire now and he could smell the powder. He leaned cautiously forward and peered around the wall. The sanctuary was dimly lit. There were some 30 men dressed flamboyantly in reddish and orange attire looking like Shriners on parade, hanging themselves out broken windows and off ledges, firing their rifles and shotguns. Others ran haphazardly around in a nervous attempt to keep busy.

Just in front of Ruby was the Reverend Frederick Holmes. He was leaned over a large, dark, maple-stained table. There looked to be a body on the table; it was draped in white linen. Behind the reverend to the right, sitting straight up, tensed and somewhat out of kilter in a deacon's chair, was Julius. Whatever he wanted or had in mind to do didn't happen and with the looks of things he never had a chance.

The Reverend Holmes was not affected by the gunfire. He stood over the table crying and chanting in a loud, broken voice incoherent passages that sounded like something Ruby had heard many times before at the Home. "'Vas doumal. Vas doumal. Vas doumal,'" the Reverend Holmes chanted, arms raised. "'Eabetta un nanoon Seadrea, Enatoo valsia chanti Eclusea.'"

Gunfire rang out continuously with the periodical inaudible squelching from bullhorns and loudspeakers filtering in from the street through the broken windows.

"'Comodrae dea Nalla,'" the Reverend Holmes chanted louder. "'Redrinea fallau un dea Seadrea.'"

Julius sat forward in the deacon's chair and yelled, "Who are you?"

The reverend did not answer.

"'Redrinea fallau un dea Seadrea eabetta un dea brata cessa. Vas doumal. Vas doumal. Vas doumal.'"

The deacons pulled Julius back into his seat. As Julius looked over at one of them he saw Ruby. At the same time, a barrage of tear gas canisters and incendiary smoke bombs came whirling through the windows. The incendiary smoke bombs hit the plush red carpet and immediately ignited into flames. One of the canisters hit the Reverend Holmes in the chest and knocked him back. The two deacons that stood guard over Julius ran forward to help him. On the table, to Ruby's sheer disbelief and amazement, dressed in white linen and unmistakably dead, was John Carter.

Julius saw the opportunity and took it. He ran past the podium, past his father and the two deacons, over the banister to where the choir stood on Sunday mornings, over a small ledge and into the baptism pool. One giant baptism of a cannon ball, soaking the mural and Ruby simultaneously. It was unorthodox and uncalled-for, but it was spontaneous and no other irrevocable repercussions came from it. Ruby helped Julius out of the pool and they descended the rickety steps out into the hallway.

Masonic brothers ran past them in a frantic hurry, throwing down their rifles and shotguns, stripping off their flamboyant costumes. They had tear gas in their eyes and were now crying. A very humbling thing for anyone to see.

"I can't leave without the reverend," Ruby said.

"He's in the fellowship hall," Julius said.

Down the hall and to the left, first through the kitchen and then the dining hall. The reverend sat in a metal foldout chair with his hands and feet bound with duct tape. His eyes were closed. He was praying. "Reverend," Ruby said, slapping him lightly on the face.

The reverend opened his eyes and looked out at Ruby as if he were seeing the Holy Ghost for the first time. "Our Father who art in heaven," the reverend cried. "Ruby!"

"No time for that," Ruby said.

They untied the reverend then exited down the hall, through the door and into the tunnel over to the Smith and Buckner Funeral Home. They cut down the alley, across the street, and over to the blue Mercedes. The reverend cried once more when he saw the condition his car was in.

Ruby, Julius, and the Reverend King sat in the blue Mercedes and watched as the First Baptist Church burned. All the while, the Reverend King told Ruby the story Reverend Holmes had told him. Ruby listened and watched the flames as they gradually made their way out the windows. Masons shuffled out from all corners with their hands raised. The gunfire had long since ceased and it was now a game of attrition. "We don't have to sit here," Ruby said to Julius, interrupting the reverend.

"No, it's fine," Julius said; he seemed to be taking the situation rather well now.

The river of water down Second Avenue was up to a good foot. The Reverend King continued to talk.

He explained to Ruby how he and John Carter were part of one grand experiment, that it was Reverend Holmes's mother, Eva, who got caught up in it. And he told Ruby of how Reverend Holmes followed him to Siler City and eventually, through Masonic channels, had John Carter transferred to the Sunbridge Psychiatric and Rehabilitation Center.

"That explains a lot," Julius said. "My father gave up everything for this pastoral job. He left my mother."

"Don't you see," the reverend said. "It was set up from the beginning to be one great family reunion."

Flames licked up the side of the church and smoke billowed out from the roof.

"That makes you my uncle," Julius said to Ruby.

"Not just any uncle," the reverend said. "The holiest of uncles."

"Don't you think that's a little much?" Ruby said.

"You tell me," the reverend said. "Are you or are you not who he says you are?"

Ruby looked at the reverend then out at the church. He ran

his hand by the collar of his shirt and felt over to the right side of his chest to where the tattoo was. He couldn't see it, but he knew it was there, as always, as far back as he could remember. His foster mother told him it was special and that it made him special. She never said why and the topic seemed to fade, along with the tattoo, the older he got. It was now barely recognizable, stretched and faded, yet impenetrable; and all the mystery that it held was nothing compared to that which surrounded it. "What happened to John Carter?" Ruby asked.

"Dead," Julius said bluntly.

"And your father?"

"I think he died with him."

A few more Masons staggered out of the church holding their arms up and coughing, floodlights sterilizing their every move. A few minutes passed then the Reverend Holmes appeared on the front steps of the church. He was nearly limp with a deacon under each arm. His Masonic suit had been blackened and his hair wildly singed. Ruby saw him first then pointed him out to Julius. "I never thought he'd come out," Julius said.

"Me neither," said the reverend.

They watched as the two deacons and the reverend stood on the top steps of the church, flames reaching out around them. Five deputies dressed in full riot gear ran up the steps and cuffed them then escorted them, heads hung, across the street to the Sheriff's Department.

A few minutes later the church's roof combusted into one great ball of flame, sending fire out the front door and windows. It was no longer a church. No plush, red carpet. No baptismal pool. No deacons and no reverend. "That's it," Ruby said.

"Yep," said the reverend.

Julius took one last look then fired up the blue Mercedes and headed it slowly back in the direction of the Brookwood Apartments.

THE BIG FRESH

It was a brilliant morning that woke Ruby. Beside him lay Lisa, beautiful and young, her breasts naked against the linen. He arose, naked himself, his clothes lying in a wet pile on the floor beside the bed. He wrapped himself in a towel, picked up his clothes, and went to the living room. On the couch was the reverend. He was shirtless and snoring. On the floor was Julius, wrapped in a single sheet, a couch pillow under his head. Ruby walked to the front door and opened it. A flood of light lit up the room. He stepped out on the deck and took a deep, satisfying breath. There was no rain. There was no Cloud. There was only one big, blue, perfect sky. Ruby looked down at his chest and at the tattoo. He ran his fingers over it and smiled.

Up the hill, the Sunbridge Psychiatric and Rehabilitation Center sat deserted with only a few random cars parked in the employees' parking lot. There was no Crowd, no news crews with their vans, no cops, no cop cruisers. The Cross was the only thing left. It stood there in the middle of the parking lot, cemented, untouched, and unwanted. A sight of uncertain beauty.

Ruby took another deep breath then went back into the apartment, grabbed up everyone's dirty, wet clothes, and threw them into the washing machine. He then took a long cold shower to purge himself of the night before. As the cool water hit his head and ran down his face he thought of the woman he had never known, the woman who bore and birthed him. He thought about the man who loved her but never more than his work and how he played God and lost. He thought of the night at the Home when he woke to find John Carter standing over him, staring at the tattoo on his chest; how insane he was; how insane he probably had always been. He thought of the Reverend Holmes, his other estranged brother—pissed off at the world for what? Ruby couldn't understand him, but neither did the world. It didn't matter now.

It all seemed too real and connected rather well in a conspiratory way, but Ruby was beyond all that. He had no use for it. It was the fresh, new day that had captured him the most. He, after all this time, could now put his wife to rest along with the man he used to be. He needed not to be the sportswriter with dreams of writing a best-selling novel. He needed not to be God. He only needed to be himself; and with the cool water from the shower running down his face he accepted all this with a smile.

It was a beautiful awakening and Lisa joined him in the shower without saying a word and they kissed and wrapped each other up in their arms. As automatic as breathing, her beauty was his and vice versa.

The shower was long and comfortable, and when they got out Ruby took the clothes from the washing machine and placed them in the dryer; he then took Lisa outside to show her the beautiful, new day. They stood there in their towels and marveled at it. "It is so beautiful," she said.

And even through the mugginess of the early summer morning, Ruby had to agree with her.

They went back inside and cooked breakfast. Bacon, eggs, grits, toast. The works. Julius and the reverend woke up one by one, and Lisa directed them to the shower. They all ate at the kitchen table in their towels, not saying much, laughing generously though. Afterwards, Ruby took their dry clothes and scattered them out on the couch. They gathered what was theirs and got dressed.

"What are you going to do?" Ruby asked Julius.

"I don't know," he said.

"What about you?" Ruby asked the reverend.

The reverend smiled. Ruby understood the situation completely and took complete responsibility for it, with or without the reverend's consent. He couldn't change the past, but he could give direction to the future.

"Well," Ruby said to Julius, "Lisa and I and the reverend here, are going to Wilmington. We're going to lay low on the beach for a while. You want to come?"

"I'm supposed to be at work."

"There is nothing there for you," Ruby said.

"I know," Julius said. "That son of a bitch."

"We'll check on him later—once we get there," Ruby said.

Julius looked at Ruby apathetically.

"Come on," Ruby said. "We are family."

Julius smiled. "When you leaving?"

"As soon as possible."

"Can you give me a few minutes to run by the house?"

"You know we can," Ruby said.

"Be careful," said the reverend.

Julius rushed down the drive, fired up the blue Mercedes, and was gone.

"You know, I never found your book," the reverend said to Ruby as they watched Julius drive off.

"That's okay," Ruby said. "I don't need it anymore."

Lisa packed a few last minute things while the reverend and Ruby sat at the kitchen table drinking coffee. Within no time, a horn blew out front of the apartment. It was Julius, riding high and smiling behind the wheel of his father's Cadillac.

"Come on," he yelled. "I don't think he'll miss it."

They all piled into the Cadillac, the reverend and Julius up front, Ruby and Lisa in the back. They drove off slowly down through the Brookwood Apartments. The Hispanic children were out front playing and they stopped to watch as the Cadillac made its way through the heart of the complex. Julius made a left at the bottom of the hill onto Raleigh Street and drove through the devastated historic downtown Siler City. There was no more smoke, no kids running half-naked, only piles of soaked debris, broken glass, and one abandoned cop car. Julius made a right onto Highway 64 and headed east.

They had the windows down and Ruby felt the wind in his face and the freshness of the air and was not tempted once by the irrelevant concerns of anything. He did not care that the car was stolen nor that they had no place to stay once they got to Wilmington. It would all fall into place as it had before, as it had for him and his wife all those years.

He could now see, even after her death and his injuries, that things had a way of fixing themselves. And with the sun and the warm summer breeze and a blue perfect sky, with him free of the Home and all it represented, with Lisa beside him and the reverend and Julius navigating and driving, Ruby felt as if he could do anything. And no matter what happened, he knew it would surely, somehow, work itself out.

THE END

Epilogue

Neena Moore found Ruby's manuscript. She read parts of it while she was still under the influence. She read the rest during her flight back to New York. Within a week she had a front-page story. Headlines reading:

THE BIG FRESH

Jesus found in small town America
under Cross and Cloud. He writes science
fiction novel and makes it rain!

The Big Fresh was her idea. It came from some old newspaper clippings she ran across while browsing the archives at the Wren Memorial Library. The Big Fresh was the name of a flood that hit Siler City in 1883. There was no explanation for it but many believed that it too had biblical properties far beyond comprehension.

She found representation for Ruby's book and published it under the pseudonym, Jesus. It was her intentions to find Ruby and give him credit, but that never happened. The book went on to receive moderate and mixed reviews.

As for Josef and the German connection, he could not sleep that beautiful, cloud-covered night in 1943, thinking of the bronzed vessel and all that Father Marcus Ramos had told him earlier that evening. The words from Father Marcelino's suicide note rang through his head: *Let no mortal man ever be endowed with such powers.*

Josef got up and got dressed, took one look at himself in the mirror, and then walked across the cool courtyard to his office. The bronzed vessel sat in its brass and glass case under its black cloth in a locked vault. Josef took it to his office and placed it on his desk. He admired its beauty once more then pried off its lid with a set of surgical instruments. He found nothing inside. Nothing at all. He went to where Father Marcus Ramos was sleeping. He woke the Father up and told him of what he found. Before Father Marcus could reply, Josef took out his pistol and shot him once through the crotch, once through the head, and once more through the heart. He then reholstered his pistol, made that long, cool walk across the courtyard to his house, took off his clothes, and lay down to bed, falling asleep almost immediately.

photo: Jeremy Thompson

Scott Morgan was born and raised in rural North Carolina in the small town of West End. He spent a few years in the army national guard as a combat medic and now lives in Chapel Hill, North Carolina, with his wife Shannon. Scott plays guitar and sings in a band called Memphis, which plays many of his original songs. Scott has written several novels. This is his second published one.